PRAISE FOR *OVE*

"Susan Walter is a master storytell[...]m business, and her novel glints with danger and brilliant insight into the hopes and dreams of an aspiring actress. I read it in one sitting, guessing the whole way through, stunned by the conclusion."

—Luanne Rice, *New York Times* bestselling author of
The Shadow Box and *Last Day*

"A devilishly fun romp, full of eccentric characters and unexpected twists, *Over Her Dead Body* will keep you turning pages, as it pulls back the curtains on Hollywood from the point of view of a struggling actress caught up in a mystery laced with darkly comedic beats. Thoroughly enjoyable!"

—Ben Mezrich, *New York Times* bestselling author of
Bringing Down the House, *The Accidental Billionaires*,
and *The Midnight Ride*

"Susan Walter swerves the reader back and forth and around blind corners in a page-turning domestic psychodrama that will twist your sympathies and drop your jaw. An A-list Hollywood thrill ride, right through to the breathtaking end!"

—Dr. Judy Melinek and T.J. Mitchell, *New York Times*
bestselling authors of *Working Stiff*, *First Cut*, and *Aftershock*

"With its eccentric ensemble cast and all the family drama of *Knives Out*, *Over Her Dead Body* is darkly funny and highly entertaining, with more twists than a bus tour through the Hollywood Hills. Fans of Janet Evanovich and Elle Cosimano will be delighted."

—Tessa Wegert, author of *Death in the Family*

"*Over Her Dead Body* is a whodunit with more twists and turns than a boardwalk roller coaster, where secrets abound and nothing is what it seems. If you're looking for a book that will keep you turning pages deep into the night, Susan Walter has absolutely written one."
—Barbara Davis, bestselling author of *The Keeper of Happy Endings*

"What a clever, fun, twisty, juicy ride! *Over Her Dead Body* will keep you guessing over and over with its kaleidoscope of conflicted characters, crisscrossed allegiances, and masterful point-of-view shifts. *Knives Out* has nothing on this quintessential LA story of ambition, greed, and good intentions gone wrong. You've never read a mystery quite like it."
—Gary Goldstein, author of *The Last Birthday Party*

PRAISE FOR *GOOD AS DEAD*

"Susan Walter's debut novel is so full of surprises it should come with a warning label. From the daringly original premise to the shocking climax, you'll never see the plot twists coming until you turn the page. I cannot wait for her next book!"
—W. Bruce Cameron, #1 *New York Times* bestselling author of *A Dog's Purpose* and *A Dog's Courage*

"Susan Walter's *Good as Dead* had me holding my breath through every thrilling twist and turn until the downright explosive ending. Fearlessly tackling themes of love, wealth, personal responsibility, and life and death, it was pure pleasure to read, and a brilliant debut."
—Alethea Black, author of *You've Been So Lucky Already* and *I Knew You'd Be Lovely*

LIE

BY

THE

POOL

OTHER TITLES BY SUSAN WALTER

Good as Dead

Over Her Dead Body

LIE
BY
THE
POOL

A NOVEL

SUSAN
WALTER

LAKE UNION
PUBLISHING

Text copyright © 2023 by Susan Walter
All rights reserved.

Published by Lake Union Publishing, Seattle

www.apub.com

Amazon, the Amazon logo, and Lake Union Publishing are trademarks of Amazon.com, Inc., or its affiliates.

ISBN-13: 9781662505102 (paperback)
ISBN-13: 9781662505119 (digital)

Cover design by Amanda Kain
Cover image: © Jacobs Stock Photography Ltd / Getty

Printed in the United States of America

PART 1

OCTOBER

CHAPTER 1

BREE

I knew what I was doing was wrong, but I was just so tired. The kind of tired that seeps into your bones and makes your limbs feel like they're filled with cement. After three months of (barely) sleeping in my car, my body was starting to fail me—my eyes wouldn't focus, my tongue slurred my words, my ears could hear sounds but my brain couldn't process them. I needed sleep.

The exterior of the house was a sleek coupling of cool concrete and warm mahogany. Unlike neighbors that hid their bones behind paint and stucco, this house had walls of glass that let you see into its soul. It wasn't the grandest house on the block, but it held a special fascination for me. I remember when it was being built—at one point the pile of dirt was three stories high. I remember thinking they'd better hurry up and get rid of it before it rained. *Can you imagine? A hundred tons of mud coursing over the neighbor's prized roses? What a disaster that would be!*

I remember wondering how the people next door felt about the swarm of bright yellow diggers and dirty dump trucks buzzing and beeping from sunup to sundown. I didn't know any super-rich people, but I imagined they came in two varieties: up at dawn, too busy chasing their ambitions to notice; and worked their whole lives, ready for some peace and quiet. Were the neighbors grateful someone was finally tearing down the old eyesore that had sullied their block for the last half century? Or annoyed?

I found it amusing how Beverly Hills people built whatever they wanted—an ultramodern house of glass next to a buttoned-up Colonial next to an English castle. The area felt more like a life-size museum of architecture than a neighborhood. This brazenly eclectic block had always been a favorite of mine on my daily jog, back when I had the energy to jog. Running for pleasure seemed like such an indulgence now. I was trying to conserve calories, not burn them. Plus, with no place to take a post-workout shower, reading and daydreaming were more practical pastimes.

I knew I could get into the backyard from the alley. The neighborhoods in the flats of Beverly Hills were serviced by alleys that were as wide as streets, because Rodeo Drive is for Louis Vuitton and Montblanc, not wheelie bins and garbage trucks. The gate would be locked, but all I had to do was hop up onto a trash can and hoist myself over it. I was not particularly athletic, but it was only a six-foot drop into the yard—I was pretty sure my twenty-five-year-old knees could handle that.

Normal people my age were leaving for Saturday-night dinner dates or drinks with friends when I slung my legs over that alley wall and peered into the resort-like backyard. I know in the movies prowlers wait until the cover of night to break into houses, but they also know how to disable motion-activated floodlights with their handy wire cutters. I had no such tools or know-how, so I made my move in the dull gray light of dusk.

I didn't want to linger on top of the wall, so as soon as I saw there were no growling dogs or armed guards with guns pointing at me, I dropped in. The overwatered sod squished like a wet sponge as my feet, knees, and hands plunked onto it. I stayed crouched on all fours for several seconds, listening . . . waiting. I didn't have a cover story if someone came, because what could I possibly say? *"I lost my key?" "Oops, sorry, wrong house?" "I'm running from a bear?"* Even the truth wasn't credible.

Not every house in Beverly Hills has a pool, but where there's a mountain of dirt, there's a big hole, so no surprise this minimansion had a sizable one. Like the house, the pool was minimalist, with smooth concrete coping that was flush with the emerald lawn. The eight-foot-tall granite waterfall wasn't currently running, so the surface was as still as glass. If you chose to, you could gaze down into that water and see your whole life looking back at you, that's how clear it was . . . not that I dared to look.

I stood up and scanned the yard. The late-October sun had just slipped below the horizon, casting an unbroken shadow as far as the eye could see. I used to be a person who craved sunlight on my face, but the silhouettes that defied the sun were much more enticing these days. *If you can't see me, maybe I can't see me* . . . At least that was the hope.

The pool house was an indoor-outdoor space, with heavy curtains you could pull for privacy. It had a kitchenette, a fireplace, a driftwood dining table with six wicker chairs. The vaulted ceiling had recessed can lights I wouldn't turn on and a skylight with a shade I wouldn't open. There was a powder room with a marble-top vanity and a tiled outdoor shower. For the last three months, the closest I'd gotten to showering was washing my parts one at a time in the hip-high sink in the handicapped stall at the mall. So yes, I was tempted by the shower. But the pool house's most appealing feature *by far* was the glorious double-wide chaise on the open-air patio. With a flick of a lever, you could recline it all the way flat like a bed, rest your neck on one of the shirt box–size pillows, and stare up into the darkening sky.

If the stars came out that night, I really couldn't tell you, because I was asleep before night had the chance to reveal them. I dreamed of him, as I always did. In my waking hours, I agonized over why the universe would give me such a great big love only to take it away. But in my dreams, we were together again. We danced barefoot in the sand, our bodies woven together like hungry vines climbing toward forever. When the morning sun stirred me from my sleep, I would have to face the white-hot sting of losing him.

And so I slept.

CHAPTER 2

BREE

I heard it before I could see it: the whoosh of water flowing into water. I could feel it in my chest, steady and eager as a drumroll. Some waterfalls are violent, like claps of liquid thunder, crashing and churning and spitting every which way. But this waterfall sounded peaceful . . . inviting, even . . . like the looping bass line of a favorite song.

Luke took my hand and gave it a squeeze, and I felt my wedding band press into my middle finger. I had never worn a ring on that or any finger before, so the feeling of the metal band connecting with my bone surprised me, but not in a bad way. From that day on, every time I felt that sensation, I was reminded of this moment: the very first time I felt like a wife.

We had checked into the hotel the day before as Mr. and Mrs., but it felt like a game—I almost wanted to giggle. Luke was perfectly cast as the confident groom to the awkward, young bride. The hotel clerk didn't look like she doubted we were really married, but I couldn't help but feel like an actress in a play. This was the kind of happiness from fairy tales or the dreamy rom-coms my mom used to watch; it couldn't be real life. At least not *my* real life.

Maui's lush tropical forest was otherworldly to someone from the arid Okanagan Valley. As I breathed in the sweet smell of honeysuckle, my eyes devoured flowers so colorful I felt like I'd fallen into a kaleidoscope. The path grew narrow, but my husband didn't let go of my hand when he eased in front of me, just readjusted his fingers to thread them through mine like yarn on a loom. The earth was soft under my feet as I followed in his footsteps, lengthening my stride to match his exactly. I played a game in my mind that if I could fit my shoe in his footprint without going outside the lines, nothing bad would ever happen to him: a grown-up version of "step on a crack, break your mother's back." Which I had played once before to its inevitable, tragic end.

The path wound around a rock the size of a school bus, then past a cluster of leafy trees. And then there it was: a waterfall as enticing as sweet pale ale flowing from a tap. I folded into Luke's chest, which was warm and damp against my smile. If there were such a thing as heaven on earth, I was sure I had found it. But of course there's no such thing. Because heaven is forever.

Luke kissed the top of my head, then wiggled free. I tried to reach for him, but I couldn't lift my arms. His face became the sun, and I felt radiant heat on my cheeks. A bead of sweat rolled down my temple, and I opened my eyes to see the majestic waterfall of my dream was just a mundane tumble of pool water pulsing down a granite slab. I wanted to cry, because once again my sleep had betrayed me, and even though I felt that crush of disappointment every time I woke, it still hurt every time.

I read in some scientific journal that the brain doesn't know the difference between a fantasy and a memory, that they both leave the same signature. I also read that a memory isn't stored like data on a hard drive or a jar of olives in the pantry. Rather, it's re-created from scratch every time you conjure it. Luke wasn't here, but that gold band on my finger told me the memory was real. And I felt immediately both better and worse.

I fumbled for my phone to check the time: 8:02 a.m. *What day is it?* It took me a moment to remember. *Sunday. It's Sunday.* I didn't have anywhere to be that morning, but I also couldn't be here. So I sat up, rubbed the sleep out of my eyes, silently raised the chaise back to its upright position, and returned the pillow exactly where I'd found it.

I gazed out at the pool. If it were my house, I would have peeled off my sweat-stained shirt and jumped in, then put my head under that pretend waterfall to let it sweep the tangles from my hair. I would have taken a deep breath and swum the whole length of the pool underwater, just for the thrill of it. I would have climbed up the ladder and lain spread eagle on the smooth, slate-gray pavers, like a snow angel minus the snow, and let the sun bake me dry.

But it wasn't my house. And I had to leave. *Now.*

But where to go? I ran through my options, as I did at the start of every day since the eviction. I didn't want to just sit in my car—it was so depressing, not to mention smelly, in there. I could go to a park; there were certainly plenty to choose from, but I didn't have a book, and the library was closed. There were coffee shops, but that meant buying coffee that I would drink too fast, leaving me craving more. I needed to wash my hair, but the mall wasn't open yet, so my choices were the twenty-four-hour car wash or the big sink at the Laundromat. What I really wanted to do was *go home*, to the things that made me feel like me—smooth hardwood under my bare feet, the patter of coffee brewing, the sweet scent of a vanilla candle burning on my bedside table. But that's the thing about being homeless. There's no place to kick back away from the watchful eyes of strangers. No place to just *be*.

I hadn't brought anything but my shame and exhaustion over that wall, so there was nothing to gather. I'd even slept with my shoes on in case I needed to make a quick escape. Getting out was easier than getting in because I could open the gate from the inside and walk on through, no wheelie bin required.

I told myself I wouldn't come here again. It was too dangerous. This wasn't just any old house, and I wasn't your typical trespasser. But that river rock in the planter was just too perfect.

So I wedged it under the gate, leaving just the tiniest crack in case I changed my mind.

CHAPTER 3

CARTER

The letter wasn't addressed to me, but I opened it anyway. I knew what it was. All property deeds came in that same oversize white envelope with aggressive block lettering that made you afraid to open it but also afraid not to.

The deed said we'd bought the property one month ago, on September 23, but that wasn't what got my attention. It was the zip code: 90210. Dad hadn't told me we'd bought a house in Beverly Hills—on *the* Rodeo Drive, no less—and he's supposed to tell me everything.

I figured it was a tear-down like all the other houses we bought to flip and resell. That was his business—*our* business. I was his partner now. Well, not partner, exactly, but he was grooming me to take over, so *future* partner. Or better yet, future *CEO*.

I'd been working at the family business for three years now, since I was nineteen. Mom had wanted me to go to college, so I went. It didn't take very long to discover it wasn't for me. I had hustle, not book smarts. Plus most of my fellow incoming freshmen just wanted to party. Back then, I was six foot two and 140 pounds soaking wet—not the kind of guy who scored at parties. So halfway through my second semester at Cal State Small Town, after I proved college would be wasted on me, Dad pulled me out and put me to work.

The family business was "real estate development." Dad taught me the basics—find the worst house in the best neighborhood, buy it and fix it up, or tear it down and build a badass one. It wasn't rocket science. And I didn't need to understand the Black-Scholes model to do it.

Dad didn't go to jobsites anymore; he had me to do that. He also used me to scout potential new investments—*Is it a good lot? Where's the nearest school? What are the zoning restrictions?* The questions were mostly common sense. He bought me a dorky Ford pickup that he called "the company car" even though I was the only one who drove it. We had our logo and phone number painted on the side, because why drive a cool truck when you can drive a billboard on wheels?

Most of the properties I scouted were pretty crappy. I put some serious miles on that truck, driving out to fringe neighborhoods like Altadena, Reseda, Torrance, Long Beach. The idea was to find houses in neighborhoods on the rise, flip them quickly, cash out before the interest on our loans ate into our profits. Most of what we bought was uninhabitable—leaky roof, crumbling foundation, devoured by termites—stuff we could get dirt cheap. So when I found out we'd bought a house in upscale Beverly Hills, let's just say I was curious.

I found the clicker to the garage in Dad's desk drawer when he was out playing golf, along with what I presumed was the code to disable the alarm. I didn't tell him I was going, but he didn't tell me not to, so I'm not sure why I was nervous about it.

The sun was a bright yellow dot in a cloudless blue sky when I got in "the company car" to visit our September 23 acquisition. I wouldn't be interacting with any vendors or contractors, it being Sunday and their only sure day off, so I wore my typical weekend attire—plain white T-shirt, shorts, and Nike slides with socks. Dad made me wear a company polo shirt when I went to jobsites, and hard-sole boots. It only took one rusty nail and a visit to the ER to understand the boots part. As for the shirt, we didn't have a marketing department, so I guess that polo and truck were it.

There was traffic on the 405 like there always is, but I made it to Beverly Hills from our house in the hilly part of Sherman Oaks in about twenty minutes. My favorite deli, Nate'n Al's, was just down the street. I figured I would check out the house, then surprise the fam with fresh bagels and egg salad. My sister, Sophie, liked their everything bagels, which made the kitchen smell like garlic when you toasted them. Mom was partial to the bagel chips, which were thin and crispy and, in my opinion, tasteless. But I never made it to Nate'n Al's that morning, because what I saw at our Rodeo Drive "investment property" made me forget all about breakfast.

Unlike the other houses we bought, this one was already renovated, and I knew for a fact we hadn't done it. Everything was new. The sod in the front yard had barely set. The stainless-steel mailbox was shiny (and locked). The exposed concrete walls were still buttery smooth and smudgeless.

I waded through the succulents around the perimeter to try to look through the windows, but they had some sort of reflective covering on them that made it impossible to see inside. It was unseasonably warm for October, a balmy eighty-three degrees, but the AC wasn't running, and no inside lights were on. At first I thought no one lived there. And then I opened the garage.

Sometimes the garages of newly renovated houses have stuff in them—leftover building materials, discarded boxes, bags of cement. But this garage contained something I didn't expect: not one but two cars. And not just any cars. *Nice* cars—a vintage convertible Porsche 911 and a newish Ford truck. *As if someone were home.*

I wasn't someone who watched those dumb movies on Lifetime about guys who had two families, but seeing this house and those cars got my wheels turning. I mean, those stories wouldn't be called "true crime" if they weren't true, right? My dad definitely owned this house, and there was definitely someone else's stuff there, and he definitely had never mentioned it.

I was tempted to snoop around the garage for clues, but if my dad's other wife was home, I didn't want her to catch me riffling through her glove box. Not that I was sure my dad was doing anything sketchy.

Which of course he was. I just got the particulars wrong.

CHAPTER 4

CARTER

"I went to the Rodeo Drive house today," I told my dad as we all sat down for dinner. Mom had made ribs and potato salad, Dad's favorite. We always ate together as a family on Sundays—Mom, Dad, me, and Sophie, who graduated from USC a year and change ago. Despite getting a degree in accounting or something to do with money, she couldn't seem to make any, and was back living at home.

"You're allowed to take a day off, you know," Dad said, missing the point, probably on purpose. Yes, I was living at home, too. But I was working. Just because it was the family business didn't mean it wasn't a real job.

"Do we have to talk about work?" Sophie asked, like we had something better to talk about. Of course Sophie didn't want to talk about work when she didn't have a job. Dad had gotten her a bookkeeping gig for a contractor we sometimes worked with, but that had petered out. She was supposed to be looking for a permanent, full-time job, but mostly she just did her nails and scrolled TikTok.

"The house is pretty swank," I said, ignoring my sister. "Was it a flip?"

"I guess that's a yes," Sophie grumbled.

"We don't have to talk about work," Dad said. But I wasn't ready to let him off the hook. If he was going to buy a house and not tell me about it, he was at least going to have to answer my questions.

"They did a good job, from what I saw," I pressed. Dad looked up from his plate. He didn't glare at me, exactly, but I could tell he was annoyed.

"Yes, it's a nice house," he finally offered.

"Who wants a corn muffin?" Mom asked, holding up the basket of muffins she'd made from a mix. Mom was a nurse—a nursing manager, now, actually—and worked long hours. But she still found time to cook for us. I wondered if Dad's other wife was so generous.

"I'll have one," Dad said. "Thanks, honey."

"Did we buy it as a rental property or something?" I asked. My cheeks were getting hot. I didn't like being ignored. "Because it looked like there were people living there." OK, I admit it. I was hurt that Dad hadn't let me in on whatever this Beverly Hills deal was. I worked on commission—10 percent of every sale made. If he had cut me out of a big one, I wanted to know.

"It's a new house. I bought it as a tax write-off," Dad said. "The owner needed cash, I needed to park some of our profits somewhere. Thanks to you, we're having a very good year."

I don't know if I bought his answer because he'd wrapped it in a compliment or because it sounded plausible. I didn't know much about tax law, but I did know that rich people moved their money around to avoid paying their fair share. If they had taught a class on that at college, I might have stayed. Anyway, it made more sense than Dad having a second family. My dad wasn't a slob or anything, but he was no George Clooney.

"So we're renting it out?" I asked. I decided not to mention seeing cars in the garage. If the place was legitimately tenanted, I didn't want to get in trouble for invading anyone's privacy.

"Still talking about work," Sophie mumbled.

"It's not sitting empty," Dad said sternly, and I knew the conversation was over. It would take what my sister told me later to realize Dad's answer was odd. I wanted more details—*Why did we buy it? How much are we renting it for? Why didn't he tell me about it?*—but Mom had made us all dinner, and I could tell by her face she didn't like being excluded from the conversation.

"Sophie, why don't you tell us about your plans for the week?" Mom said, passing her the salad, knowing it was the only thing she would eat. My mom's ribs were delicious, but I always felt like I needed a shower after eating them. The sauce got everywhere—on my cheeks, up my nose, under my fingernails. Sophie wouldn't touch them, but she barely ate anything these days. I don't mean to be critical of my sister, but, as Mom constantly reminded her, she was "a beautiful woman with a college degree—it was time to stop puttering her life away." Sometimes I heard my parents arguing about how to force the issue: *"Tell her to get a job or get out"* versus *"She needs support, not threats."* Mom thought they were enabling her, letting her sleep until noon every day. Dad thought she was depressed and needed a hug. I didn't know what to think. Maybe she was just smarter than me. She was the one with a college degree.

Somehow we made it through dinner without bickering. Dad bragged about his golf game, Mom talked about her new crop of volunteers at the hospital, and Sophie just stayed quiet, at least until the meal was over and we were alone in the kitchen.

"Dad lied to you," my sister said as she set our dirty plates on the counter by the sink. Sophie and I always did the dishes after our Sunday dinners. She cleared and wiped down the table, and I washed the pots and loaded the dishwasher.

"What about?"

"The house. There's no one living there." How the hell would she know that? She didn't work for the company, never had.

"How do you know?"

"Jared told me." Jared was our pool guy. I know it sounds fancy that we had a pool, but pretty much every house in our neighborhood had one. Summers were long in LA, and the Valley got super hot.

14

"How would Jared know?"

"He's there twice a week. Dad hired him to clean the pool." And that surprised me for a different reason.

"Since when do you talk to Jared?"

"Since when did you become a snob?" I didn't mean it in a "we're better than him" way. Dad worked at a lumberyard before he started flipping houses. I just had never seen Jared and my sister talking.

"I didn't mean it like that," I said.

"Jared said it has a really nice backyard. The pool has a waterfall."

"How does Jared know that nobody is living there?" I asked, recalling Dad's strange remark: *"It's not sitting empty."*

"Because Dad gave him a mailbox key and told him to clear away any flyers from the porch. He's been doing it all month."

What my sister was saying made no sense. *Why would my dad buy a house just to let it sit empty?* "I guess it doesn't matter," I said, even though it kind of did.

Sophie suddenly gasped and grabbed my arm. "We should have a Halloween party there!" she said, her eyes lighting up. "When Mom and Dad are in New York!"

As soon as she said it, I knew it was a terrible idea, and also that she would talk me into it.

CHAPTER 5

BREE

"Do you know what 'presto' means?" I asked my student at the beginning of our Sunday afternoon lesson.

"Fast?"

"It means really, really fast."

"I can play fast," she said, like she wanted to prove it.

"Let's hear it."

I leaned back in my chair and closed my eyes. I had chosen Beethoven's *Moonlight Sonata* for twelve-year-old Ellie because her mom wanted her to play something "harder" than twirly Mozart and by-the-numbers Bach. I tried to tell her it was hard to play any piece well, but Mom wouldn't have it. I couldn't afford to lose my job as Ellie's once-a-week piano teacher for $125 an hour, so Ellie got Beethoven and Mom got bragging rights.

I knew after the first measure that Ellie was in over her head. Her left hand was weak and unable to sustain the complex syncopated rhythms. Her right hand was clumsy and overpowered the left, making the piece feel uneven and muddled.

I opened my eyes. I was about to yell for Ellie to stop when I saw her mom watching from the doorway, hands curled into fists like Ellie was a racehorse and we were at the track. To the untrained ear, Ellie was killing it. So I bit my tongue and let my student gallop toward the finish line.

Besides Ellie, I currently had two other students—one girl, one boy. I tried to book them all on the same day and wash my hair accordingly. I had the kind of hair that looked dirty even when it was clean—dark and straight and in desperate need of cutting. But with the boy student prone to cancel and only two students I could count on, I didn't splurge on anything nonessential like a haircut. So I either let it hang or pulled it back into a slick ponytail that shone without the help of hair gel from a jar.

Ellie started speeding up. This midsection was easier, but a reprise of the more complicated opening was ahead. My teacher would have stood up and started clapping his hands like a human metronome to keep me from rushing. But Ellie's mom was enjoying the show, and I didn't want to ruin it for her. If I'd thought Ellie wanted to be great at piano, I might have been tougher on her. But she was not destined for a career in music. Her mind drifted, and while I would never call her on it, it was obvious she barely practiced. She played to please her mom. As, once upon a time, I had, too.

Some people might think it a waste that I studied piano for twenty years but never fulfilled my "destiny" of becoming a concert pianist. But it was never my dream to be on the stage. Like Ellie, my most important audience was the person who made me breakfast, took me to school, tucked me in bed. Mom gave me everything. I gave her music. My schoolmates had club soccer and team barbecues. I had the smile on Mom's face when I played for her. She encouraged me by telling me the piano was my ticket to fame and fortune, not knowing her smile was all the reward I ever needed.

"Brava!" I shouted as my young student banged out the final chord. Her mom was looking at me, so I met her "I told you so" gaze and just nodded like, "You were right."

"How did that feel?" I asked my student.

"I think I messed up a little," Ellie confessed.

"I thought it was really inspired," I offered, not just because Mom was listening. People take up musical instruments for all different reasons; who says being great is more noble than playing for the ones we love?

"I forgot to go to the bank," Ellie's mom said as she walked me to the door. "Can I give you a check just this once?"

"I can swing by tomorrow," I offered. It was embarrassing that I didn't have a checking account. But everything had been in Luke's name. I didn't come to the marriage with any assets beyond my virtuoso piano playing, which, until recently, had seemed like enough.

I thought she would say "Sure, what time?" so I was caught completely off guard by what she said instead.

"Is everything OK with you, Aubrey?"

It wasn't the question that scared me. It was her tone: muted and serious, like a school nurse talking to a child. *Where does it hurt, honey? Do you want me to call your mom?* I wondered what had tipped her off. *Was it my hair?* I hadn't been able to wash it that morning—there were too many people at the Laundromat, and there were rules about these things. *Do I smell?* I'd washed my pits and put on deodorant. *Is it my shirt?* My scoop-neck cotton tee was clean . . . ish . . . but wrinkled, like when you pull it out of the dryer ten minutes too soon, which I had. *Is it the bags under my eyes?* I didn't have a stitch of makeup on, but I rarely wore makeup these days, given that it had all melted when I'd left it in my car, because where else could I have left it?

"Yes. Of course," I lied. "I just don't trust banks." It was a ridiculous thing to say, and I immediately regretted it. I was not prepared for this moment. *Obviously.*

She glanced down at my hands. I was twirling my wedding ring, my new nervous tic. "My sister-in-law is a social worker," she offered. "If you don't feel safe at home . . ."

She didn't finish her sentence. *Why wouldn't I feel safe at home?* I shook my head like I didn't understand.

"How does your husband feel about you teaching piano?" she asked gently. And then I got it. She thought I was a battered wife. I didn't have the heart to tell her I was something even more tragic.

"I don't have a husband," I said. She was still looking at the ring, so I clarified. "Not anymore."

"Oh. So . . . you're divorced, then?"

I shook my head. It took her a second to figure it out. And then she let out a little gasp. "Oh, Aubrey, I'm so sorry," she said, her hand floating over her heart.

I would not let her see me cry. I didn't trust myself to speak, so I held my head high and forced a tight smile.

"Wait here."

She disappeared down the hall. Ellie was staring at me. I made a funny face but she didn't smile. A few seconds later, her mom reappeared with a wad of cash that looked like stripper money—small bills, lots of fives and ones.

"It's our earthquake money," she explained. "Ellie's dad thinks no one will be able to make change." She rolled her eyes a little, then pressed the money into my hand.

"If you need anything . . . ?" She said it like a question.

"Thank you," I said, because how could I tell her what I needed was *everything*?

I didn't talk about what happened to Luke because I didn't want to open myself up to questions like, *"Were you there when it happened?" "Didn't you see it coming?" "Was there nothing you could have done?"* Plus if Ellie's mom knew what I was, that would be the end of our weekly lessons, and I was barely getting by as it was.

"See you next week," she assured me.

And I nodded, grateful to have somewhere to be.

CHAPTER 6

BREE

Ellie's mom gave me three twenties, two tens, four fives, and twenty-five ones. My tank was nearly empty, so I decided to unload some of those singles at the gas station up the street. If the attendant was surprised by the fat wad of one-dollar bills, he didn't show it. I imagine he saw every kind of desperate person through his plexiglass barrier at the highly trafficked Chevron on the corner of coming and going, and I wasn't any more remarkable than anyone else.

I didn't like carrying that much cash around, so I stuck a twenty in my pocket and put the rest in my hiding spot. I kept my money in a ziplock bag in the tire well of my trunk, under the spare. With the addition of today's earnings, I had a little over $800, plus three rolls of quarters for meters and laundry. I know that doesn't seem like a lot, but I had worked hard to save it, and had a plan for how I could use it to save me.

It was dinnertime, and I was hungry, so I drove to my favorite pizza place and had a slice and a Coke. The three-dollar soda was a splurge, but I loved the sensation of sweet bubbles in my mouth after a salty, greasy bite of pizza. One thing about having only $800 to your name: you come to appreciate the simple things.

I lingered at my table as long as I reasonably could, licking my fingers and crunching my ice until the cup was empty. It was getting dark, and that nervous feeling was starting to take hold. I never parked on the same street twice, but I didn't want to waste my five-dollars-per-gallon gas looking for a new neighborhood to call home for the night. Twilight used to be my favorite time of day, with its moody, romantic skies. Sunset was no longer an invitation to wind down, but a call to action. *Time to find a place to sleep.* I sucked back my last bit of ice, tossed my cup in the trash, and headed outside to meet my nightly challenge.

The cicadas were singing rat-a-tat-tat as I walked to my car under the darkening sky. Unlike birds and mammals, who make music with their mouths, a cicada's whole body is his instrument. Quick contractions of its tymbal muscle rattle the circular membranes on its back, shaking them like tiny maracas. There's a percussive instrument called the timpani (also from the Latin *tympanum*) that makes a similar sound, but of course, unlike the insect, the timpani cannot play itself.

"Rat-a-tat-tat back to you," I whispered to my cicada friends as I slid behind the wheel of my aging Prius. Luke bought me the powder-blue hybrid right after we got married so I could learn how to drive in the big city. He said we could trade it in for a new one once I got comfortable in LA traffic, but I never saw the need. The steering wheel was flaking, and the undercarriage rattled when I went over bumps, but it still got me from A to B, and for that I was grateful. It probably needed an oil change, but I was afraid if I took it in, they would find a bunch of other stuff that needed fixing, and then what would I do? Every dollar I made was accounted for. I put seventy-two dollars aside every month for my cell phone. I told myself my students needed a way to reach me, but more than that, scrolling kept me from spending too much time with my thoughts. I allotted fifty dollars per week to eat at restaurants, mostly so I could enjoy the air-conditioning. I put another fifty into my ziplock piggy bank, because if I was going to get off the streets, I needed money for an apartment. The rest I spent on gas, toothpaste, soap, and bean burritos from 7-Eleven. I used to be a coffee snob, but I never went out for coffee now. And there was no wine with dinner. I tried not to think about all the food I'd wasted in my pre-vagrant life—apples allowed to turn brown, milk gone sour, the rest of last night's shrimp scampi left to rot in the fridge. *What I would give for last night's shrimp scampi now.* If I ordered food, I finished it, because my car smelled bad enough without yesterday's tuna sandwich stinking it up, and I couldn't bear to let anything go to waste.

More than food, I missed my bed. I missed the smell of fabric softener, the feel of cotton sheets against my cheek, the whipped-cream softness of my goose-down comforter. But most of all, I missed my bed-mate—the warmth that radiated off his body, his feet hooking around mine, his hands reaching for me in the dark. I missed feeling wanted. I missed feeling loved.

Being a musical prodigy is supposed to be a gift: a ticket to fame and fortune. But being born with a gift comes with the obligation to use it. If I didn't have this "gift," I might have had friends, and I sure could have used a few friends. But recipients of "God-given talent" aren't allowed to have friends—only admirers, who stop admiring you when you fail to put your talent to good use. Family loves you uncon-ditionally, but it was just my mom and me, until Mom's cancer took her and it was just me. Mom left me just enough to give her a proper burial and buy a plane ticket to New York. And with no friends to talk me out of it, I went.

I was eighteen when I left British Columbia for the Big Apple on a full scholarship to Juilliard. People dream of careers in music because they think musicians are the life of the party. But there are no parties for conservatory students; we're in classes or practicing from the moment we get up until the moment we go to bed. Woodwinds, strings, and brasses have opportunities to mingle in chamber groups, band, and orchestra. But playing the piano is not like playing the violin—there are no string quartets to join or standmates to befriend. In a cruel twist of irony, the only way to escape the loneliness of your soundproof cubicle is to crawl deeper into the music, where there is no space or time or pain, only sound that you can ride like a rocket through the ocean. You are at peace only when you are the music and the music is you. People envy you for your superpower as you envy them for their ordinariness. You don't want to be a phenom anymore. You just want to be a friend.

I turned on the car and started driving west, toward Beverly Hills. I told myself I was going to find a quiet street to bed down for the evening, but I could have done that here in Larchmont Village. I don't know what I was looking for beyond a good night's sleep . . . *A sign? A miracle?* Luke had always been the man with the plan, solving my problems before I even knew they existed. I never had to worry about mundane things like utility bills (gas, electric, water, internet) or home repairs (unclogging the sink, changing that light bulb way up high) because he took care of all that. I had my teeth cleaned before my gums started hurting. I had health insurance before I knew it costs money to see a doctor in America, and a doctor before I got sick. Luke knew my life had been hard and wanted to erase all struggle. But the problem with letting yourself be saved is that you forget how to save yourself.

I hadn't always been so helpless. I wasn't looking to play in a band when I arrived at Juilliard with only a tattered suitcase and a pocket full of toonies, but when I saw the craigslist ad for a "cute female keyboard player," I jumped on it. They paid me fifty bucks a gig, all cash, and we had shows almost every weekend. The chord progressions of pop music are pretty simplistic, and I could play their ragged covers of Elton John and Journey with one hand tied behind my back. I couldn't have found an easier, more enjoyable job if I'd tried.

Like all keyboard players, I was off to the side of the stage. I thought no one noticed me there, tucked between the bass player and the drummer. But one cold January night someone did, and one month before graduation, as soon as I'd passed my exams, I headed west to marry him.

And why not? Life in New York was brutal—noisy and dirty and crowded, *so crowded!* You can't walk anywhere without someone touching you—bumping shoulders on the sidewalk, dodging elbows on the subway. Life in LA with Luke meant warmth, space, sunshine, and love. What did I need with a grueling career when I had him? Being a professional concert pianist requires constant travel. Luke and I were eager to start a family, and we couldn't do that if I was away all the time. We figured once I got my green card, I could get a teaching job at a conservatory, or maybe even start my own school. Yes, it's an honor to play for well-heeled audiences who marvel at your technique. But being on the road is no life for a new wife. So with no friends to impress or parents to disappoint, I let myself enjoy my new man and my new life.

I had no idea the enjoyment would be short lived. Nobody tells you when you're twenty-two that you should have things like life insurance, a bank account in your name, an equity line of credit in case of emergencies. I thought I'd already had my share of bad things, but maybe I'm a magnet for them. Because more bad things were coming. I was literally driving straight toward them.

I parked and made my way toward the house like a homing pigeon returning to the nest. The river rock was right where I'd left it, which meant no one had walked through the gate all day. Not an invitation to come on in, exactly, but it sure made things easy.

It was dark this second time I entered the backyard. I don't know what I would have done if lights came on, but none did, not even when I stepped onto the pool house patio. It was cooler tonight, but the oversize towel I snatched from the cabana was just enough to block out the chill.

Once again, I fell asleep as soon as my head hit the pillow. I wasn't proud to be squatting in someone else's yard, but I told myself it was no big deal. Yes, I was trespassing, but I wasn't hurting anyone. That would come later, and it would hardly be my fault. I didn't really believe death followed me wherever I went.

Until someone wound up dead.

CHAPTER 7

SOPHIE

Unlike most Gen Z women, who live their lives on social media—showing off their fab new hairstyle, found puppy, how their butt looks in their jeans—my life was as buttoned up as a bank vault. Being discreet was a point of personal pride. I wanted to be someone you could trust. If I knew what you did last summer, I kept it to myself. Because everyone knows if I tell you someone else's secret, you can't trust me with yours. And I wanted you to tell me yours.

I was a cheerleader in high school; I knew what everyone was up to—the players, the coaches, the coaches' wives, the coaches' girlfriends . . . or boyfriends. I never spilled. Secrets are a currency. Their value is not just in knowing them—it's people *knowing* that you know them. I never threatened to tell Coach Zolak's wife that he was sleeping with my statistics teacher; it was enough that he *knew* that I knew. I think I could have gotten an A in that class either way—I'm pretty good at math—but it was a nice insurance policy. Plus I had nothing to gain by blowing up his life, and my stats teacher was in a better mood after those after-school meetups in the teachers' lounge.

So yeah, I knew how my dad had come to own a house on fancy-schmancy Rodeo Drive, and why it was filled with someone else's stuff, but I had no intention of telling anybody. I know keeping my brother in the dark when he was already feeling left out seems cruel, but it was for his own good. And, if I'm being honest, for my own good, too.

I used to love our family dinners. But it was getting harder and harder to face questions about what I was "actively" doing to find a job. I knew my family thought there was something wrong with me that, a year and a half out of college, I was still slumming in my childhood room. But I didn't want any old job; I was holding out for *the* job. And I was "actively" working to get it. I just couldn't tell anybody. So I let the world think I was a slacker, then played the part to perfection.

Rome wasn't built in a day, and jobs like the one I was chasing wouldn't land in my lap. I knew it would take time, but that didn't mean I wasn't restless. I hadn't seen my friends in ages, and I was lonely. So I waited until Mom and Dad were in bed, then knocked on my brother's bedroom door.

"Can you talk?" I asked, poking my head in.

"What about?"

"The Halloween party!"

I could tell from his eye roll that he'd hoped I was kidding when I floated the idea during our Sunday dinner cleanup a few hours ago. I hadn't pushed because I didn't want him to say no. Not that I needed his permission or his help. Jared knew his way around the house, and I knew how to throw a party. But it would be selfish not to include my brother. The poor guy worked his butt off—nobody deserved a party more than he did.

The timing was perfect. Mom and Dad would be out of town, it wasn't crazy cold yet, so we could do the whole thing outside. It was the perfect venue for a party. We could set up the bar in the pool house and people could bring lawn chairs and blankets, Frisbees and Hula-Hoops. I didn't think anyone would want to swim, but if we made a mess of the pool, Jared would help me clean it up. He was taking care of it after all, and he'd obviously be invited.

Carter sat up in bed and waved me in. I could tell he was nervous about it, but he was nervous about a lot of things. While I'd been a cheerleader, he was a band nerd, so not exactly one of the cool kids. Poor guy played the clarinet. There was an action shot of him in the yearbook, busting out the melody of "Smooth Criminal" at homecoming, cheeks puffed up like Alvin the chipmunk. I knew the girls on the yearbook committee were mean, but that was beyond. To make matters worse, he had tragically bad acne. The scars weren't visible anymore, but I knew they were still there.

"I think we should do it on Friday night, when they're on the plane," I said. Mom and Dad were taking a red-eye. I knew that because they'd asked me to take them to the airport. "That way if a neighbor calls about the noise, they won't be able to reach them."

"How long have you known about this house?" Carter asked.

I didn't know what that had to do with having a party. "What difference does it make?"

"I'm just curious," he said, and I could hear the defensiveness in his voice. "Dad never told me we bought a house on Rodeo Drive."

I didn't want to stir up any father-son drama, so I just shrugged. "Jared told me about it," I said, not only because it was credible but also because I wanted to squash any jealous thoughts like, *Why did Dad tell her but not me?* My brother was prone to jealousy, especially when it came to Dad. He was a sensitive kid who often disappeared in books or anime or his clarinet. I, on the other hand, was obsessed with all activities that required a ball—football, baseball, basketball, tennis—just like our dad. I had (OK, *still* have) a poster of Cody Bellinger on my wall (*That hair, I could die!*). I cheered all four years in high school and in college. Not competitive cheerleading, the real kind, on sports fields with players and pom-poms. Dad and I had an easy rapport. Sports was our common language. Before joining the company, Carter never had much of a relationship with our dad, and it was obvious he still felt like he was playing catch-up.

"You don't think it's weird that he would buy this super expensive house and not tell me about it?" my brother asked. Of course it was weird. But I was good at secrets, remember?

"Who cares?" I said, evading the question. "The house is ours—let's use it!" I didn't mean to exploit his anger, but throwing a party in the house Dad neglected to tell him about would be the ultimate "screw you," and he was clearly upset. I just wanted to have a party. I missed my friends. Nobody tells you when you graduate college that getting the gang back together is like extracting troops from a war zone—*"Sorry, I work weekends now"; "I can't, I have an early morning"; "I'd love to, but we're fasting / have yoga / can't leave the dog."* But a Halloween party at a mansion in Beverly Hills? Now that's something that would make your former cheer cocaptain call a dog sitter.

"You're sure there's nobody living there?" *Ha! I got him!*

"We can go by there if you want, make double sure."

"When?"

There was only one weekend left in October. If I was going to have a Halloween party, I had to start planning.

"Let's go now."

CHAPTER 8

SOPHIE

We entered the house through the garage. Jared hadn't told me there were cars in there, but I wasn't surprised, given what I knew about the place.

"Nice wheels," I said, running my finger along the hood of a sporty-chic Porsche convertible.

"Don't get any ideas," my brother warned.

I stuck my tongue out at him, then reached for the knob on the door to the house.

"Wait!" Carter called to me. "Maybe we should knock."

"Why?"

"In case Jared's wrong." Jared wasn't wrong, but I couldn't tell him how I knew that.

"What's the worst that could happen?"

"I don't know," my brother said, "someone greets us with a shotgun and blows our brains out?"

"This is Beverly Hills," I said. "Only gold-plated revolvers here." Then, before he could stop me, I turned the knob and pushed on the door. It swung open into darkness. An alarm beeped, but Carter pushed past me and entered the code on the keypad and the beeping stopped.

"Nice job, bro," I said, clapping like a posh operagoer.

I groped the wall for a switch. "I can't find the light." Carter took out his phone and lit up the wall in front of me.

"There," he said, pointing to a dimmer switch. I stuck out a finger and eased it all the way up.

"Whoooo-eeee!" I catcalled as overhead track lights warmed to life and the grand cook's kitchen lit up like a stage. "Look at that fridge!"

"Which one?"

Turned out there were two refrigerators in the *Architectural Digest*–worthy wood-and-steel kitchen—a slim beverage cooler with a glass door, and a double-wide stainless Sub-Zero. Light pooled on the onyx countertops, and the ceilings were so high there was headroom for a giraffe. I'd imagined doing the whole party outside, but that was before I'd seen the inside.

"This place is dope," I said, plopping down on a leather stool at the island big enough for a whole family. I glanced at my brother. He looked uneasy. "Will you please stop worrying?"

"If no one lives here," he whispered, "why is there food?" I knew the answer, but I didn't want to make him worry more.

"They must have known we were coming," I joked, doing a quick inventory of the groceries that had been left behind: clear canisters of dried beans, coffee, sugar, a box of elbow macaroni, a jar of mixed nuts.

My brother was shaking his head like he wanted to get out of there, so I tried to reassure him. "It was probably staged to look inviting; real estate agents like to do that."

He looked down. I followed his gaze to where a bowl of uneaten cat food was sitting on the floor.

"Looks like someone had a cat," I offered.

"Real estate agents don't put out food for the cat."

"Will you please stop worrying," I said. "It's *our* house. We own it. We have every right to be here. And have a party!"

I stepped over the cat bowl and peered out the floor-to-ceiling windows overlooking the backyard. It was dark except for a sliver of moonlight bouncing off the pool. That's when I saw it. A blur of movement, just in front of the pool house. At first I thought I'd imagined it. But then I noticed something on the ground. Something that couldn't have gotten there by itself.

"What are you looking at?" my brother asked. I didn't want to freak him out, but I confess I was a little freaked out myself.

"I think I just saw the cat," I joked.

"What?"

"Just kidding," I said, taking a breath to steady my nerves. "Let's check out the backyard!" I wasn't a head-in-the-sand kind of girl. If there was something out there, I wanted to find out before it crashed my party.

"Fine."

My brother reached up and flipped a small brass lever. Turns out that floor-to-ceiling "window" was a sliding door to the outside—the fancy kind that disappears into the wall. I remembered they call that a pocket door, because it fits in the wall like a phone in your pocket.

The heavy door slid smoothly on the track, and I stepped out into the cool night air. As I was thinking about heat lamps (*Where does one rent heat lamps?*), Carter saw what I had seen and pointed to it.

"What's that?"

There was a switch on the wall behind me, so I flipped it. Cool blue light flooded the yard as futuristic-looking underwater orbs lit up the pool, illuminating the pool house and the object we both had seen.

"It's just a towel," I said, then walked over to pick it up. The striped bath sheet was strangely . . . warm. *But how could that be?*

"What the hell, Sophie?"

"There's a whole stack of them right there," I said, pointing to a tower of towels just inside the pool house. There was no door, and the heavy drapes were pinned back, so the towel didn't have to pass through walls or anything. But I concede, it was a bit of a mystery how something so voluminous could have migrated all the way to the other side of the double-wide chaise. I didn't want my brother to change his mind about the party, so I did my best to downplay my befuddlement.

"An animal probably dragged it off the pile," I said. "Those Beverly Hills squirrels can be quite industrious. I once saw one steal a whole bread basket off the patio at Spago." OK, that last part was a bit of an exaggeration. The squirrel swiped a piece of bread, not the whole basket. But he was a burly little sucker—I wouldn't have put it past him.

"Why is there furniture and food here if the house is vacant?" my brother said. "And cars in the garage."

"You want to search the place?" I asked, not sure what I wanted the answer to be.

"I mean, if we're going to have a party here . . ." It was still an "if." So I had no choice.

"Fine," I said. "Let's go squirrel hunting." Knowing full well if we found something, it wouldn't be a squirrel.

CHAPTER 9

———

BREE

The outdoor shower was on the side of the pool house, between the north wall and the property line. It had a door, but there was no point closing it. There was a solid foot of empty space between the stall wall and the ground—just like the toilets at the mall, so you could look for feet before you pushed on the door. Plus hinges squeak, and latches make noise, and if I was going to be a sitting duck, I wanted to be a quiet one.

I'd woken up when the kitchen light went on. I knew it was the kitchen because when I sat up, I saw the gleaming stainless appliances through the floor-to-ceiling glass door. I slept with one eye open now, as people who are living on the edge do. If I had known the late-night snackers were coming outside, I would have retreated to the alley, but it was too late now. They were already in the yard.

"What's that?" I heard a male voice ask. He sounded far away . . . *at the threshold of the house maybe?* My heart was beating presto, keeping time with my panicked, shallow breathing. This was my first trespass, but not my first crime. If they decided to press charges, things could get really bad for me.

"It's just a towel," a woman said. In my scramble to flee the scene, I'd kicked off the towel and left it balled up on the ground. It never occurred to me they would come outside, but I was new to squatting—anticipating what a homeowner might do was not my forte.

I heard the sound of hard-soled shoes on concrete, click-clacking toward the pool house. *Please don't come back here, please don't come back here . . .* I held my breath and stayed still as stone.

"What the hell, Sophie?" the male voice said.

"There's a whole stack of them right there," the woman said. If she was on the pool house patio, all she had to do was peek around the side of the house and she would see my shoes. The shower was small. I was pressed all the way back against the cold tile wall, but my feet were as visible as a wart at the end of your nose.

"You want to search the place?" the woman asked, and I felt my heart rise up into my throat. I tried to think what would happen if they found me. *What would I do if I found me? Scream? Call 9-1-1? Attack me with the pool skimmer?*

I was about to make a run for it when I heard the sound of sandals clip-clopping toward me. My skin tingled with fear. I flashed back to the day I arrived in New York—clutching my suitcase in the back of the cab, not knowing if the funny-looking bills in my pocket would be enough to pay for the ride and what I would do if they weren't. I had gotten through dicey situations before, I told myself. I would get through this, too. As I held my breath and prayed for a miracle, ten manicured toes appeared five feet from where I was standing. *If I could see hers, she could see mine . . .*

"Let's go squirrel hunting," she said, and those toes gripped smooth leather insoles as their corresponding feet rounded the shower stall. And then they stopped, right in front of the open door, and I found myself face-to-face with a woman who looked like a Kardashian sister—the young, pretty one with perfect eyebrows and lips that protruded from her face like a cartoon fish.

Terror seized me by the throat. "It's not what it looks liiii—" I started, but she stopped me with a finger to her Instagram-perfect pucker. If she was alarmed to find a stringy-haired homeless person hiding in her shower, she didn't act like it.

"No squirrels by the pool house," she called out, then winked at me. She mouthed the words "Stay here," then made a stop sign with her hand like you would to a dog. I was too stunned to speak, but when she nodded, for some reason I nodded back.

"Five minutes," she mouthed, then held up five fingers, and I didn't know if that meant she was leaving in five minutes or coming back in five minutes. She gave me a thumbs-up, so I mirrored the gesture, even though I had no idea if I'd just agreed to leave or wait.

She turned her back to me, then disappeared around the side of the pool house. "I'll ask Jared about the towel," I heard her say to the man. "He probably went for a swim and forgot to put it back."

"Does he do that?" the man asked.

"What, forget to put things back?" the woman said. "All men do that!"

"No, I meant does he go swimming in the pools he cleans?"

"Only the ones where there's no one living in the house," the woman said. "Like here." She said the "like here" part a little too loud. And I couldn't help but think it was for my benefit. But why would she want me to know that no one lived here?

"Still doesn't explain the cat food," the man said. And I felt a pang of sadness. Luke and I had a cat. We called him our love child because when we got him, we weren't ready for human children. His name was Wolfgang Amadeus Mozart—Wolfy, for short. Our rented bungalow didn't allow pets, but Luke said people who didn't like pets were psychopaths, and if they kicked us out because of Wolfy, then we were better off somewhere else. "We'll be moving soon anyway," he'd said. "To a house, where we can have as many pets as we want." I knew my husband had big dreams, and I believed him when he said we would someday have a house. But I still lived in fear that the landlord would find out about Wolfy, even though there were other things I should have feared more.

"We can come back when it's light out," the Kardashian twin said, as the sound of her sandals faded to a faint clicking sound. *Was that for my benefit, too? To make me believe they were leaving?* I heard the sliding door clunk shut. And then, silence.

I had no idea why that woman asked me to stay, but I didn't wait to find out. I was trespassing; for all I knew she was going inside to call the police and wanted me to stay put so they could catch me red handed. As soon as I was sure they were inside, I slipped out into the alley and ran back to my car, not knowing that woman had already blown up my life, just as I was about to blow up hers.

CHAPTER 10

—

BREE

I woke up to a dull ache in my neck and a parking ticket on my wind-shield: eighty-five dollars, for parking on a street that was "by permit only." I could only turn my head in one direction, but the ticket hurt a whole lot more. Finding free overnight parking is a major pain. Good neighborhoods have restrictions and cameras and neighborhood watch-ers that record and report any vehicles they think don't belong there . . . like an aging Prius with bald tires and a dented passenger-side door. And bad neighborhoods have worse problems, especially if what you're seeking is a good night's sleep.

If I weren't so panicked about the eighty-five dollars, I might have been mortified that the meter maid had seen me conked out on my back seat under a blanket as tattered as the life huddled beneath it. But all I could think about was the money. Eighty-five dollars was a night in a motel. It was new sneakers. It was a week's worth of lunches at Subway, a haircut with a blow-dry. I didn't indulge in those things because I was trying to save money to rebuild my life. I didn't have the credit history for my own apartment, but if I kept putting money away every week, a roommate situation would soon be within reach. With a home address and a place to reliably sleep and shower, I could start applying for jobs at music schools that could sponsor my work visa. That eighty-five-dollar hit was a huge setback to someone counting every penny.

Luke used to tell me not to sweat life's little mishaps, like a flat tire or a toothache. *"In the construction business we call them 'contingencies,'"* he'd said. *"And we budget for them."* He'd tried to teach me how to read a spreadsheet, but I never had much aptitude for math, except when it came to calculating how many quarters I needed for the laundry machine—that I learned right away. *"If you set money aside every month for loss and damages, they won't hurt so much when they happen,"* he'd said. He never mentioned what to do if the whole thing blew up in your face. Turns out there's no contingency for losing everything.

I considered ripping up the ticket, but I knew if I didn't pay it, they would just tack on more fines. And if you don't pay those, they take the car, which—until I got that apartment—was also my bed, my bank, my dressing room, and the only place on earth where I could be alone. I tucked the ticket in my visor, then dug out a clean shirt and what was left of my shampoo and headed for the mall for a desperately needed hair washing. It was only ten thirty; it wouldn't be crowded yet, and I could clean up in relative peace. If I was lucky, some of the food kiosks would be sampling their offerings and I could score some teriyaki chicken and a few Wetzel's bites—not the healthiest lunch, but I could be choosy when I got back on my feet.

The Westfield Mall had underground parking, but I found underground garages disorienting—I preferred to park outside by the loading dock. There were always spots there, and unfortunately today was the day I was going to find out why.

I walked through the food court to find the bathroom gloriously empty. The sink in the handicapped stall was low, but the water was warm, and my hair squeaked when I rinsed it clean. I didn't bother with conditioner—it made my fine hair too greasy. But I took my time with the blow-dry, tipping the dryer nozzle up and letting the warm air toast my scalp like a dinner roll.

I made a makeshift lunch out of samples of vegan (not) chicken, pita triangles smeared with red pepper hummus, and Dixie cups of kombucha, then wandered the mall. I didn't care much about the clothes; they all looked the same to me—stovepipe denim bottoms, slouchy sweaters, black boots with buckles. The people walking through the mall all looked the same, too, even though it was obvious by how they winged their eyeliner that they wanted to be noticed. I wasn't a fashionista or anything—I mostly just wore leggings and T-shirts. I'm just saying that if you're going to dedicate a whole city block to selling clothes, you should offer some variety.

I weaved through kiosks hocking phones and sunglasses and hair extensions, marveling at the idea of wearing someone else's hair—*what a trip!* If I could have gotten that eighty-five dollars back, I might have gone into Foot Locker; I was desperate for new sneakers. But instead I averted my eyes away from the rows of colorful swooshes so I wouldn't feel tempted. And then I arrived at Nordstrom. Which was where I was headed all along. Not to wind through the maze of purses, perfume, and cosmetics—those things held no allure for me. No, I was there for what was at the top of the escalator, between the designer jeans (which looked like everybody else's jeans) and the in-store café.

There was never anybody sitting at the majestic Kawai grand piano on the second-floor landing, and I couldn't help but wonder how long it had been since someone had played it. Pianos don't like just sitting. As beautiful as they are with their graceful curves and shiny pedals, they are not made to be looked at. A piano sitting unplayed is like a sandwich sitting uneaten. Left alone too long, it will dry up or become the snack of pesky vermin. It made me want to scream to see a six-foot-two conservatory grand grow stiff and stale like that. It deserved a better fate than being prostituted as a space filler; it deserved to be played.

The lid was all the way up on the long prop because the second-floor landing was big and barren, and if you're using a musical instrument as an art piece, you want to display it in its most visually impressive state. But keeping the lid open like that was terrible for it. The prop is not meant to be up all the time—that lid is heavy, and the wooden leg could warp or even fail. And without the lid to protect them, the strings are exposed to dust particles that burrow their way under the hammers and hamper the action of the keyboard. The ebony wood gleamed like the surface of a frozen lake, and I cringed when I imagined what sorts of chemicals they sprayed on it to make it shine like that. If that piano could talk, it would be crying right now. Which of course it could. It just needed a little coaxing from someone like me.

I circled the magnificent creature like it was an animal at the zoo. "I'm so sorry," I whispered. "I wish I could save you." The keyboard cover was open, and the sight of eighty-eight ebonies and ivories standing at attention made my fingers twitch. My fingers played on their own sometimes, when I listened to the radio or hummed in my head, my right hand twirling out the melody, my left hand pounding out the counterpoint. I closed my eyes and let the magnificent opening chords of the Grieg piano concerto echo through my body as my hands pantomimed the progression. *Bum, bum-bum-bum, bum-bum-bum, bum-bum-bum—*

"Hey!" a shrill voice said, snapping me out of my trance. "You can't sit there." I popped off the bench with an embarrassed nod. I didn't remember sitting down, but I guess I had, and someone who couldn't care less about that poor shackled beast apparently didn't approve.

"Sorry," I mumbled to the woman in the navy pantsuit, then cast my eyes downward toward her shiny black sling backs.

"It's not a plaything," she admonished, like I was a stupid kid, when in fact she was the stupid one, because that's exactly what it was. A plaything. As in something that should be played.

I backed away from her, then turned and fled down the escalator. I didn't feel like hanging out at the mall anymore, so I made for the exit. I figured I would go pay that parking ticket. If I didn't pay it, I might lose it—there was no point putting it off.

At first I was confused when I saw the window glass on the ground by the dumpster where I thought I'd parked my car. *There was no glass on the ground where I parked. Am I at the wrong dumpster?*

But as I looked around and saw that no, there were no other dumpsters, I realized not only was that glass freshly scattered, but the car with the window missing was mine.

"No, no, no . . . ," I wailed as I pulled on the driver's-side door handle, setting off the *whoop-whoop!* of my car alarm. The window was broken, but the car was still locked and armed. *What a stupid security system!*

"Shut up!" I hissed, hitting the unlock button on my remote. I peered into the back seat, which was a jumble of recently ransacked clothes and shoes. The floor of the trunk was propped open. Which meant whoever had broken into my car had opened the tire well.

"Oh God, no."

I ran around the car, popped open the trunk, and pulled up the cover.

The donut spare was still there, but the money was gone. Every last cent. I looked up to see my parking ticket on the visor, flapping in the breeze that was blowing in through the hole where the window should be. The image blurred as my eyes filled with tears. I thought of Ellie's mom; what had she said? *"If you need anything?"* And I almost laughed. I needed everything: food, shelter, a job, a life. But I couldn't ask for help. Because asking for help meant answering the question on the tip of everyone's tongue: *"What happened to your husband?"* Which I couldn't tell them . . . because the most awful thing about it was that it was all my fault.

CHAPTER 11

———

Bree

I spent my last twelve dollars on duct tape and a candy bar—a SNICKERS, because it fills you up, and I knew I wouldn't get a proper meal until after my next payday. The orange apron guy at Home Depot must have felt sorry for me when I asked him what he would use to stand in for a car window, because he gave me a remnant of clear plastic sheeting for free. "It sells by the roll," he explained, "but I have a little piece left over that you can have." I didn't like to accept handouts, but he insisted he was going to throw it away, plus that duct tape was ten dollars, so what choice did I have?

I taped up the window the best I could, then sat on my back bumper to try to drum up some work. Hello, I texted the mom of my boy student. It's Aubrey, just wanted to check in to see if David might like a lesson this week? Cindy, my other student, was scheduled for Wednesday—just two days away!—so I confirmed that with a little prayer. (Please don't cancel, please don't cancel.) Cindy's mom texted back almost immediately (yes, confirmed!), and my chest flooded with relief. It was almost six o'clock, which meant I only had to get through two nights and one full day until my next payday. I'd gone longer than thirty-six hours without a meal plenty of times, plus I knew how to get free coffee at the Toyota dealership—they always had some out, sometimes popcorn and apples, too. And with my broken window I was credible as someone in the market for a new car.

I took some time to reorganize my clothes, rolling the dirty T-shirts and leggings into tight spirals and folding the clean ones into squares and laying them flat. I stuffed my toiletries into my backpack—shampoo, bodywash, razor, toothbrush, toothpaste, dental floss, tampons—grateful they hadn't been stolen because of how much it would have cost to replace all those things. It was getting dark. I needed to find a place to sleep. And now that I was one window short of a full complement, my car was not an option.

People might think that twenty years of pounding on a piano would have deadened my hearing, but the opposite was true. Ears trained to discern the difference between finger staccato, wrist staccato, close-to-the-keys staccato, and whole-arm staccato can hear a pin drop in the ocean. The sounds of the city were like an orchestra playing five symphonies at once. I heard the rumble of tires on pavement, the whine of hydraulic brakes, the chug of a distant commuter train, the songs of birds, dogs, crickets, people, planes, police sirens, trucks backing up. And of course, thanks to the nice man at Home Depot, the crunching of my plastic window when the wind blew. There was no way I was sleeping in my car. Not tonight. Not anymore.

I waited until the neighbors' lights were out, then parked in the shadow of an elm tree and hoped my car would make it through the night undisturbed. It would only take one swift stroke of a butter knife for a thief to separate me from everything I owned, but there was nothing of value left in there. Plus I was cold and tired. So I took the chance.

Like the last two nights, I snuck into the yard with only the clothes on my back. It was cool, so I dressed warmly, in a long-sleeved Henley and fake-down puffer. I knew it was possible that couple would come back, but it was also possible they wouldn't. They weren't living there; the woman had announced it loud and clear. I had no idea why she'd done that; she had no way of knowing what this house meant to me. But I believed her pronouncement, mostly because I wanted to.

I tiptoed around the pool house like a predator in a spy novel, letting my trained ears lead the way. The house was dark, but I still dropped to hands and knees to crawl across the patio. The lounge chair was in the head-down position, just as I'd left it when I'd scurried off.

At first I thought the rectangular mass at the foot of the chaise was the towel—that the Kardashian look-alike had folded it and left it there. But as I approached, I saw it was too big to be a towel. Also it had handles, with a thick black ribbon tied around them in a droopy bow. It was a shopping bag. There was something written on it in loopy cursive letters. I couldn't read it in the dark, so I took out my phone and clicked on the flashlight. "To my shower buddy," it read. And I got a chill down my spine.

I turned off the phone light and stood completely still. My first instinct was to run, and maybe I would have, if I'd had somewhere to go. If this was a trap, I'd walked right into it. But why would anyone set a trap for me? I had nothing to give, and while I'd done bad things, I'd already paid the price for my crimes.

I peered up at the house, which was quiet and dark. I gazed into the pool house—also quiet and dark. I closed my eyes to invoke my superpower but heard nothing but the hoot of an owl and the hum of a neighbor's compressor. All indications were that I was alone. But I couldn't shake the eerie feeling that someone was watching me—the unfortunate imagining of a perpetually guilty conscience.

I eased my butt onto the chaise and peeked in the bag. Whoever had packed it did so with great care. There were maybe a dozen items, all wrapped in crisp white paper. I dipped my hand in and pulled out an eight-inch flat rectangle: a bar of chocolate. Not a cheap one from the drugstore—a fancy one, with a name I couldn't pronounce. There was a sachet of macadamia nuts, a bag of granola, a small sack of tangerines. There was a bottle of wine, a corkscrew, a block of cheese, a box of water crackers, a small knife, a stemless wineglass. Then, under all that, to quash any doubt that this windfall was meant for me, was a handwritten note, folded in half, with "Pool House Friend" written on the back in those same loopy cursive letters.

I unfolded the note. I had to use my phone light to read it. "Things will get better," it said. "Please accept these gifts to help get you through. The costume is for Friday night. The party starts at ten. I hope you will come, there will be lots of food and nice people. No big bad wolf, I promise!"

I peered back into the bag. There was a bundle of what looked like clothes swathed in tissue paper. I unwrapped them to see a white peasant blouse, a strappy black corset, and a red velvet hooded cape. If not for the big bad wolf reference, I might not have known it was a Little Red Riding Hood costume, and that it was meant for me.

Under any other circumstances I might have seen this as a gesture of friendship. But I knew better than to think anyone would want to be my friend. *So what is this all about?* I thought about the prospect of going to a party, with people, music, food, and beer. *How long has it been since I've had a beer?*

If I were thinking straight, I would have taken that food and gotten the hell out of there. But I had already uncorked that wine and slugged back half a glass. I tore open the cheese and cut off a two-inch hunk. Then I sat under the stars and imagined what kind of shoes Little Red Riding Hood might wear to a party.

CHAPTER 12

————

SOPHIE

"The water is freezing!" I said as I dipped my foot into the pool. My party was in two days, so I asked Jared to meet me at the house to get his opinion on how to set everything up.

"Yeah, it's October," Jared said as he grabbed the pool skimmer to sweep some fallen leaves off the surface.

"Thank you, Captain Obvious," I snarked. "Can we warm it up?"

"Sure, but it will cost you guys five hundred bucks."

"What!?" *Five hundred bucks to heat the pool? Is he kidding?*

"It's twelve dollars per hour to run the heater," he said. "If you want it warm by Friday, I have to crank it all the way up and keep it running for the next forty-eight hours." I did the math in my head. He was right. Heating the pool would cost almost six hundred bucks. That amount would not go unnoticed by my dad, who was the one who would get the bill. Not that he had the right to go accusing anyone of anything. But I didn't want to get my brother in trouble—their relationship was fragile enough.

I slunk down on the pool chaise. I had no way of knowing if our squatter had gotten the bag of goodies I'd left for her, but the odds were good, given that it was gone and no one else had been back here except for a few squirrels. I imagine it startled her to see a care package on her bed, but I wanted her to know the owners were friendly. Plus I needed her to know we were having a party on Friday, in case she was planning to crash here that night . . . and what better way to tell her than to invite her!

All but two of the twenty-three friends I'd invited RSVP'd "yes." At least half of them would be bringing a plus-one. Some might even sneak in a plus-two. I calculated there'd be about forty people total, including Jared, Carter, me, and Ms. Shower Squatter, if she showed.

"It's not that cold," Jared said, dipping his foot in the water.

"I dare you to jump in," I said.

"I will if you will." He peeled off his shirt. The man was all muscles and sex appeal, and I knew the first time our eyes met that I would wind up in bed with him. Our flirtation started months ago, not long after I moved back home, but there weren't any opportunities to consummate it at my parents' house with my brother always lurking, and Jared lived in Santa Clarita with a roommate, and I wanted no part of that. But once Jared got this gig, our problem was solved.

"I'm not wearing a bathing suit," I said.

"Me neither." He slipped his thumbs under the waistband of his shorts and slid them down. A moment later his naked body disappeared under the water with a splash. I felt a tingle of excitement as I watched his rock-hard physique glide across the bottom of the pool. He popped his head up and shook the water from his hair, then flashed that dimpled Harry Styles smile that he knew I couldn't resist.

"You're crazy," I said.

"Crazy for you."

He swiped at my feet and I let out a little scream as I hopped back out of his reach. A second later he popped out of the water and reached for my waist with sopping-wet arms.

"Don't!" I laugh shouted as his fingers found the small of my back and he pulled me into his chest. "You're getting me all wet!" And of course he went for the cheesy retort.

"That was the plan."

He slipped his hands up the back of my dress, and I felt my cheeks blush red hot. We left a trail of my clothes on the patio—sundress, bra, sandals, panties—as we groped and kissed our way into the pool house. We used to close the curtains, but we didn't bother anymore. There was no one here to see us. At least that's what we always presumed.

I hadn't told Jared about our squatter. I liked our biweekly pool sex—there was no reason to spook him. Plus I had no idea how long she'd been coming here or if she was coming back. All I knew was that she must've been desperate, and that you should be kind to desperate people, because you might be one yourself someday.

We bumped up against the table, then tumbled onto the couch— not a couch really, more like a booth with cushions, like you'd find on a boat. There was storage underneath—I'd peeked in there once. It was empty except for a couple of blankets and extra towels, which I'd clocked because I thought Jared and I might need them once the weather turned. Assuming he didn't do or say anything to mess up our arrangement, which was always a looming possibility.

He looked down at me as we moved together on the not-couch. "Sophie . . . I love . . ." *Please don't say it, please don't say it.* ". . . being with you." I was into Jared, and we had fun together, but I didn't want him to fall in love with me. My life was complicated enough without a boyfriend who I would have to lie to about what I was doing (and not doing) with my life. I trusted Jared, but I couldn't tell anyone what I was up to. And it's impossible to get close to someone when there's a giant lie between you.

"Shhhh," I cooed. "Don't talk." I said it to him, but of course it was a command for me. Because if I wanted to survive my secret, I had to keep my mouth shut.

CHAPTER 13

―――

SOPHIE

"Any plans this weekend?" my mom asked as we crested over Mulholland Drive on our way to the airport. My parents' flight wasn't until ten o'clock, but they liked to get to the airport early, thank God, because I needed time to get ready. Carter and Jared were already at the house, setting up the bar and arranging the heat lamps. But I still needed to do my makeup and get dressed; I didn't want to drive to the airport in my Cleopatra costume with my boobs popping out.

"There's a Halloween party," I said, because there would be pictures, and you never knew whose mom might see them and repost for all the other moms to see. "Besides that, not much." I had mastered the art of lying without lying—a useful skill for someone in my situation.

"Who's having a party?" Mom asked, and I got to use my special skill again.

"Just someone in my old friend group," I said, knowing she wouldn't push. At one point Mom knew all my old friends, but she hadn't seen them for years; I doubt she even remembered their names.

"It will be nice to see everybody," Mom said, then mercifully changed the subject to their pending adventure in New York—a Broadway show, brunch at the Russian Tea Room, and of course the bar mitzvah for the son of some friend of Dad's. That was the main reason for the trip. If things went as planned, they would never know I'd thrown a rager at Dad's secret acquisition. But plans have a way of coming unraveled, as I was about to find out the hard way.

"Have a great time," I said as I hugged them at the terminal. And they said something about being safe or having fun—I'm not sure, I wasn't really listening. I had planned to wear that Little Red Riding Hood costume myself until a few days ago, and the makeup for Cleopatra was much more involved: fake eyelashes, cat eyeliner, shiny red lip. I'd bought everything at Sephora the day before but hadn't done a test run. *Is the red I picked too pink? What if the alabaster foundation makes me look like a corpse?*

Traffic on the way home was stop and go, but I still got back with an hour to spare. I had made the dress from a plain white top sheet, which I wore double belted at the hip and under the boobs with thick gold Christmas ribbon. I repurposed the blunt-cut black wig I'd bought to play Mia Wallace from *Pulp Fiction* a few Halloweens back and made a headdress out of an old coin necklace from Pandora. I wasn't great with liquid eyeliner, but after fifteen minutes I was satisfied my cat eyes were even, and the fake eyelashes went on with minimal struggle.

I glanced at the clock: it was nine thirty. *Time to go.* I texted the boys (on my way!), then called my Uber. I had bought two cases of wine and enough rum for ten pitchers of mojitos—there was no way I was driving.

It was a warm night, with light Santa Ana winds blowing from the east—which was good, because Cleopatra wouldn't wear a hoodie, and I didn't have any animal skins lying around. I got to the house in twenty minutes, tipped my Uber driver, then clip-clopped up the front walk in my chunky gold heels, which I would come to regret.

"Nice legs!" I catcalled to Carter, who met me at the front door dressed as a gladiator in a black leather skirt and sandals that crisscrossed up his calves. My brother had always been so skinny and awkward, it was nice to see him showing off his bod, which had finally filled out.

"It's your skirt," he said, modeling it for me.

"You wear it well, bro."

"Jared's inside," he said, "trying to figure out the stereo." He leaned into the word "stereo," presumably to prod me to offer an explanation why the house our father bought came with a stereo. But I didn't take the bait.

"Great." I could tell he suspected I knew more than I was saying. Siblings can be intuitive like that.

I crossed through the atrium with a sky-high ceiling and a crystal chandelier from Neiman Marcus. I knew it was from Neiman's because I'd seen the bill. Just like I saw the checks for the wide-plank oak flooring under my feet and custom floating staircase that led to the primary suite, home office, and two guest bedrooms. Jared was in the sitting room off the kitchen, futzing with the receiver, looking ridiculously sexy in the skintight *Saturday Night Fever* leisure suit I'd helped him buy off eBay.

"We should have gotten you some stick-on chest hair," I said, eyeing the triangle of smooth, tanned skin between his pointy lapels.

"Are you saying I'm not manly enough?"

"No, just not hairy enough." I wanted to bend over and grab a kiss, but Carter was heating Swedish meatballs on the stove and had a clear line of sight. I knew my brother wouldn't approve of me hooking up with Jared, but that's not why I didn't tell him. He worked for our dad, too, and had no right to play the I'm-better-than-you card. Plus, unlike Jared, who'd had to interview for the job, Carter got his EVP position as a consolation prize for failing out of school. So yeah, I couldn't care less what Carter thought. But there was no point ruffling his feathers over a fling. So I kept it under wraps and asked Jared to do the same.

"You look hot," Jared whispered, his eyes devouring my glittery cleavage. I pretended not to hear, even though I wanted to jump his bones, too.

"I made a playlist," I said, nudging him aside with my hip and plugging my phone into the USB connector. He kept his hip touching mine, and I could feel the heat radiating off his polyester-clad leg.

"Don't," I warned as I pressed a gentle elbow into his ribs and opened my Spotify app. I didn't need to keep my phone on me; there would be no selfies or Instagram stories of this party, at least not by me. Dad didn't check my socials, but Mom did. I didn't think she suspected there was anything wonky about Dad's Beverly Hills property—Dad had bought dozens of houses over the years, and Mom had her own demanding job. But better not to broadcast that I was having a party in one of them.

I got my playlist going—Rihanna, Arctic Monkeys, Lady Gaga—then went out to the pool house to inventory the bar. The mojitos were premixed, so I helped myself to a red SOLO Cup and poured myself a tall one. It was ten after ten, but I didn't expect my friends to start arriving until at least ten thirty—no one wanted to be the first.

"The Adults Are Talking" by the Strokes was blasting as I took a sip of the tangy, minty concoction. My heart swelled with excitement and happiness. I had been so lonely for so long, the thought of dancing and drinking with my friends made me smile so wide my cheeks hurt. I was about to put the pitcher back in the fridge when I heard the back gate open and close. I had told my guests to enter the yard through the side gate, not the alley, but maybe someone was confused?

I put my drink down and stepped out of the cabana. I figured it was Jenna, my friend with a new baby, who said she "probably couldn't make it," but even if she could drag her butt out of the house, she "couldn't stay late." *Famous last words.* She was the only one who I thought might try to slip in from the back, because she couldn't fit into her costume, or any of her other clothes yet, thanks to that baby, and was embarrassed to be seen looking like a "giant cream puff." When I'd offered her my extra white sheet and suggested she come as Casper the Friendly Ghost, she'd blanched, even though it was kind of a brilliant idea.

"You don't have to sneak in through the back like a cat burglar," I called out as I rounded the side of the pool house. "No one else is here yet." And then I stopped talking. Because my punctual arrival was not Jenna.

"Oh. It's you," I said to the wide eyes staring at me from beneath a heavy crimson hood. "Welcome."

She didn't say anything. So I asked, "Would you like a drink?"

She closed and opened her hands in and out of tight fists, and for a second I thought my Reluctant Red Riding Hood might flee.

"I made mojitos," I offered.

And after a tense beat, she finally nodded. "A mojito sounds great."

CHAPTER 14

───

BREE

I did something completely irresponsible with the $125 I got from
Cindy's mom after our lesson. I got a haircut. Not a seventeen-dollar
haircut at Fantastic Sams—a real haircut, with proper layers and a blowout to show them off. Turns out without all those split ends to weigh
it down, my hair had a bouncy, flattering natural wave. At least that's
what the stylist said. *And who was I to disagree?*

Emboldened by my new do, I went to Sephora. After spending
eighty dollars at the hair salon, I couldn't afford to buy any makeup,
but that didn't mean I couldn't let the nice lady in the black apron talk
my ear off while teaching me the secrets of a smoky eye and contoured
cheeks. It would be rude to show up for a party looking washed out
or ill, especially after the hostess had gifted me with such a nice outfit
to wear. I normally gravitated toward spooky Halloween costumes—
witches and goblins and other undead beings. But I confess I kind of
liked how the velvet corset cinched my withering waist, making my
modest B cup look almost formidable. And that red wool cape conjured
fantasies of superheroes, which was eerily fitting, given that I was about
to walk into a crime scene.

I snacked on what was left of my cheese and water crackers as I sat
in my car counting down the minutes until ten o'clock. I didn't want to

be early, but if there was food, I wanted to make sure to get there before it was all gone. I know that sounds low class, but I was too hungry to be proud. As I dusted cracker crumbs off my fingertips, I looked down at my ring. I don't know if I thought it didn't go with the costume, or something else, but I had a sudden urge to take it off. Whether it was the end of something or the beginning of something, I wasn't sure. I just knew, at least for one night, I wouldn't have to worry about someone asking me where my husband was.

I parked two blocks away, under a leafy maple tree, then started walking toward the sound of upbeat rock music. My band had never covered the Strokes, but my hands still instinctively pantomimed the predictable chord progressions. *G minor resolves to C major . . . Step down to F major . . . C becomes Bb.* I hummed along as I rounded the corner. Not dancing, exactly. More like walking in time to the beat. I had no business being buoyant, but I still couldn't stop that flutter of nervous excitement about going to a party—*an actual party!*—from taking flight in my chest.

The front porch light was on, but I decided to slip around to the back of the house and enter from the alley. I didn't think my hostess was foreshadowing my demise by dressing me as Little Red Riding Hood, but I wanted to scout the scene for wolves before showing myself. Plus, even with a perfect red lip and expertly styled hair, I was still a vagrant and not worthy of walking through that regal front door.

The backyard was empty when I pushed through the gate, which they had unlocked, and stepped onto the lawn. I should have known when I showed up at ten after ten that I'd be the first one there. This was a party, not a concerto competition—of course people would be fashionably late. I was about to turn around and do a lap around the block when I heard a voice.

"You don't have to sneak in through the back like a cat burglar. No one else is here yet," the voice said, and suddenly I was standing face-to-face with a cat-eyed Cleopatra. Her eyes registered surprise, and as they dropped down to my cleavage, I instantly regretted tying that corset so tight.

"Oh. It's you. Welcome," she said brightly, and I suddenly realized she hadn't expected me to come. "Would you like a drink? I made mojitos."

What I really wanted was a steak sandwich, but I said yes, and she beckoned me to follow her into the pool house.

"I spent all day chopping mint; I'll probably smell like a pack of Trident for the rest of my natural life," she said as she handed me a drink, as if the rest of her natural life were going to be a long time. "Cheers!"

I put the cup to my lips and poked my tongue into the pungent concoction. It tasted like floor cleaner, but I forced down a sip.

"Oh my God, it's terrible, isn't it?" She looked genuinely mortified, so I tried to reassure her.

"No, I just . . . haven't had hard alcohol for a while," I said, because I couldn't think of any other way to explain my grimace without hurting her feelings.

"I used that lime juice from a bottle instead of fresh—I think it's too sour!" I didn't know why she was talking to me like I was an old friend, but nobody needed a friend more than I did, so I played along.

"It's not too sour," I said, then took another sip. "I like it."

"I spent a fortune on the ingredients, so people are going to have to choke them down." She smiled, revealing a mouth full of teeth so perfect they looked almost fake. I squeezed my lips together so she wouldn't see my crooked jumble. Luke had told me I could get braces if I wanted, but I didn't care about pleasing anyone except him, and then it was too late.

"That costume looks great on you," she said. "I knew it would. Your waist is so tiny!" My "tiny" waist was not a source of pride for me, but I knew she meant it as a compliment.

"Thank you for inviting me," I said. "And for the care package."

"We all need a helping hand once in a while." She adjusted her shiny jet-black wig, tugging the blunt-cut bangs down over her eyebrows. "Ugh, this thing is so itchy!"

"I love your dress," I said, admiring her flowing white gown trimmed with gold.

"Thanks! I made it myself." She spun around like Cinderella at the ball, and her sheet-skirt fanned out to reveal strappy gold heels. I wasn't remotely as elegant in my black leggings and knee-high leather boots, but my feet were warm and dry, which I never took for granted anymore.

"Sophie! When do you want to bring the food out?" a man called to her from the house, and I recognized the voice as her fellow squirrel hunter from a few nights ago.

"Now!" she shouted back, then lowered her voice to add, "I'm Sophie, by the way."

"Bree."

"I know my friends. They're all going to come at once and ask me where the food is! Come help me carry it out?"

"Yes, of course."

She smiled at me like your mother when you get an A on your report card. "I'm so glad you came." I thought for a second she might hug me, but she just turned and headed for the house. "Come on!"

I followed her across the lawn and onto the sleek wood-and-fiberglass deck canopied with twinkly lights. The sliding door to the kitchen was open. I marveled at the understated opulence as I stepped inside and gazed up at the soaring ceilings dotted with space-age light fixtures.

"This is my brother, Carter," she said, pointing to a gladiator, who stared at me like I was the wild beast he was going to have to face off against in the arena. If I weren't still in love with my husband, I might have thought he was cute, with his Joseph Gordon-Levitt dimples and lean runner's physique. Luke was tall and lean like that, too. And stared at me exactly the same way.

"Carter, this is Aubrey."

"Hi," he said as he extended his hand to shake. But it wasn't the oddly formal gesture that made my blood run cold.

"Hi," I said, shaking his hand, because it would be rude not to.

"Nice to meet you, Aubrey."

"Actually, my friends call me Bree." And I glanced at Sophie. I don't know if it was the heat from the bubbling pot of meatballs that had reddened her face, or what I'd just said to her brother. Because we both knew I had introduced myself to her as Bree, not Aubrey.

Which meant she had known my name before I'd told it to her.

CHAPTER 15

CARTER

If I got in trouble with Dad for having this party, it would be worth it for a few minutes with the woman who just walked in from the backyard.

"Nice to meet you, Aubrey," I said, then for some unknown reason offered my hand like a slimy used car salesman.

"My friends call me Bree," the most beautiful woman I had ever seen said. Her hand was small, but her grip was strong, and I felt a jolt of electricity up my arm when her palm connected with mine.

"OK, I put a sign on the door telling people to enter through the side gate," Jared said as he walked in from the atrium. "Oh!" he blurted in a "where did you come from" way when he saw Bree. And of course I was wondering the same thing.

"That's Bree," Sophie said.

"Nice to meet you, Bree. I'm Jared."

He didn't offer his hand because only a moron would do that. Plus he probably didn't want to do anything that might make Sophie jealous, like trying to shake the hand of a beautiful woman at a freakin' party, then holding it two full seconds too long. Not that Sophie was the jealous type. But any guy with half a brain knows better than to pay too much attention to another girl in front of their girlfriend.

"Let's take this food outside," Sophie commanded, handing me the Crock-Pot and nudging me toward the door. I hadn't known she and Jared were sleeping together until a few minutes ago, when I saw her grab his butt as he was adjusting a heat lamp, but it made sense. Why else would she have his number and then call me a snob when I asked her why? She obviously (correctly) thought I wouldn't approve of her sleeping with an employee of the family business, so I pretended not to see the butt grab. There was no point confronting her about it—the alcohol would reveal all in a matter of hours.

I took the Crock-Pot out to the pool house and plugged it in. It was an amazing party house, and seeing it all lit up with Christmas lights and candles stirred my outrage at not being told about it. This was a significant property, the crown jewel of our holdings. *Why hadn't Dad mentioned it? And why is there still cat food in the bowl and cars in the garage?* All I could think of was that the occupants had left in a hurry . . . or were imminently coming back.

"Yo, yo, yo!" a flock of my sister's friends called out as they traipsed into the backyard: Wonder Woman, Cinderella, a sexy witch, and (gasp!) another Cleopatra.

"Hey, ladies," I said, because I couldn't remember their names. There was no point in learning them—I would always just be "the little brother." Not that I cared; the perfect woman was already here.

"Samantha! You bitch!" Sophie shouted from the porch steps.

"I thought you were going to be Dora the Explorer!" the bitch shouted back. And someone made a joke about "who wore it better," and then there were hugs and mojitos and more people coming through the gate.

"Hey, Carter," a guy dressed as Tom Brady said, offering a fist for me to bump.

"Hey, TB12," I said, because I thought his name was Ryan but wasn't 100 percent sure.

"Are these meatballs edible?" he asked, peering into the Crock-Pot.

"They're from Costco," I offered, and let him decide for himself. I had something—or rather *someone*—more important on my mind than meatballs, and I didn't want another party guest making a move on her before I got the chance.

I scanned the crowd, which seemed to be doubling every ten seconds now. I could see through the glass door that Bree wasn't in the kitchen anymore. *So where did she go?*

Sophie was standing by the waterfall talking to a couple dressed as Thing One and Thing Two, so I made my way over to her. "Clocks" by Coldplay was blaring from the outdoor speakers. People were dancing and laughing and yukking it up. By all measures the party was a success. I could have relaxed and joined in on the fun, but I was a man with a mission.

"Hey! You guys remember my little brother," my sister said to Things One and Two as I approached.

"Where's Bree?" I asked, not acknowledging the Seussian duo, which I know was rude, but I was too panicked to care.

"Don't go there, bro," Sophie said as her friends took the hint and moved off into the crowd.

"I just want to talk to her."

"Her life is complicated." I was tempted to tell her that me talking to Bree couldn't be more complicated than her hooking up with the pool boy, but I held my tongue, because that would be mean. And, as I would soon discover, also not true.

"How do you know her?" I pressed. And her answer confused me even more.

"I don't. Not really. I just know she's trouble."

"Then why did you invite her?"

"Sometimes I like trouble," she snarked, and then peered into her empty cup. "Speaking of which, I need another drink."

She glided off toward the bar, and I suddenly felt like a total idiot in that leather skirt and sandals that pulled on my leg hair. What my sister was really saying was that Bree, and probably everyone else at her stupid party, was too good for me. *Why had I let her talk me into this?*

There was a cluster of people dancing on the lawn and a swarm crowding into the pool house, refilling their SOLO Cups and munching on chips and cheese. And then there was me, standing alone by the deep end, cursing myself for being such a nerd all the time.

I was about to drown my self-pity in a drink when everyone suddenly gasped. It wasn't the lights going off that was jarring—there was plenty of light from the candles we had set out. It was the sudden, deafening silence. No music. No waterfall splashing into the pool. Not even the hum of the refrigerator working to keep those mojitos cold.

"Jeez, you guys," one of the guests murmured. "Didn't you pay your electric bill?"

And it suddenly occurred to me that maybe we hadn't.

I looked at Sophie. Her face was panicked, because it wasn't a party without music, hot food, and cold drinks. As bad as I felt for myself, I felt worse for her. Because she hadn't seen her friends in months. And now they would leave. Maybe not instantaneously, but soon. The heaters we got were electric, and it was cold and getting colder. Sophie's eyes found mine, pleaded with me to "Do something!" But I was the marketing guy, Dad was the builder; I didn't know jack about how a house worked.

People were slugging back their drinks and eyeing the exit. Sophie looked like she wanted to cry. But then, just as we both thought the night was over before it even started, the sweet sound of Coldplay came tumbling out of the house. Those famous opening upside-down arpeggios, syncopated triplets against half notes. I knew the chord progressions from band practice. Except it wasn't a band. It was a solo piano. And it was coming from inside the house.

CHAPTER 16

BREE

I spotted it in the shadows of the sunken living room the moment I stepped into the house. Unlike the one at the mall, this beauty was properly buttoned up, protected from the elements, cared for, loved.

As the party hosts filed out, arms laden with Crock-Pots and cheese plates, I lingered behind to steal a closer look. I didn't dare turn the living room light on—didn't need to; I knew every curve of the magnificent creature by heart.

I approached it slowly—not out of caution, but reverence. The piano was a mahogany Steinway baby grand, just under six feet in length, regal, fit for a king. As I walked the length of the keyboard, I raked my fingertips along the cover, leaving four shallow, parallel troughs in the thin layer of dust that had settled there. The feel of polished wood against the pads of my fingers was deliciously familiar, like stroking the fur of a beloved pet. I wiped the particulate onto my pant leg as I circled the rim, savoring the instrument's gentle curves and virtuoso craftsmanship. After rounding the bow, I dipped into the hourglass cutout, then gripped the lid with both hands. I wouldn't be able to see the orderly grid of strings, knobs, and hammers in the dark, but I didn't need my eyes to experience their perfection. As I hoisted the piano's heavy wooden cover above my head, I leaned into its belly and breathed in the sweet swirl of spruce and iron. The smell brought me back to happier days—the loving arms of my mother, the cocoon of my practice room, the warm smiles of attentive listeners at my childhood church recitals, the approving nods of teachers and concertgoers.

The long prop beckoned to me, so I reached for it, levering it straight up toward the sky with one arm, then setting the heavy lid down on it with the other. With the instrument's mouth wide open like a lion midyawn, I reached in and put my palm to the strings like a doctor taking a pulse. And pulse they did, vibrating in sync with the music pouring from the speakers: *A, E, C#, F#* . . . The piano loved the bright overtones of A major, and I smiled to myself as I imagined it singing along to the catchy pop song.

The bench was tucked under the keyboard, so I slid it out and floated down onto the tufted leather, flipping my crimson cape behind me like I was a soloist at Carnegie Hall. The final bars of Vampire Weekend's "This Life" gave way to the cascading arpeggios of "Clocks" by Coldplay, and I opened the keyboard cover and pantomimed playing along. I had never performed the song, but I knew the chord progressions by instinct. Pop music was deliciously predictable, and I had played enough of it to anticipate what was coming next. *Eb, Bb minor, F minor* . . . the tumbling V chords washed over me like ocean waves, and my fingers reveled in their stunning simplicity.

My eyes were closed, so when the lights went out, I didn't register it. The music may have stopped for everyone else, but for me it played on—not just in my chest, but also in my hands, which went from hovering over the keys to connecting with them: *1-2-3, 1-2-3, 1-2, 1-2-3, 1-2-3, 1-2* . . . The Mixolydian flat-seven progression was more common in blues riffs than rock songs, and its refusal to resolve to the root chord gave the song a haunting quality that perfectly complemented lyrics about closing walls and ticking clocks. The vocal had dropped out, so I picked up the melody with my right hand. As the music coursed through me, I lost all sense of time and place. I was no more a homeless rag doll than I was Chris Martin himself. Was I playing for millions, or just myself? And what's the difference when music is all there is?

At first I thought I was imagining the voices singing the chorus. But then I opened my eyes and saw that the voices belonged to actual people—partygoers who had gathered around the piano to sing along. There was a football player, a Laker Girl, a Playboy Bunny, a pirate. The drumbeat came from a guy dressed as Batman using chopsticks as drumsticks and the coffee table as a drum. So I kept going. The music was a life raft and we were all riding it together. The shore was a blur as we coursed through rushing rapids, then crested over a waterfall of pure sound. And then it was over, and people were clapping, and I remembered my life had a purpose; I just had to find a way back to it.

"That was awesome!" my new pirate friend said, and I met his smile with one of my own. Next to him, Sophie nodded in gratitude at me, and I nodded back because we both knew the person she had invited out of pity had just saved her party. In that moment, I forgot to wonder how she'd known my name. It would take the events of the next forty-eight hours for me to realize her impulse to invite me did not rise from pity, but from guilt, because she not only knew why I was homeless, she was the one who had made me that way.

"Play something else!" a girl's voice rang out.

"'Free Bird'!" someone shouted, so I played a few bars and the room exploded with laughter.

"Go get your clarinet!" Danny Zuko from *Grease* shouted, and then everyone was looking and laughing at Sophie's little brother. And even in the dim light I could see his face flush crimson to match my cape. I felt a sudden kinship with him. Because, true to the cliché, jocks always picked on music nerds, and I knew the clarinet to be a brutally difficult instrument to learn, and not cool like drums or electric guitar.

"Come here," I said to my gladiator friend, sliding a few inches to my right and patting the left side of the bench. And for a second he hesitated, like he wasn't sure I meant him.

"Carter, right?" I said, remembering his name, and how his hand felt warm and welcoming when I shook it.

Someone in the crowd let out a low whistle as he eased down on the bench next to me, and I saw his blush grow darker.

"You play piano?" I asked, ignoring the whistle.

"A little. I took a few lessons before I switched to the clarinet."

"That's a tough instrument," I said. "Good for you."

I put my left hand to the keys and played the simple opening bass line to Journey's "Don't Stop Believin'": *Bum . . . bum-bum-bum . . . bum-bum-bum . . . bum-bum bum.* Then indicated for him to give it a try.

His hand shook as he put it to the keys, but I pretended not to see. *E major, B major, C# minor, A major.* He got it almost immediately.

"Yeah, baby," the football player encouraged, so he started playing faster.

"Don't rush," I soothed, like he was one of my students, which in the moment I guess he kind of was. "It's not a race."

I put my left hand on the keys one octave above his and played along, slowing him down as I set the tempo. "You got it?"

He nodded, so I scooched over and put both hands on the keyboard a few octaves above his, waiting for him to finish the cadence so I could join in. The New York pub scene loved the classics, and if you could play one eighties soft rock hit, you could play them all. Carter and I sat like that for the next two hours, hips touching, my left elbow dodging his right. I taught him the bass lines to all the crowd favorites—Earth, Wind & Fire; Elton John; Toto; the Doobie Brothers. I didn't realize how starved for music I was until the feast of that party, and I didn't want the night to end. And neither did Carter, but not for the same reason as me.

Our act finally ran its course, as all acts do, around 1:00 a.m. I didn't realize I needed food until Sophie brought me a plate of meatballs with an apology: "Sorry they're not really hot anymore." And then she hugged me, and I was so stunned by the first meaningful human contact I'd had in over three months, I forgot to hug her back.

I was on my third meatball before I realized Carter was still sitting next to me. He caught me peeking over at him and he smiled.

"That was so fun," he said. "You're amazing."

"Thanks," I said, a little embarrassed for him that he thought my clunky rendition of "Crocodile Rock" was praiseworthy. But he quickly redeemed himself.

"This kind of music must be so easy for you."

"I enjoy it," I said, because I do. Yes, Rachmaninoff is orders of magnitude more difficult, but performing for a bunch of buttoned-up symphony goers isn't any more satisfying than playing for a tavern of bawdy bar patrons, especially when they sing along.

"How long have you been playing?" Carter asked as I sucked back another meatball.

"I can't remember ever not playing." My childhood home came with a piano because our landlady's daughter played and it was too expensive to move it. My mother had viewed the aging Yamaha upright as an inconvenience, not a luxury. The room was small, and she would have much preferred a sewing table. But, as the story goes, I took to the instrument like a fish to water, plucking out my nursery school ditties—"Ring around the Rosie," "The Wheels on the Bus," "I'm a Little Teapot"—often improvising on the melodies and harmonies like a baby Dave Brubeck. Our church paid for lessons in exchange for my performing on Sundays and at Christmas. My becoming a pianist was as inevitable as a bird learning to fly. Sitting at that pockmarked Yamaha is not only my earliest memory, it's one of my happiest.

"So, do you, like, play professionally?" Carter asked, and I felt my throat tighten.

"I mostly teach now," I said, as if my life didn't depend on it.

"See ya later, little man," a towering Abe Lincoln in a top hat and muttonchops said, offering Carter a fist for him to bump. All around us, people were hugging and saying their goodbyes. Phone lights flickered in the dark as partygoers looked for purses and coats and eventually the door. Sophie looked every bit the queen, bidding everyone adieu in her golden headdress and heels, and I felt a swell of satisfaction that I had been able to earn my keep. As the last of the party guests trickled out the door, my overfull heart sank like a stone. Because it was bedtime. And I had no bed.

"There's no point trying to clean up in the dark," Sophie called to her brother as she put on her coat. "I'll come back in the morning. Can you lock up?"

"Sure," he said. And a few seconds later the pocket doors closed behind her and we were alone.

"Do you live near here?" Carter asked. And it was all I could do to not start crying.

"Not far," I managed.

"I can give you a ride?" There was a version of this night that ended with me going home with him. He was nice, and pretty good looking. And chances are, had a bed.

"I have a car," I said. Because I was many imperfect things, but I was not a whore.

We sat there in awkward silence, him in the chokehold of attraction, me in the gully between two unpalatable options: sleeping in my car, or sleeping with him.

"I'm just going to check the back gate," Carter finally said, standing up, so I stood up, too. "Then I'll walk you to your car?" I nodded, because it would have been rude not to, and watched him slip out the sliding doors. And that's when it occurred to me that I had a third option.

I glanced at the stairs: thick wooden planks that disappeared into blackness. My next move was so obvious I almost laughed. For the first time in three months, I would be gloriously alone, in a bed, with no garbage trucks rumbling by at dawn or wind whistling through my broken window.

I would sleep real sleep that night, not knowing I'd wake up to a nightmare.

CHAPTER 17

CARTER

Best. Night. Of. My. Life. And it wasn't over yet.

I didn't care if the back gate was open, closed, missing, or on fire—I just needed to step outside for a minute to keep my heart from flying out of my chest. As I sucked in a mouthful of cool night air, I raced through my possible next moves. *Reach for her hand to help her up? Offer her my arm like a gent on* Downton Abbey? *Grab her and pull her into a kiss?* She already made the first move when she beckoned me to sit next to her, so the store was open. This should be a lock. We already practically made love on that piano bench: her leg touching mine, our chests expanding and contracting in perfect unison. If I couldn't close this, I didn't deserve to get laid, now or ever.

There were a handful of red SOLO Cups dotting the deck, so I picked them up as I exhaled through my mouth to keep from hyper-ventilating. Any other night I would have been irritated that grown-ass adults would just drop their garbage on the ground, but that night I was grateful for an excuse to catch my breath. In fairness to my sister's friends, the whole place had been plunged into near-total darkness—maybe they couldn't find the trash can?

If I weren't so lovestruck, I probably would have been more curi-ous about why the power went out. I would have noticed that the streetlamps were still on and the front porches of all the other houses were still lit, that it wasn't a whole-neighborhood thing. I would have remembered that it's not like Dad to miss a payment; he had everything on autopay, down to my zit cream and Sophie's weekly shrink visit. And I would have realized that he wouldn't shut the power off on purpose; that sod needed to be watered, and the pool water would turn icky and green in a matter of days without the filter running. Dad may not have wanted me to know about this house, I would have reasoned, but he wouldn't intentionally have let it fall into disrepair. But I didn't think of all that, because, like I said, I had love on the brain.

The yard was black except for a few flickering candles in the pool house, so I started across the lawn to go snuff them out. I had just stepped onto the pavers at the shallow end of the pool when I heard the back gate open and close. *Who's that?* I figured someone forgot something—car keys, a sweater. I was about to call out when I saw a silhouette in a flowing white gown step into the yard. I wasn't sure it was Sophie until I heard her voice.

"There you are," my sister said. "I was afraid you left." I couldn't see who she was talking to, but I had a strong suspicion.

"You asked me to wait," Jared answered, and my suspicion was confirmed.

"Everybody's gone now," she said. "We're all alone." She took a step toward him, and their silhouettes merged into one. I got a nervous feeling because Sophie was my sister and I didn't want to think about what she and Jared were going to do in that pool house. I thought about announcing myself with a cough or a *"Hey, what's up?"* but if I said anything now, they would know I was spying on them, so I just stood there like a post.

"Sophie, I care about you," Jared said, then surprised us both by adding, "but I can't do this anymore." Their bodies separated as he took a step away from her, and I felt uncomfortable for a different reason.

"I'll wear the wig," Sophie teased, cupping the bottom of the bob with her hands. "You can't say no to the queen of the Nile." She reached for his waist to pull him toward her. But he stood his ground.

"I'm serious, Soph. I really like you, but I don't want to be your dirty little secret anymore." I felt a flash of guilt for disapproving of their relationship. Jared was a good guy. And making a connection with another human being is hard—who was I to say what was appropriate and what wasn't?

"I want to be with you," Jared continued, "but if you're ashamed of me—"

"What? No! That's not it!"

"Then what is it?"

She lowered her voice. "I just need my private life to be on the down low right now." It was a strange thing to say, but I was too preoccupied with my predicament to psychoanalyze it. I had to get out of here and back to Bree!

"I want to be your boyfriend, Sophie. Out in the open. No more sneaking around."

"I want that, too," Sophie said. "I'm just not ready, not yet."

I tiptoed backward toward the house, hoping they were too engrossed in each other to notice me. My sister would be pissed if she knew I was eavesdropping. I told myself I would confess to her in the morning, not knowing that would be too late.

I heard her say his name, then something hushed that I couldn't make out. She leaned into his chest, and he wrapped an arm around her in a gentle hug. I didn't know how this was going to end, but it was none of my business. I wasn't even supposed to know they were together. Plus I had my own love story to write and was eager for the next chapter to begin.

I crept up the deck stairs, grateful there were no lights to reveal my presence. As I reached the door, my heart pounded with anticipation. I told myself not to scare Bree off with a cheesy line, like, *"Your place or mine?"* Ugh, *what would I say? I'm so bad at this!*

As I slipped into the house through the sliding glass door, I made a decision. I would take it slow with this girl. I wanted more than a hookup; I wanted something lasting. The dating scene in LA sucked. Most of the women I met wanted an Instagram moment, not a relationship. Bree was different. She was gorgeous, kind to me, and crazy talented. I didn't want to blow my chance of having something real with her by coming on too strong.

I turned my gaze to the sunken living room. Even in the dark, I could see that the piano lid was down. The keyboard cover was closed. And the woman I wanted to make my girlfriend was gone.

"Bree?" I called out, panic rising up my throat. "Are you here?"

No answer.

"Bree?"

I groped my way down the hall, opening every door I found: a laundry room, a closet, a powder room, all empty. My disappointment turned to rage. First my dad, then this girl; did I have a sign on my back that said BETRAY ME? *I told her I'd be right back. And she just takes off, without saying goodbye? What the hell?*

In that moment, I hated everything about this night, not knowing the morning would be a whole lot worse.

CHAPTER 18

BREE

"Luke, come closer, you're too far away," I said without opening my eyes, because I wasn't ready to wake up yet. I reached for him, and a puff of cold air snuck in under the comforter. If he was sleeping, he wouldn't come to me; I would have to abandon my side of the bed and wriggle over to his. He always slept on his back with one arm over his head like he was hailing a cab. Or waiting for me to snug into the gentle valley of his armpit and rest my head against his chest.

I didn't want to leave the little patch of bed that I had worked so hard to warm, so I retracted my arm and wrapped it across my body. *Why is it so cold in here?* Luke and I often sparred about how low to drop the thermostat at night. "You're from Canada!" he used to tease. "Shouldn't you like the cold?"

"I came to California to get away from the cold," I would remind him. And he would look all hurt and say something like, "I thought you came here for me," and stick out his lower lip in an exaggerated pout.

"Of course I came here for you, you big dope," I would say. And then he'd make this goofy frowny face to keep from laughing, and I would slip my hands into his back pockets and go on tippy toes and kiss him on his fake-sad mouth. And he would try not to kiss me back, just for a second, to draw the game out a little longer. And then inevitably we would wind up here, in this big, beautiful bed, under sheets of every color except for white, because, according to my husband, white sheets were for hospital beds, and this bed was for loving.

I opened one eye. A whiff of daylight was rising over the window-sill, threatening to roust me out of my dream. I hadn't known what color the sheets were when I crawled into bed in the black of night, but now the sliver of blue rising up from under the sand-colored comforter appeared to me like a peekaboo ocean view. I smiled a little, because given the choice, I would always choose blue. Luke's mom gave us Tiffany-blue sheets on our wedding day—not cotton, as I'd thought all sheets were made of, but bamboo. Luke told me people like them because they don't hold the heat, which I guess is a good thing, under different circumstances.

"I miss you," I said out loud, even though I knew my husband wouldn't answer. Luke was a really sound sleeper; one of those people who could fall asleep anywhere—in the car, at church, on a lounge chair by the pool. He slept like a person who worked hard all day and never had to worry about demons dropping in. I always envied him for that.

"You forgot to close the blinds, Luke," I murmured, knowing he wouldn't answer. Dawn was starting to reveal the objects in the room: a midcentury modern teak and tweed chair, a three-legged coffee table with a clear bowl of marbles on it, a lowboy dresser, a wedding photo framed in silver—him in a black Armani suit, her in lace and diamonds. My wedding dress was bright white silk charmeuse with an overlay of Chantilly lace. I hadn't planned to wear a tiara, but my husband had insisted. He started calling me his snow princess after we watched *Frozen* together and I learned all the songs and played them on the piano. I was more an Anna than an Elsa, with my round face and freck-led nose. My face had hollowed since then, and that off-the-shoulder wedding gown would hang on me now.

I drifted off into the memory of the most perfect day of my life. I didn't have anyone to give me away, so we skipped that part, just walked down the aisle arm in arm. He could have invited more people, but he didn't want me to feel bad for not filling up "my" side of his tiny childhood church in rustic Ojai, where he'd grown up. "My friends will be your friends," he'd said. But then we crawled into our little nest and never saw much of those friends. And then he was gone, and there was no way to get them to want to be my friends now.

The reception was at an indoor-outdoor banquet hall with a view of the whole world. We dined at long picnic tables covered with white tablecloths and rose petals and danced to Sinatra and Lady Ella until my bare feet were black as coal. Except for the walking down the aisle part, we did all the things people getting married were supposed to do—tossed the bouquet, cut the cake together, let the guests shower us with rice and hang tin cans off the bumper of Luke's pickup truck. The something old I wore was my mother's heart-shaped gold locket with a picture of me when I was a baby. The something new was the dress we'd bought at a proper bridal store, because, as Luke said, you only get married once—you should wear the dress you always dreamed of. The something borrowed was that tiara. Luke had a cousin who worked at Hancocks of London; if I had known the diamonds were real, I never would have dared! And the something blue was my powder-blue undies I ran out to PINK to buy that very morning. When I told Luke about my eleventh-hour excursion, he teased me for being superstitious. In the end, he was right; it didn't matter that we did everything by the book, because our marriage was short lived, even with that something blue.

My stomach was empty and my bladder was full, but I didn't want to get up and break the spell being in this bed had cast on me. The memories swirled around me like fog on a mountaintop: sharing a whiskey with my very first groupie, who'd shyly admitted he only stayed for our second set because of me; letting him take my hand on the walk home, then saying yes when he stopped in the middle of the sidewalk to ask if he could kiss me; not wanting that kiss, or that walk, to ever end; eating like royalty every night that week—pastrami sandwiches at Katz's, pizza at Lombardi's, dim sum in Chinatown. I had never known such extravagance. Or so much love. He loved me with food, with words, with his touch, with his whole heart. He didn't coerce me to come to LA—I went because even my music couldn't save me from the pain of being away from him. My reward for coming west was a promise of forever. And he would have kept that promise if it weren't for me.

As I drifted in and out of sleep, memories of the blissful beginning gave way to memories of the blistering end. I was in the grocery store when the call came in. "I'm going to make a lasagna!" I'd chirped into the phone, assuming it was Luke, because it was too early for any of my students to be calling. I'd become quite the domestic goddess since becoming Luke's wife, cooking and organizing and keeping house. I wanted to take care of him like he took care of me. I'd found the veggie lasagna recipe on Instagram and had filled my basket with all the ingredients: button mushrooms, yellow squash, broccoli, zucchini, four kinds of cheese. I never used a trolley—it felt silly to buy more food than I could carry. Besides, I liked going to the market every day; planning our dinner had become a daily ritual—along with making the bed, practicing my études, getting books from the library, and making love to the man who filled my heart with joy.

"I'm so sorry," the voice on the phone said, and a moment later the hard tile floor was covered with what was supposed to be lasagna but was now the last time I ever shopped for two.

I forced my eyes open and sat up in bed. The sound of rain on the roof was a gentle cymbal roll: steady, smooth, and unrelenting. The morning light was muted by cloud cover. As my eyes adjusted to the gauzy, gray dawn, I took in the room. My eyes landed on the framed wedding photo. My wedding. It was a picture of Luke and me. Because who else would it be? This was our house; at least it used to be. Being back here in the bed I shared with the most beautiful man I'd ever met, under those bamboo sheets, looking at the nightstands I'd bought at Wayfair and the books I'd ordered from Amazon, was surreal. I would have thought the place would be cleared out by now, but it was exactly the same as the last time I'd slept here. That was almost four months ago. The only thing that was different now was that Luke wasn't here, and I wasn't supposed to be, which I guess is a pretty big difference.

I leaned over and pressed my face into Luke's pillow to breathe in the smell of him. He wasn't a cologne guy, but he had a distinctive scent—Irish Spring peppered with wood chips swirled in tenderness. More painful than the staggering loss of everything I loved was knowing it was all my fault. If it weren't for me, he'd be here with me, in this big, beautiful bed, under these sheets the color of a perfect bluebird day.

I closed my eyes and tried to disappear back into the memory of him beside me. I knew my best days were behind me. What I didn't know was that the worst were yet to come.

CHAPTER 19

———

BREE

It took every ounce of effort I had to pull myself out of that bed and back into reality. The bathroom I'd once shared with Luke was spacious, with two sinks and a built-in vanity. Dim light leaked in from a high window above a soaking tub big enough for two. My Herbal Essences shampoo was still on the shower caddy next to Luke's Head & Shoulders and a shriveled bar of soap. I turned the water as hot as I could stand it and let my tears disappear into the stream like candlelight in the sun. As the water swept away the memory of my perfect life, I turned my thoughts to where I would go from here. The nights were getting cold now. I couldn't sleep in a car with no window, and it would be a while before I could get it fixed. And without the money I'd been saving, there was no getting an apartment now. I had to find shelter. *But how?* I wasn't going to prostitute myself for a place to sleep. And there was no way Carter would let me stay here once he found out what I was.

I dried off and went into the bedroom to find some clean clothes. I had taken most of my stuff, but Luke's drawers were full. As I dipped in and pulled out a pair of joggers and a plain white tee, I caught sight of something in the pool. Something diaphanous and white, like a tablecloth or a plastic bag. Except it wasn't floating—it was on the bottom like it was anchored there with a bag of rocks.

I crossed to the window and peered through the rain-streaked glass. It was coming down harder now, stirring the water, distorting the object. There was a black smudge at one end of the mass, undulating with the choppy waves. The way it fanned out, it looked almost like snakes, writhing against an invisible current. As the image of Medusa flashed in my head, I realized it wasn't snakes, it was hair. *Cleopatra hair.*

I stumbled back. My fingers shook as I dialed 9-1-1. I spit out the address as I ran down the stairs and out the sliding back door.

The cold nearly stopped my heart as I dived headfirst into the deep end. I frog kicked to the bottom of the pool. Sophie's fingernails skimmed my forearm as I reached out and grabbed her wrist. Her hand was rigid; her fingers curled in toward her palm like a bear claw. I gave her arm a little tug; her elbow didn't bend. Horror seized me like a vise. I was too late . . . *way too late.*

Chlorine stung my eyes as I shot to the surface and gasped for air. I kicked and flailed my way to the shallow end. Cold rain pelted my body as I crawled up the pool steps and pressed my face to the pavers. Sharp, silent sobs rose up from the bottom of my belly. It was in that moment I knew I must be the devil, because why else would everyone who was kind to me suffer and die? My mother was barely fifty when she was devoured by cancer; she was so emaciated when she passed you could strum her ribs like guitar strings. And then there was Luke, who dared to love me, not knowing how much he would suffer for it. Maybe it was hubris to think this had something to do with me. Or maybe I should have expected it by now.

A police siren howled in the distance. I tried to remember what I had said to the 9-1-1 operator: *There's been an accident? I need help? Send an ambulance?* I peeled myself off the ground as the siren grew louder. I was shoeless and sopping wet, and my car was two blocks away. I knew I shouldn't run, but after trespassing in the house I'd been told in no uncertain terms to stay away from, I knew I couldn't stick around, either.

The siren chirped, then abruptly stopped. I heard banging on the gate. The sound of the gate clanging open. Heavy footsteps. A voice announcing, "Gate unlocked, proceeding into the backyard." A response over an open mic: "Copy that." I had three seconds to decide what to do. The pool house was ten steps in front of me. So I ran barefoot through the puddles and slipped inside.

CHAPTER 20

SOPHIE

My face was sticky from crying as I climbed into the Uber. Jared had offered to drive me home, but I told him Carter was waiting, even though I was sure he'd be long gone. I was getting good at lying—*too good*. Jared deserved someone who could be honest with him, and I was living a lie, playing Gen Z underachiever while sitting on a ticking time bomb. I couldn't tell him what I was up to, but if we were together, I couldn't *not* tell him. Which is why, when he insisted we come out with our relationship, I had to let him go.

I could tell from the look on my driver's face that, contrary to what it said on the package, my eyeliner was not waterproof. I peeked at my reflection in the rearview to see it streaking down my face like prison bars. At this point I looked more like a zebra than Cleopatra, but I didn't have a tissue, plus I figured a guy who drives all night has probably seen worse.

Jared's ultimatum had taken me by surprise. I tried to tell him that it wasn't him, it was me—that I had some things to figure out—but he didn't buy it. *"Your brother never went to college, either; I have my own business, I'm not a slouch; I could make you happy if you let me."* I wanted to grab him and tell him "I know! I believe you!" but it wouldn't have made any difference. If I told him I was trying to protect him, I would have to tell him what I was protecting him *from*, thereby not protecting him anymore. He thought I was ashamed of him, but the opposite was true. I thought he was amazing. He was gorgeous, funny, and smart, and we had unreal chemistry. He was the only person I felt connected to these days. *Ugh! Why can't this whole ordeal be over already?*

With Jared out of my life and no party to plan, I would have to find something else to bolster my sagging spirits. I wanted to help Aubrey—or Bree, as she apparently liked to be called—but sneaking her food and blankets wasn't exactly a full-time job. It was good for my conscience, though. I know it sounds heartless, but I hadn't considered what would happen to her after she lost her house. Once I discovered her husband's dirty secret, I thought she deserved the same fate as him. But then it occurred to me that husbands sometimes do things without telling their wives, and maybe she was a victim, too.

I hadn't meant to reveal that I knew her name. I didn't want to scare her. But then I slipped, called her Aubrey after she'd introduced herself as Bree. Not to worry—if it came up, I would just tell her I had a childhood friend named Aubrey who went by Bree, and I just assumed she did, too. It was a credible lie. And I was a practiced liar.

I'd googled her right after I saw her name on the deed. That's how I recognized her. Apparently she was some sort of child prodigy—there were photos of her at every age, sitting at pianos all across the continent, from churches in Canada to Carnegie Hall. I had seen so many photos of her that when we were standing nose to nose in that outdoor shower, it was almost like looking at an old friend. I hadn't expected her to return to her marital house, but I wasn't surprised to see her, either. All her stuff was there—who could blame her for wanting it back? I didn't regret what I'd done, but seeing her face-to-face, all skin and bones and sadness, made me question what her role in all this was. Good people sometimes do bad things, just as bad people sometimes do good. I didn't know which variety she was, just that she needed help, and I needed to feel helpful.

Inviting her to my party was a crazy idea, but also kind of brilliant. I wanted her to know the house was empty, that she was safe there. Winter was coming; if she had no other place to go, it would be cruel not to let her stay, at least until my dad decided what he was going to do with it. I had no intention of telling her I was the reason she was homeless now. She would know me simply as the new owner's daughter. The other stuff would come out later, as would answers to my questions about her part in it all.

A few sad Halloween fireworks pop-popped in the distance as my driver crested over the top of Mulholland Drive and dropped down into the Valley. I would be home in a few minutes, thank God; I couldn't wait to get out of this costume and into a hot bath. I hoped Carter wasn't waiting up for me. I didn't want him to see my pin-striped face and ask a bunch of questions. Maybe I was kidding myself that he didn't know about Jared and me. If he didn't, there was no point telling him now.

My dullsville suburban neighborhood was predictably dead when we turned onto my street. Our block was a series of tract homes built in the sixties, and many were still occupied by their original owners, now in their eighties. There were no sidewalks, so we rarely got foot traffic, except for the occasional coyote. There were also no streetlights. Once the Uber drove away, it would be completely dark. So I took out my phone to have a light at the ready.

"Thanks for the ride," I said to my driver as I got out and clicked on my phone light. He nodded and pulled away, and I shined the beam on the ground to light my path. They hadn't repaved our street for decades, and some of the potholes were so big you could go fishing in them.

I was so focused on not turning an ankle in my heeled sandals, I didn't notice the black sedan parked next to my driveway until I was passing by the front of it. I felt a whiff of heat off the hood but was too in my head about my breakup with Jared to think anything of it, so I just walked on by. Not that my reflexes were fast enough to fend off the attack, even if I hadn't been caught by surprise. The gloved hand was over my mouth before I realized that the clomping sound was footsteps and the hard thing pressing into my back was a gun.

I heard a clack as my phone smacked to the ground. I tried to call out but the hand was clamped too tight. I couldn't pull it off but because I couldn't move my arms—my attacker had pinned them behind my back.

"Nice and slow," a male voice said, and suddenly I was in a head-lock being dragged toward that black sedan. I could feel hairpins digging into my scalp as his hard bicep pressed into the base of my skull. I heard the engine turn over—*there are two of them!* Another set of hands grabbed my feet—*no, three!*

I felt my body being lifted off the ground, and an instant later I was in the car. I tried to take in as many details as I could: black seats, black shoes, hairy knuckles gripping my ankles . . . *Ugh! Why didn't I pay more attention when I walked by the car?*

I had always known if the wrong people found out what I'd done, things could get dicey. As a hand gripped my neck and forced my face into the sticky leather seat, I realized I'd just met the wrong people.

CHAPTER 21

Bree

I pulled the heavy pool house curtain closed all but a crack and peered out into the backyard. I was grateful for the rain because it camouflaged my footprints. If it was bad to be caught alone with a dead body, it was worse to be caught running away from one, but as usual, my knee-jerk reaction was to hide. I wasn't a murderer, but I was far from innocent, so I guess I was behaving in a manner fitting who I'd become.

As I stood there huddled in the pool house like a wet rat, I flashed back to the night before, sitting at the piano surrounded by people and music and joy. For a few glorious hours I was in my pre-Luke life again, playing pop music for listeners who reveled in singing along. The band I played with in New York called itself Killing Time, which I never quite got, because "killing time" implies there's somewhere you'd rather be, and I never felt that way when I was playing music. It didn't matter if I was in the practice room or onstage; if people were listening or I was alone; if it was Bach or the Beatles. Music was never what I did to pass the time—it was how I transcended it. Luke used to worry that I spent too much time alone, but how could I explain that when I was making music, there was no such thing as time? You know the feeling, when you are so immersed in something you don't need food, you don't need sleep, you look up at the clock and the whole afternoon is gone and you have no idea where it went. That's how I felt about music, and how I felt about Luke. Luke was my soulmate. Music was my soul. Everything else was just going through the motions of being human. *Killing time, I guess.*

The wind picked up, and the heavy curtain arched inward in the breeze. I tucked myself behind it and peered through the sliver between the panels. I heard a voice say "On scene" and someone on the other end of a walkie-talkie say "Copy that," and a second later two firefighters in mustard-yellow jackets appeared in my sight lines.

One of them called out, "Hello? Anybody home?"

They had helmets on, presumably to shield them from the rain, which was coming down in sheets now. Luke had installed a lock on that side gate, but Sophie and Carter had opened it for the party, probably because they didn't want people tromping through the house. Everyone wound up in the house anyway, thanks to me, Chris Martin, and Steinway & Sons. I guess after all that music and drinking and drama they had forgotten to lock it—not that it mattered now; Sophie was dead, I was trapped, and the firefighters were just the first of many people who were about to storm the scene.

I watched as one of the men in yellow circled the pool and peered into the water.

"Aw, crap," he muttered as he saw why he'd been called.

"I'll go," the other one said, then shed his jacket and hat and waded into the pool. As he disappeared under the water, the other firefighter stripped down to his T-shirt, too, and then they were both in the pool, one retrieving, one waiting to receive. Several seconds passed, and then the submerged one popped up out of the water dragging what looked like a life-size Barbie doll. From behind the safety of my curtain, I saw legs that looked more crab-like than human—stiff and white and bent just so. I saw an arm, jutting stiffly out to one side. And then I saw that fan of black hair, and I had to look away, because I didn't want to see the face of the woman who had been so kind to me and now was gone just like the others.

The two firefighters set the body down beside the pool. I was so spellbound by the rain bouncing off that snow-white corpse that I didn't hear the chorus of sirens until it was right outside. The responders were streaming in like soldiers now: EMTs in navy-blue windbreakers pulling a gurney, police in shiny black raincoats and those signature black hats. I didn't know why they needed so many people to help a woman who was already dead. I counted eight, not knowing the important ones were still coming.

I shuddered as pool and rainwater ran down my shins onto the cold tile floor. I thought back to the last time I'd seen Sophie alive—standing in the doorway, saying goodbye to her friends. She'd looked so happy, there was no way she'd done this to herself. *So an accident, then?* Even if she'd slipped and fallen, surely she could swim. Yes, she'd had a few drinks, but she wasn't drunk. So how had she wound up at the bottom of the pool? The police would be wondering the same thing. And then they would want to know why I ran away, and I would have to tell them the truth, and my heart raced with fear because that meant facing it myself.

"Cover her up," I heard someone bark, and a moment later there was a pale yellow tarp on Sophie's body and a policeman standing guard like a dog over a bone. The EMTs left without her, which I thought was strange, but also logical, as there was nothing they could do to help her now. I'd watched enough crime shows in my life to know that in a suspected homicide they try not to disturb anything until the forensic people arrive and comb the place for evidence in their bunny suits and Mickey Mouse gloves. My fingerprints would be everywhere. But so would a lot of people's, thanks to the party. If they brought bloodhounds, it would be perfectly logical to find my scent all over the house, given that I used to live there. You didn't need to be a detective to know that. There was nothing to connect me specifically to Sophie's death. All I had to do was wait it out, and then I could go back to my piss-poor existence in peace.

Now that I'd spent one night in a bed, I was more determined than ever to get off the street and into an apartment. It had taken me three months to save that $800, but if I didn't make any more stupid mistakes, maybe I could do it again in two? I really didn't need much, just the occasional tank of gas and tube of toothpaste. Food was pretty easy to come by, if you weren't too proud to ask for it. Now that I'd lowered myself to hiding from police in my former pool house, nothing was beneath me.

I backed away from the curtain, then grabbed a towel from the tower by the couch-bench to blot my wet T-shirt and hair. The joggers were hopelessly waterlogged and cold against my skin, so I slipped them off and wrung them out in the sink, then draped them over the edge of it so they could dry. There was a trail of water across the floor, so I used the towel to mop it up. Then, wearing only my wet T-shirt and under-wear, I tiptoed back over to the curtain. The rain had washed away the trail of pool water that would have led them right to me, and for that I was grateful. I'd had enough police interviews to last a lifetime; I didn't want to endure another interrogation, today or ever.

I peered back out into the yard. One policeman was still standing over the body like he was afraid it might get up and walk away. The other three (I think there were three?) were huddled under the eave, trying to stay dry. It was one of them who pointed at the object on the deck, then went over to examine it. He looked like he was about to pick it up, then thought better of it.

"What is it?" one of the other cops called to him.

"A phone."

The blood rushed to my face as fear seized me like a bear trap, because of course that phone was mine.

CHAPTER 22

———

CARTER

I woke up to three missed calls from my dad. For a second I was confused: *Couldn't he just knock?* Then I remembered he and Mom were in New York and we'd had a party, where I'd found and then promptly lost the woman of my dreams.

I glanced at the time: seven thirty. The sun was up but had been swallowed by heavy clouds. Rain was pelting the roof and blurring my windows. I was tempted to turn my phone off and go back to sleep, but I didn't want to wake up to more missed calls, so I unlocked the phone and dialed.

"Carter?"

"Hey, Dad," I said, making no attempt to hide the scratchiness in my morning voice.

"I know it's early there, but I got a power outage alert at the Beverly Hills house. I need you to check it out, OK, buddy?" *Buddy? That's a new one.*

"Yeah, no problem."

"It went out in the night sometime." Of course I knew that, but I didn't say so.

"OK, I'll check it out."

"The breaker box is in the garage, hopefully something—a power surge maybe—just tripped it and you can reset it. You know how to do that, right?"

"I'll figure it out." If I knew how to do it, I would have done it last night. But like I said, I'd figure it out.

"Don't wait too long. If there's a problem, we have to get on it. It's got a pool—"

"Yeah, I know, Dad." I didn't mean to sound defensive, but I'd been the EVP of the company for three years; I may not have known my way around a breaker box, but I knew why a house with a lawn that needed watering and a pool that needed filtering couldn't go without power.

"You'll call the DWP if you can't get it sorted?"

I felt agitated that Dad expected me to take care of the house he hadn't even told me about. But then I realized if we didn't want him to find out about the party, it was probably a good thing that he asked me to be boots on the ground.

"Yeah, Dad, don't worry, I got it."

I hung up with a promise to keep him posted, then rolled out of bed. Waiting around for the Department of Water and Power was not how I wanted to spend my Saturday, but the universe didn't seem to care what I wanted these days, so I sucked up my annoyance and got dressed.

Sophie and I shared a Jack-and-Jill bathroom, and the door to her room was open. I peeked in to see not only was she not there but her bed was still made and covered with yesterday's clothes. I flashed back to her conversation with Jared. I hadn't stayed until the end—maybe she'd agreed to come out as a couple and then left with him? It was the only reasonable explanation why she wasn't home, and I wasn't ready to go down the road of unreasonable. I texted her (U good, sis?), then went downstairs to suck back a Nespresso shot. As I got behind the wheel of my truck, I checked my phone to see my message hadn't been delivered, which was weird, but not enough to make me nervous yet.

I drove on autopilot, rolling through the neighborhood stop signs. Heavy rain pounded my windshield as I got onto the freeway. It hadn't rained like this for months, but it was almost November; we were overdue for some weather. As my wipers squawked across wet glass, my brain was a merry-go-round of self-loathing. *Why did Bree just leave like that? What did I do wrong?* If I were a glutton for punishment, I could ask Sophie for her number. She didn't approve, but she'd probably still give it to me. But then what? If the woman wanted to go out with me, she'd had her chance. I'd told her I was coming back, I'm sure I did. *Is it possible she didn't hear me? Or misunderstood? Or is she just rude and self-absorbed, like every other woman in this town?*

I saw the emergency vehicles as soon as I turned right off Sunset Boulevard onto Rodeo Drive. My first thought was that something must have happened to one of the neighbors, because why would there be police cars at our place?

There were two squad cars, an unmarked sedan, and a fire truck parked in front of the house. I tried to cling to my theory that something must have happened to a neighbor, but the fire truck was blocking our driveway.

I flashed to Sophie's bed, still made from the night before. I looked down at my phone, at my text to her from earlier this morning: still undelivered. *Stay calm, Carter, stay calm . . .*

I texted Jared because, as far as I knew, he was the last one to see her. Hey man, sorry to bother you, but do you know where Sophie is? I figured if she was with him, he would tell me, because wasn't that the point of his ultimatum, to start telling people? He texted back right away: No I haven't talked to her since the party, sorry.

I pulled over and jumped out of the truck and into the rain.

There was no point trying to get in through the front door—there was a cop standing guard, and I didn't have a key.

The gate to the side yard was cordoned off with yellow police tape, but unguarded. I sprinted over to it, flipped the latch, and ducked underneath the tape.

"Hey!" I heard a voice call after me. "Hey!"

My heart was pounding as hard as the rain as I tore along the side of the house toward the backyard. I heard police chatter over walkie-talkies—"perimeter breach . . . side yard . . . intercept . . ."—but I kept going. *Sophie, where are you . . . ?*

I reached the threshold of the backyard and stumbled to a stop. I saw the body immediately, lying supine on the side of the pool. It was covered with a tarp the color of butter, but its shape was unmistakable.

"Oh God," I wailed. An arm reached out to grab me as my legs gave out.

"You can't be back here, sir."

"No, no, no . . ."

I felt another set of hands grip my arm. "Let's get him inside."

I couldn't feel my legs as I walk-floated up the porch stairs into the kitchen. Somehow I wound up on a stool at the marble-top island. A few seconds later a bald guy in a dark suit was standing over me with a glass of water.

"Here, take a drink."

I shook my head as I waved it off.

"The body, I need to see . . . ," I started, but then choked on my words. *Maybe I don't need to look under that tarp. Maybe if I don't see, it might not be true.*

"We're waiting for the coroner," the bald guy said. "She gets the first look." And I didn't know whether to be furious or relieved.

"My sister didn't come home last night." My voice cracked. I felt tears burn my eyes, and the confession tumbled out of me like a landslide. "We were here, we had a party." It wasn't much of a confession; the trash can was overflowing with red SOLO Cups, the counter was littered with chips and soiled paper plates—the evidence was everywhere.

"Tell me about your sister," the cop said as he sat down on the stool across from me. "How old is she?"

I saw that he had a notebook open. *A detective.*

"Sophie," I said. "Her name is Sophie."

"And you are?"

"Carter."

I thought back to the night before. Spying on Sophie and Jared from the deck. Coming back inside to collect Bree.

Bree.

What happened to Bree?

I glanced toward the front door. When I left last night it was locked—dead bolted from the inside. I knew that because I was the one who locked it. Which meant she hadn't gone out that way, because how could she have locked it behind her without a key? She couldn't have gone out the garage because that was closed, too. She would have needed a clicker and power to the house to shut it behind her, neither of which she had. And she couldn't have gone out the back—I'd come in from there, and she hadn't walked past me. But when I came back inside, she was gone. *So where did she go?*

"Tell me more about Sophie," the detective urged. "What does she look like?"

Jared told Sophie he wanted her to be his girlfriend, out in the open for the world to see. She hadn't said no, just that she "wasn't ready." He adored her, and I had every reason to believe he'd give her a chance to come around.

There was only one other partygoer still there after all the other guests had left. I thought back to what Sophie had said about her: *"Don't go there, she's trouble."* I'd brushed it off in the moment, but now that warning haunted me. Because if I hadn't seen Bree exit the house, it could only mean one thing.

"She slept here," I said.

"Who?" the cop asked, so I told him my bone-chilling realization.

"The woman who killed my sister."

PART 2

———

MAY

(FIVE MONTHS AGO)

CHAPTER 23

—

BREE

"Happy anniversary!" Luke said as he held up a bar-of-soap-size cardboard box tied with a shiny red ribbon. I was making breakfast—poached eggs on sourdough toast—in our cozy galley kitchen, like I did every morning before Luke went off to work.

"You know you didn't have to get me anything," I said. Getting gifts always embarrassed me because we never had much growing up and I knew every time Mom bought me something it was taking money for things we needed, like food and soap and gas for the car.

"It's not what you think," he warned, and I wiped my hands on a dish towel and took the box from his outstretched palm.

"Is it a puppy?" I asked.

"I hope not!"

I held it up to my ear and gave it a little shake.

"Don't shake it, you'll scare him!" Luke joked, and I swatted him with the dish towel.

"Ha ha."

"Just open it!"

I pulled on the ribbon, and the bow melted into the palm of my hand. I lifted the top off the box. There, in a bed of cotton, was a plain brass key.

"It's a key," I said.

"That's right."

"Um, thank you?"

"You're welcome."

My egg timer went off, so I skimmed the eggs out of the pot and put them on the toast. Luke and I ate breakfast together every morning at the bistro table by our kitchen window. We had lived in this little bungalow since the day I arrived here, and I knew it so well I could navigate it with my eyes closed. After breakfast, Luke would go off to a jobsite or to meet a customer, and I'd clean up, practice, then either head out to teach a lesson or shop for dinner. I know it doesn't sound like much of a day, but everything about my LA life was new and exciting to me, and I was savoring getting to know my new husband and my new home.

"So?" I asked as I sat down across from him at the breakfast table. "Are you going to tell me what this key is for?"

"Nope. I'm going to show you."

It was our third wedding anniversary. The first one, he'd gotten me two dozen long-stem red roses and I cried because I knew how much they cost and that they'd be dead within a week. Our second was diamond earrings, because, as he reasoned, unlike those roses, diamonds are forever, so I didn't have to cry. But this year there was no crying, and no explanation—even though it arguably called for one more than either of those other gifts did.

I put the dishes in the dishwasher and wiped down the counter. Our bungalow apartment was small but in a nice part of town, walking distance to good Thai food, a French bakery, a pub with live music. It was just Luke, me, and Wolfy the cat; we didn't need more than the one bedroom. Not yet, anyway. We weren't trying to get pregnant, but we'd just stopped *not* trying, so maybe soon?

Luke was waiting for me in the living room with his car keys in hand. We had space for a piano or a TV but not both. Luke had insisted on buying me a baby grand the moment I arrived in LA, and it took up more than half the room. We had a TV in the bedroom but barely watched it. If Luke wanted to watch sports, we went to the pub.

"Why are you making that face?" I asked when I saw Luke standing at the front door wearing a big Cheshire Cat grin.

"What face?"

I made the face.

"Would you prefer this?" He pursed his lips together in an exaggerated scowl.

"Now you look constipated." He laughed and opened the door for me.

"Do you have the key?"

I held it up.

"Then let's go."

He followed me outside, and I waited for him to lock the door. We had a small, one-car garage that was just big enough for my Prius, but the landlord let him park his truck in front of it, which was fine because he always left before me.

"You want to drive?" he asked.

"Sure."

He opened the door for me, and I hopped up into the cab. I liked driving his truck because you could see over all the other cars and it made me feel like a boss.

"Which way am I going?" I asked as I neared the end of the alley.

"Turn left on Doheny."

He directed me out of our funky West Hollywood neighborhood into the heart of Beverly Hills. We were only a mile from home, but it felt like a world apart. As soon as we crossed the town line, tightly packed cottages and duplexes gave way to sprawling green lawns and houses five times the size of our rented bungalow.

"Are we going to a safety-deposit box?" I asked as we approached the bustling downtown. But instead of turning toward the city, he had me turn into the residential neighborhood where I liked to jog.

"Turn right here."

"On Rodeo Drive?"

"Yup."

I wasn't a big fitness buff, but I liked to jog because I could check out the crazy-luxurious Beverly Hills neighborhoods up close and personal. Los Angeles was like a quilt; every square was different, and I loved to hop from one square to the next. Rodeo Drive was one of my favorite streets, with its parade of palm trees so tall and thin they seemed to defy the laws of physics. I had never seen palm trees before I came to LA, and they still made me feel like I was in a dream.

"Pull over," Luke instructed.

"Here?"

"Yes, here."

I slowed to a stop in front of a modern-looking house with big windows and a double-wide front door. I knew the house—watching it get built had been one of my favorite pastimes over the past year. That and playing *Where's Waldo?* with the mobile detailer who I knew would be somewhere in the neighborhood, because it wouldn't be Beverly Hills if someone wasn't getting their car washed.

I turned off the engine and hopped out of the truck. Luke was waiting for me on the sidewalk. He took my hand, and I'll be damned if he didn't escort me right up the front walk of that spectacular house.

"Sorry there's no grass yet," he said. "We'll do that last." I had no idea why he was apologizing for the state of someone else's front yard, so I didn't respond.

"Where's your key?" he asked as we stepped onto the front porch. I pulled it out of my purse, and he pointed to the lock.

"Unlock the door."

I didn't know what kind of trick he was pulling, but I wasn't playing.

"Luke, what is happening?" I asked, and he gave me that Cheshire Cat smile again.

"Key. In. Lock."

I relented and slid the key in the lock, turned it, then pushed on the heavy mahogany door. Light from twin skylights shone down on the polished oak floor, making it literally sparkle.

"Go on in," my husband urged.

"Are you sure we're allowed to be here?"

"Of course we're allowed to be here—it's our house."

The statement was so absurd I almost laughed. We were at a mansion on famed Rodeo Drive—the same street as Dior, Gucci, Valentino, Dolce *and* Gabbana. Why was my husband saying this was our house?

"Luke, what are you talking about?"

"Happy anniversary."

I thought back to the first time I'd jogged in this neighborhood, when this house had just been a big pile of dirt. I'd been fascinated by the process—dig a hole, pour concrete, frame the walls, put in windows, lay the roof. I'd wanted to understand what my husband did. I never in a million years thought I was actually watching his workmen do it!

"Did you . . . ?" I started, then stopped, because the notion seemed positively insane.

"Build it for you? Yes."

My hand floated up over my mouth. I knew if we got pregnant, we would have to move, but this house and this neighborhood were beyond anything I could have ever imagined. I was a simple gal from a raggedy logging town, not a movie star, and now I was moving to *the* Beverly Hills? I had no idea when I married Luke that builders got to keep all the best lots for themselves—which of course they didn't, but I knew better than to ask too many questions.

As I stood there at the formidable front door of this marble-and-glass fortress, I flashed to my mother, how she'd scrubbed the kitchen while I practiced, promising I would have a big, fat, beautiful life as long as I followed my heart. I looked up at Luke, the man who had lured my orphaned heart out of hiding, and tears of gratitude and grief spilled down my face. My mother had worked her fingers to the bone—sweeping floors, washing dishes, dusting, mopping, polishing, folding laundry for the whole neighborhood—so I could be here. I didn't know if our loved ones watched over us after they passed, but if they did, I hoped my mother could see that her sacrifices weren't in vain. No, I wasn't touring the world as she'd fantasized I would someday do, but I wouldn't have this beautiful life if it weren't for the piano and the mother who'd encouraged me to learn how to play it.

"What am I thinking," my husband said, shaking his head. "There's a proper way to do this."

And with those words he scooped me off the ground and carried me over the threshold of that magnificent house. The feeling of his arms around my legs, the warmth of his chest pressing against mine, the glow of sunlight taking us into its warm embrace . . . I felt like I'd just walked through the gates of heaven.

I wrapped my arms around my husband's neck and pressed my nose into his neck. In that moment, I knew I had married the most amazing, generous, perfect man on the planet. What I didn't know was that his gift to me would lead to the devastating end of us.

CHAPTER 24

—

LUKE

The hardest part about building the house was keeping it a secret from Bree. She never complained about our tiny rented cottage being cramped or dated, but it was getting embarrassing that after almost three years of marriage I still hadn't offered her something better. I was a contractor! I'd dragged her all the way across the country—the least I could do was give my bride appliances from this century and a two-car garage. I hadn't anticipated a supply chain jam turning what was supposed to be a nine-month sprint into a two-year marathon. With the exception of a few finishing touches, it finally came together just in time for our third anniversary, and my ego breathed a sigh of relief.

The original house was a teardown—a rare find in the flats of Beverly Hills. As a builder with connections, I got a chance to buy it before it went on the open market. Bree and I had been married for almost a year, and I knew she was obsessed with the neighborhood and sometimes went jogging there. After growing up in rural British Columbia, she'd had enough of trail running in the woods. *"You've seen one tree, you've seen them all,"* she used to joke. Beverly Hills, on the other hand, was *"better than Disneyland,"* she'd raved. *"There's every kind of house there, not just boring A-frames like we have back home."* She loved to tell me about all the *"crazy-big mansions"* and make fun of the people who lived there for how often they washed their cars. *"Nobody ever washes their car in Canada,"* she'd say. *"But I see that mobile detailing guy in someone's driveway almost every day!"*

I loved seeing Los Angeles through her eyes. As a transplant from Ojai, a small town in the mountains above Ventura, I'd always found the city noisy and congested and full of hustlers. But Bree was like a kid in a candy store here, gushing over all the different varieties of people, neighborhoods, sights, and sounds. She loved that you could get fruit on your pizza and garlic in your ice cream. She loved that there were palm trees *"right outside our front door!"* and murals that stretched for whole city blocks. It was exotic and exciting to her, and so it became exotic and exciting to me. Her enthusiasm was intoxicating, and I knew the moment I'd brought her here that I wanted to get drunk on it every day for the rest of my life.

At first glance Bree and I might seem like an odd match—the builder and the pianist. But our crafts were not so different. Bree's piano playing could transport you to another place and time. What she did with eighty-eight keys, I did with two-by-fours and cement. Building, like making music, was a mysterious swirl of divine inspiration and meticulous technique. Architectural drawings, like sheet music, are just blueprints; it takes talent and skill to bring them to life. Bree and I understood each other in the way only fellow artists can. Our connection was immediate and deep and meant to last a lot longer than our circumstances permitted.

I'd asked Bree what her favorite houses were, and she'd said *"the super modern ones"* because her town was old and quaint and she'd had enough of that. It was a great lot—perfectly flat with a pair of mature maple trees in the back for shade and privacy. I used a plan I'd done for a client in Westlake Village to save money, then made it my own with the finishes—warm mahogany and cool concrete on the outside, blond wood and bright stainless steel on the inside. If this house was going to take two years to build, I wanted to make sure it was worth the wait.

"I thought we could put the piano right there," I said, setting Bree down and pointing to the sunken living room. The house was still missing a few final touches—light switches in the kitchen, baseboards here and there, grass in the yard. I hadn't installed the sprinklers yet; I figured I could do that after we moved in. As for furniture, we'd have to start from scratch, because nothing from our little bungalow would work in the space. Except for Bree's piano, of course; if we only brought one thing with us, it would be that. Bree never talked about going on tour, but her desire to practice every day suggested she hadn't completely given up on the idea, even if she didn't know it consciously. I confess it broke my heart a little that her talent was wasted on just me. But she'd been under pressure to play for others her whole life; I had no intention of applying more.

"You know April Fools' Day was last month," Bree said, and I tried not to seem offended that my wife couldn't believe I had built us a house.

"I'm a builder. This is what I do."

She must have seen the hurt in my eyes, because she immediately took my hand and squeezed it.

"I didn't mean it like that! It just feels too good to be true."

"Babe, I've been saving up for this for a long time, since before I met you," I said, to make it make sense. I know it's a little strange that I'd never owned a house, but I was a contractor for hire, not a flipper. Plus while my mother was alive, I didn't touch my savings in case her health took a turn for the worse. I could have bought something already on the market after Bree and I were married, but the opportunity to build something for her was impossible to pass up. As for this house being "too good to be true," my wife wasn't wrong, but I couldn't tell her that.

I'd been obsessed with tools and building things since I was old enough to hold a hammer. I'd built a chicken coop for my neighbor when I was in sixth grade—that was my first paying job, and I did the whole thing myself. My dad wanted me to be an engineer, but then he left, and the prospect of going to college left with him. So I just kept building stuff: a fence for the local dairy farmer, a tree house for the preschool, a toolshed, a carport, a guesthouse, a loft. I was a master framer by the age of sixteen, a licensed electrician by the time I graduated high school. It felt good to help Mom pay the bills with my side jobs, and I sent money home until the day she died.

"Can I go explore?" my wife asked, eyes wide with curiosity.

"I'd be disappointed if you didn't."

Bree peeked into a closet, the powder room, then padded through the dining room into the kitchen. "Oh my God, the backyard is like a resort!" she cried out as she peered through the glass pocket doors that opened to the outside. I didn't have to put in a pool, but they're not that expensive to build, and good for resale. Not that I thought we'd be selling anytime soon. After twenty years in the business, that's just how I was wired.

"Oh!" she gasped. "There's a little pool house, too!"

The pool house had been an afterthought. I realized after I'd committed to the pool that there was no shower on the ground floor, and the powder room was all the way at the front of the house. I didn't want people to have to trudge through the kitchen and dining room to go to the bathroom. Plus there was the perfect spot for it at the back of the yard between those twin maple trees.

"Can I go out there?"

"Of course."

I showed her how to unlock the pocket doors and then followed her out onto the deck. She ran over to the pool house and started peeking in all the built-in compartments meant for dishes and board games and knickknacks. She lifted the bench of the built-in window seat, then climbed inside and popped out like a jack-in-the-box.

"It's like a little dollhouse!" she exclaimed.

"You're such a goofball," I said. And then as if to prove me right, she went into the kitchenette, opened the minifridge, and pantomimed finding a pitcher and pouring a drink.

"Join me for some lemonade?" she asked, offering me a pretend glass.

"I'd love to."

Some of my friends raised eyebrows when I told them I was marrying a woman thirteen years younger than I am after knowing her for only three months, but I didn't care. "You're in the fog of lust," they warned, and I'm sure what they said behind my back was worse. But they didn't know Bree. I know it sounds like a contradiction, but she was both the most angelic and down-to-earth person I had ever met. She made me see things in new ways—a pool cabana was a playhouse, a song was a way for strangers to hold hands without touching, a traffic jam was a thousand souls trying to reconnect with their loved ones at once. Her imagination was as expansive as the California coastline. I didn't marry her because I had promised her that if she moved to LA I would take care of her; I married her because every day I was with her was the greatest day of my life.

Time stood still as we sat with our feet in the pool, drinking our imaginary lemonade and letting the sun warm our faces while the water numbed our toes. I didn't want to speak, didn't want to pop the bubble of happiness that had formed around us and made me feel like I might float up to the sun.

"Do you think we'll grow old here?" my wife asked.

And I wanted to say yes, because I had built this house with enough space to have kids and pets and birthday parties all the way to forever.

But deep in the darkest recess of my heart, I feared the lies this house was built on would claw their way out and rip that dream apart.

"Time will tell," I offered, because the mood was celebratory, and I didn't want to ruin it with the truth.

CHAPTER 25

BREE

I had a present for him, too.

I'd found the car on Autotrader—a 2004 convertible Porsche 911 with forty-four thousand miles on it. Luke loved his truck, but it needed two parking spots at Trader Joe's, and city life was challenging enough. I knew he sometimes wished he had something smaller that he could zoom around town in when he had to run to the hardware store or we went out for dinner. He said he didn't mind the Prius, but I knew he was lying. Besides, the Prius was my car and, with its dented passenger door and mismatched tires, not really fit for pulling up to the valet.

I hadn't thought about what we'd do for parking since we only had the two spots, but now that we had a house (*we have a house!*), it wouldn't be a problem. Maybe on some level I'd known our living situation was about to change, because when I bought the car, I didn't give it a second thought. Or maybe I knew finding legal overnight parking was about to become my life and I wanted to get some practice.

I had the car checked by two different mechanics before I bought it, just to make sure I wasn't getting a lemon. As for how I paid for it, well, that was the sneakiest part of this story. Luke had applied for my green card so I could work legally, but we were still waiting—we were told it could take up to four years! But I needed something to do besides keep house, and I had a marketable skill. It was Luke's idea for me to start giving piano lessons. "You can take cash," he'd said. "Until your green card arrives."

I'm sure when he said it, he thought what I made would never amount to much—a haircut, a night out, a new pair of shoes. Three years into our marriage, I had seven students, all paying $125 for their lessons—some weekly, some every other week, a couple just now and again. I tried to give Luke the money, but he told me to keep it "for a rainy day." I had no idea that my whole life would soon be rainy days, but I did as I was told. He never asked how much I had, and I never told him that my stash had grown to five figures. The car did the talking when I gave it to him on our anniversary.

"Are you ready for your present?" I said as we were getting ready to leave for dinner. Luke had made a reservation at our favorite Italian restaurant. We didn't need to dress up, LA people hardly ever do, but we both wanted to look good for each other, so I wore a wrap dress with flowers on it, and he wore a tie.

"You got me a present?" he said, and I handed him the same box he had given me, tied with that same red ribbon.

"So, not a puppy," he guessed, and I laughed.

"No, not this time."

His face registered confusion when he saw the key.

"This is a car key."

"Very good."

"There's no way you got me a car."

"Go see for yourself."

His face reddened with astonishment when he saw that snow-white Porsche perched in our garage like a prince on his throne. The car was in great condition; it was nearly twenty years old, but it barely had a scratch. The engine had been rebuilt, the brakes were new, and the caramel leather seats were supple but not faded. The car had been lovingly cared for, just as my husband had lovingly cared for me.

"Bree . . . ," my husband said. "How . . . ?"

"You told me to save my money. What else was I going to do with it?" I'd been squirreling away between $300 and $600 per week for over two years. I thought it was a game—how much could I save in a week, a month, a year? It never occurred to me what I was doing was improper, and that by amassing so much cash I was putting a target on our backs.

"Does it run?" my husband asked, and if I didn't know better, I might have thought he hoped the answer was no. Because then maybe the amount of tax-free money I had hoarded might still be insignificant.

"Of course it runs! The engine was completely rebuilt." Having a car that wouldn't cost more to own than it was to buy had been paramount on my mind, so I'd done my homework, poring over service records and crawling under the hood myself. Growing up in Canada, where temperatures plunged below freezing for months on end, we were meticulous about our cars. Both Mom and I knew how to change the oil and check the radiator, the antifreeze, the brake fluid, the tires. I wasn't a mechanic, but I was no princess.

"Then let's take it for a ride."

As we drove to the restaurant with the top down and our fingers threaded together, I thought my husband was quiet because he was stunned and humbled. *He knew his little wife was talented but never in a million years thought she could pull off something like this!*

It didn't occur to me he was quiet because he was worried. I only knew I'd done a bad thing because of what happened next.

CHAPTER 26

SOPHIE

"A guy I work with needs some bookkeeping help," my dad said when I came down for dinner.

"OK . . . ," I said. "Are you volunteering me for the job?" I asked, as if he hadn't already.

"He's a contractor. It shouldn't be too complicated." I graduated with honors from USC; not sure why my dad would think "not complicated" would be a draw, but I tried not to look insulted.

"Sounds great. The more mind numbing the better," I said cheerfully.

"Your father's trying to help you," Mom said as she put a steaming basket of baked potatoes on the table, which we were meant to stuff with sour cream and cheese, because nothing like a big glob of saturated fat to top off your carbo load.

"I have a degree in forensic accounting, Mom," I said, because apparently she'd forgotten. Over the last three months, and with zero enthusiasm, I'd made a list of private firms that offered forensic accounting services in civil matters like divorces and personal bankruptcies, but I couldn't bring myself to apply for jobs at any of them. I had my heart set on working for the FBI. I checked the website every day for openings and applied every time something came up, which wasn't often, but that didn't deter me. I'd even called the local field office to ask if I could intern, because yes, I would have done it for free, that's how much I wanted it. In the beginning, I told my parents about my efforts (*"A new opening popped up," "I heard back from the recruiter," "I sent three résumés this week!"*), but when I still couldn't get so much as an interview after a year of trying, I stopped talking to them about it. I could tell by the way they looked at me that they thought it was a pipe dream. But 15 percent of FBI employees are people like me—number crunchers who bring down bad guys with pens, which turns out really are mightier than swords. Though I would have learned how to swashbuckle, too, if they told me that was required.

"Well, in the meantime you can take some part-time work for one of your father's colleagues," Mom said. I looked over at my brother, who was mashing the insides of his potato with the back of his fork. I was happy for him that he found a job at my dad's company, but I didn't like the precedent he had set by making everyone's business the family business.

"Can you pass the bacon?" he said, pointing to the bowl.

"Are there any, like, vegetables?" I asked, sliding the plate of crumbled pink-and-brown pig butt toward my brother.

"Green onions are vegetables," my brother said, offering me the bowl.

"If you want to steam some broccoli, there's some in the fridge," Mom offered.

"I'd love some broccoli," Dad said. I could feel him looking at me, but I didn't meet his gaze. I knew my parents thought I was "lost" and "lazy," but they were dead wrong; I just had no interest in settling for an ordinary life, and landing the extraordinary one I wanted was taking longer than I'd thought.

"Broccoli. Great idea. I'm on it."

I met my dad's colleague the next morning at his office in Culver City. It wasn't much of an office—just a box trailer on cinder blocks.

"Thanks for coming," my new boss said, waving me into the ten-by-thirty rectangular trailer-office. "I'm Luke." He put down his coffee, which was steaming and inky black, to shake my hand. I came to learn he drank it constantly, and always black. In fact, the coffee machine was the only personal item in that trailer, besides the mug he drank out of.

"Sophie," I said, offering my hand.

He was younger than I expected—late thirties, maybe? I had thought because he was a friend of my dad that he'd be older. He had a hunky construction worker vibe in his flannel shirt, faded Levi's, and boots, and I could tell from the calluses on his hand when I shook it that he'd been a laborer all his life. He was kind of a babe, with his sky-blue eyes and dimpled smile, and if it weren't my dad who'd sent me here, I might have thought this was a setup.

"I'm sure this job is beneath you, but I got behind on my cash flow report, and I just need some help reconciling my receipts," he said as he pulled out the chair for me. There was only the one chair, and it felt a little weird to be sitting while he was standing, but he didn't seem to mind.

"Sure, I can do that."

"Does thirty an hour sound fair?"

It sounded more than fair, so I nodded. "Sure."

He explained how he bought materials at wholesale prices, then charged the client retail. "I don't upcharge for labor, so pretty much all my profits are from materials."

It seemed like a lame business model, but I was there to do math, not judge. "Makes sense."

He pointed to a stack of files. "I think there are about twelve or thirteen different jobs there. Every charge should have an affiliated receipt; I just need you to put them in the ledger." He opened a spreadsheet on his computer. "It's basically just balancing my checkbook for me."

"Yeah, no problem." It was mindless work; a monkey could do it. But for thirty dollars an hour, I was happy to lend a hand.

He left to meet a client, so I put on some tunes and got to work. Based on the cheesy wood paneling and cheap plywood floor, I figured the operation was pretty rinky-dink, and his books proved me right. He made twenty grand for a kitchen reno, eleven grand for converting a garage, eighteen grand for a pool installation. I saw my dad's name on a couple of projects; he gave a discount to repeat customers, and Dad was one of the lucky few who took advantage.

He brought me a salad for lunch, which I thought was really nice, and I showed him what I had done so far. Besides entering the data on the spreadsheet, I had gone through and stapled the receipts to the invoices so they would be easy to pair. He had undercharged in a few places, so I asked him about it, and he looked a little embarrassed. "Yeah, I'm not much of a bookkeeper."

We called it a day around three with an agreement to meet at nine the next morning. I thought he would pay me at the end of the job, but he Venmoed me my two hundred bucks for the day's work on the spot.

"Just make sure to add it to the spreadsheet, because I'll forget," he joked.

Mom had mah-jongg that night, and Carter was at a Kings game, so Dad ordered Chinese food for the two of us (vegetables, yay!) and we ate at the kitchen island.

"So how'd you like Luke?" Dad asked between bites of kung pao.

"Seems like a nice guy," I said. "Not much of an operation."

"No?"

"His office is just a crappy trailer in a parking lot."

"Well, he owns a house on Rodeo Drive, so he must be doing something right." I had never known my dad to be a jealous guy, but the way he was moving his food around his plate suggested I might not know him as well as I thought.

"Is that why you sent me there? To see how he did it?"

"No," Dad insisted. "I sent you there to get you off TikTok for a few hours."

"Fair enough." I did spend too much time on TikTok.

Luke let me in the next morning, then announced he had to go to a jobsite. "I won't be back until end of day," he said, putting the keys to the trailer on the desk. "If you go out for lunch, make sure you lock up."

I got through the rest of the folders in about three hours, then tidied up the spreadsheet. There were a few receipts missing—items he had charged to customers (a dishwasher, a garage door, a half dozen wall sconces) that didn't have associated purchase orders, so I didn't know how much he'd paid for them. I knew the approximate dates, so I could easily get the information I needed from his bank statements, but I'd forgotten to ask him for them. The job wasn't really finished until I corroborated the cash flow report with his withdrawals and deposits, and I didn't want to leave the spaces blank. *Shoot, why didn't I think to ask him for bank statements?*

I was about to text him when I saw his keys there on the desk. I wasn't trying to be nosy when I unlocked the file cabinet—I was just trying to do my job.

The monthly bank statements were in a folder called "Business Checking." They weren't in chronological order, so I took them out and spread them on the desk. At first I thought I must have opened files for a different business, because the amount of money in the account was wildly out of proportion to the cash flow report I had just done. By my calculations, Luke had a few hundred thousand in annual gross income and netted just under $200K of profit. But these bank statements were in the millions.

I thought about my dad's off-the-cuff remark about Luke buying a house in Beverly Hills. *"He must be doing something right."* And I got an eerie feeling that maybe the opposite was true. There was no way a guy making less than $200,000 a year could afford a house on Rodeo Drive—even a teardown would be twenty times his annual salary. But the guy with the money flowing into this account could. *Does he have two sets of books? And what kind of person keeps two sets of books?*

My heart sped up in my chest. I glanced at the door, then got up and locked it. There was a puzzle here, and I was a forensic accountant—I'd be damned if I wasn't going to figure it out.

CHAPTER 27

———

BREE

We moved into our house the week after our anniversary. I'd wanted to move in right away, but Luke had to get the painter over to finish the upstairs, and I had three years of junk to sort through at our apartment. In the end we wound up taking very little—just our bed, sheets, clothes, favorite books and pictures, and of course my piano, which we hired professionals to move.

We didn't need a moving truck—Luke's truck was plenty big. He had a couple of guys from his work help load and unload, and we did the whole thing in a day. It still smelled like paint in our bedroom that first night, and I could tell Luke was worried about the fumes, so I made an inspired suggestion.

"Let's sleep in the pool house."

He looked at me sideways, like that was a terrible idea. "There's no bed in there."

"We can sleep on the chaise!"

We hadn't bought new furniture yet—we'd wanted to take our time with that—but Luke had found a cushy double-wide chaise when he was shopping for a client, so he bought it so we could enjoy the pool while we were deciding how to decorate the inside of the house.

"There's no heat out there," he warned.

"I'm from Canada!"

He laughed because we both knew I was the wimpiest Canadian on the planet when it came to cold. But something about that pool house called to me. Maybe I was drawn to it because it brought me back to my childhood. My mom and I lived in a house behind a house, though I never liked to think of it like that—to me it was just home. Most people in our town used their converted carriage houses for home offices or playrooms, but Mom convinced someone to rent theirs to us, and until I moved to New York, it was the only home I ever knew.

"It'll be cozy," I pleaded.

I'm not sure he was convinced I'd make it through the night, but he relented. "OK, let's do it."

We carried our pillows and blankets outside, then set them on the chaise and rolled it inside the pool house. There was no furniture in there yet—it fit where the table would eventually go. I lowered the headrest so it would lie flat. Luke went to close the curtain, but I grabbed his arm to stop him.

"No, leave it open."

"It's going to get cold." It was springtime, but the nights were still chilly by Southern California standards, low- to midfifties with a breeze.

"It'll be like camping!" Mom and I never took vacations to touristy places that required staying in hotels, but every once in a while we met our cousins from Alberta for camping when I was little and she still had the strength. We slept in a tent she'd bought at the Salvation Army thrift store, in mismatched sleeping bags that we pressed up against each other for warmth. I loved being close to her like that, listening to the night sounds and breathing in crisp mountain air. I knew packing the car with all the stuff we needed—pots, pans, food, clothes, flashlights, sleeping pads—was a lot of work for a person who already worked really hard, but she did it for me because she knew how much I loved it.

"I should have put in a firepit," Luke said. "Then we could roast marshmallows, too." I didn't know if he was serious or making fun of me, but I thought it was a great idea.

"That would be a dream," I said, so he knew what to get me for our next anniversary—not that he had to get me anything ever again.

When Luke told people he was a contractor, I know they saw someone with limited education whose most impressive skill was knowing his way around the lumberyard. But to me, he was a magician. Just like Beethoven could create a magnificent opus from silence, Luke could turn an empty lot into a palace fit for a king. Or a cozy cabin. Or a grand concert hall, a snazzy retail space, a sacred sanctuary. His imagination was as vast as his hands were skilled. I marveled at his ability to make something out of nothing; as much as I loved Beethoven, my husband's special skill was much more practical.

We climbed under the blankets. I looped my legs around Luke's to soak up some of his warmth. I thought he would reach for me to pull me into him like he always did, so I was surprised when he didn't respond to my touch.

"Luke, is something wrong?"

The last time Luke got quiet like this was on the first anniversary of his mom's death. He hadn't been by her side in her final days; it wasn't his fault—one never knows exactly when that moment will come, even when someone is brutally ill. But his guilt still ate away at him, a gnawing sadness that leaked out as anger. The more I begged him to talk to me, the angrier he got. I cooked his favorite meals, but he wouldn't eat them. I tried to drape him with affection, but he shrugged it off. I thought he didn't love me anymore. It didn't occur to me that he was being cruel to me because he was angry with himself.

I had nowhere to go during those tense few days except inside my music, so I played to escape my panic, just as I had when Mom was sick. I played Mom's favorites—Debussy's "Clair de Lune," Gershwin's *Rhapsody in Blue*, Schumann's *Scenes from Childhood*. Immersing myself in those pieces brought back memories of how I'd beaten myself up right after my mom died, too: *Why didn't I spend more time with her when she was sick? Should I have called that specialist? Could I have made her last days better?* I suddenly understood Luke's torment, that it wasn't about me, and that the more I pulled on those knots in his chest, the tighter they would get. So I left him alone. And eventually he returned to me, and we cried as we talked about how grief was a shape-shifter and we needed to be diligent about recognizing all the ugly forms it could take.

"Luke?" I asked again, because after that awful period, we'd promised to help each other find words to talk about scary feelings. "Talk to me."

"Do you think it's too much?" he asked, turning his head to look at me. His skin was cool blue in the light of the moon. I recognized that anguished look in his eyes, even though I'd misinterpreted it.

"What, the house?"

"You have to understand something," he said, turning onto his shoulder to face me. "Before I met you, I thought money was important. Because I didn't have anything else in my life that meant anything to me."

"I love that we're building a home together," I said, reaching for his hand and pressing it to my heart. I knew it was an incredible house and that he had spared no expense in building it, but I would have been happy living in this pool house as long as I was with him.

"When you get your green card, we're going to set your business up properly. You'll pay yourself a salary, declare your income, we'll do it all aboveboard."

"Yes, of course." My mom cleaned houses for cash. She kept her money in a coffee can. I did the same in New York, when I was playing with the band. After a gig, I'd take my fifty bucks and stuff it in a boot under the bed. It never occurred to me that taking cash under the table was improper, because that's all I ever knew.

"I didn't realize how much you were making." And suddenly I felt scared. I'd only hidden the money so I could surprise him. He had given me so much, I wanted to give him something special in return.

"I don't always have this many students," I said. "I can cut back."

"Oh, baby," he said, pulling my hand to his mouth and kissing my palm. "This is not about holding you back. I love that you're doing so well. We just have to do it on the up-and-up from now on."

I felt tears stinging my eyes. I clenched my jaw to hold them back. Two months later, when they came and took everything, I would remember this conversation. Because what I was doing—taking all that money and hiding it in my dresser drawer—was cheating the system. And cheaters eventually get what they deserve.

CHAPTER 28

BREE

I didn't rush out to buy living room furniture.

It wasn't because I couldn't decide what I wanted. After going from an overstuffed carriage house in BC to a one-room apartment in New York to a pint-size bungalow in West Hollywood, I wanted everything we got to be airy and inviting. Just because the house was modern didn't mean we had to furnish it with rigid tables and sofas that forced you to sit up straight. Our couch would be poofy and soft with lots of room for snuggles, and our dining table would be long with plenty of seats for friends and friends of friends.

I wasn't putting off going furniture shopping because I was worried about spending money, either. Luke had assured me he had been saving up for this moment and I didn't have to stress about not having enough. That didn't mean I would go crazy! I planned to buy quality items at fair prices, shop sales, be sensible about it, because that's how my mother had raised me.

I hadn't started decorating the house yet for one purely selfish reason: without any furniture, rugs, or wall hangings to dampen the sound, my piano sounded like a concert grand at Carnegie Hall. I had no plans to go back onstage. But as long as my house was empty, I could pretend.

Susan Walter

When we were living in our rented bungalow, I'd tried to be courteous—sticking to gentle fare like Mozart and Debussy and only playing at midday when my neighbors were unlikely to be sleeping. I didn't dare open the lid! And if I was playing something particularly tedious (scales or boring études), I'd lay a blanket on the strings to dampen the noise. But now that I had my very own house, I put the lid up on the long prop and indulged in all the pieces I loved, even the bombastic ones.

I was feeling particularly indulgent that morning, so after warming up with some Chopin, I played my audition piece for Juilliard: Tchaikovsky's Piano Concerto no. 1. Tchaikovsky was a crowd pleaser, with its hummable melodies and satisfying harmonies, and the chord progressions fell easily under my fingers. I was easing into the graceful second theme when the sound of the doorbell cut in like a sour note.

"Who's that?" I asked Wolfy, our orange tiger cat, who was curled up on the windowsill, warming himself in the morning sun. People say cats don't like to move houses, but Wolfy was a shelter cat; we'd saved him from spending his nine lives in a windowless ten-by-ten room, so he cut us a little slack. He flicked his tail, and I took it to mean "Go see for yourself."

I couldn't check my appearance in the hallway mirror because we didn't have one yet, so I tucked my hair behind my ears and hoped I didn't look too disheveled.

"I hope I'm not disturbing you," the slender, salt-and-pepper-haired man said when I opened the door. He was smartly dressed in a dark blue button-front shirt, suit pants, and leather belt with a shiny buckle. Judging by the laugh lines around his eyes and his graying beard, I would have put him in his late fifties—about the age my mom would be if she were still alive.

"I was just practicing," I said, assuming that he was a neighbor wanting to know how much longer he had to put up with the noise.

"Tchaikovsky no. 1 is a bold choice for a Monday morning," he said, but before I could apologize, he added, "I've always been partial to Mussorgsky. I don't imagine you take requests?"

122

I wasn't a fan of "the Five," as Mussorgsky and his Russian contemporaries were called; their music was dissonant and rebellious, not to mention difficult to play.

"I think I can still play *Pictures at an Exhibition*," I offered, still unsure if he was bothered by my playing or soliciting a private recital.

"You really are accomplished, aren't you? I'm Alex," he said, then held up the opaque plastic shopping bag he was carrying. "My wife and I live up the street. We saw you moving in; she made you a honey cake to welcome you to the neighborhood."

I was so touched by the gesture, it didn't occur to me that he might be lying, and not just about that honey cake.

"Oh! That's so kind of you."

"The Mrs. and I, we're from Leningrad"—he used the retired name of the Russian city now known as Saint Petersburg, and in a Russian accent, too—"so you understand why we are less enthusiastic about Tchaikovsky."

I did understand. Tchaikovsky was Russian, but from Moscow, and his music was derivative of the popular European composers of the time. Real Russian patriots preferred composers who dared to pioneer a new, distinctly Soviet sound. It was a bit of an acquired taste, and as such not performed as widely.

"Though I confess, Tchaikovsky is easier to swallow," he added with a wink, and I felt myself relax because I realized he wasn't here to complain. He wasn't here to welcome me to the neighborhood, either, but I didn't know that yet.

"Well, please thank your wife for the cake," I said. I was about to close the door, but then he said something that broke my heart a little.

"Perhaps someday you'll let me gaze upon your piano," he said. "I wasn't able to bring my Steinway over when we emigrated, and it felt silly to buy another—my paltry talent isn't worthy of the investment."

"You play?"

"Well, not like you!"

"Can you sight-read?"

"Are you inviting me to try?"

I didn't have many duets in my library of sheet music, but I was able to dig up some Schubert for four hands, and I let him pick which part he wanted to play.

"I didn't catch your name," he said as we sat down at the piano together. Playing four hands was a rather intimate affair—it was probably time to introduce myself.

"Bree," I said, because I foolishly thought we might become friends.

He was not wrong about his talent—he dropped the left hand after just a few bars and barely managed to plunk out the right. But it was fun, and he laughed when I pushed his hand out of the way to reach my notes.

We played for about twenty minutes, at half tempo, but we made it to the end. He made a million mistakes, and apologized after every one of them, so there was as much talking as playing. But I love Schubert, and it's always fun making music with someone; I so rarely got to do it these days.

"This has been an absolute pleasure," he said as he got up to go. "If I can find a place to practice, I'm going to insist you give me lessons. You're magnificent!" I hadn't told him I gave lessons, but I figured he just assumed it by how I bossed him around (*"Pianissimo here! Right hand staccato!"*). The thought that he'd been spying on me was too absurd to enter my mind, and I wasn't the suspicious type back then. Of course I've since learned not to trust anybody, even if they bring you honey cake.

CHAPTER 29

———

LUKE

"So I have a story," Bree said as we made dinner together. She was an excellent cook. She let me do noncritical things like chop and stir, but I wasn't to be trusted with anything that required judgment or skill.

"Do tell," I said, sneaking a carrot from the pile that was supposed to be for the stir-fry. I had a terrible habit of eating the food before my wife had a chance to cook it. If she saw me, I'd get a swat with the dish towel.

"I made a friend today."

For most people, hearing your wife say she made a new friend was probably no big deal. We lived in a city with a population over six million. There were endless opportunities to connect with like-minded people: at museums, yoga classes, coffee shops, a concert in the park. But my wife didn't partake in any of those offerings. I'd tried to encourage her to find a book club or a running group, but she wasn't interested. "I have my piano," she would say. "And you and Wolfy."

In the beginning, I'd tried to engineer double dates with my friends and their girlfriends or wives, but nothing ever clicked. Bree wasn't into small talk. She wasn't a big drinker, and though she'd join me for a beer and a ball game every once in a while, she didn't grow up on American sports and wasn't inspired to cheer along. Plus my friends were all ten to fifteen years older than Bree—she was midtwenties; they were pushing forty. We were of a different generation and from a different country. She never said as much, but I think my friends were boring to her. And as a result, they became a little boring to me.

"You made a friend?" I tried not to sound shocked, but I wasn't much of an actor, and it was pretty shocking.

"Don't sound so surprised!" She looked over at my pile of carrot wheels and nodded her approval. "Why don't you cut some broccoli?"

She dropped some raw chicken strips into a pan of sizzling oil, then sprinkled them with spices—white pepper, ginger, salt, garlic powder. She was clearly enjoying stringing me along, but I wasn't cutting any broccoli until she fessed up. I put the knife down and crossed my arms in front of my chest.

"It's not going to chop itself," she said.

"Not chopping until you spill."

She laughed, not because she knew she'd piqued my curiosity, but because I'd turned this into a game, which was normally her thing.

"Well, he's older," she said as she poked the chicken with the back of her wooden spoon.

"Older than me?" I asked. I made the mistake of occasionally complaining about an ache or a pain, which earned me the nickname "old man."

"A little bit. But he had a lot more gray hair." I suspected she wanted to make sure I knew he was older so I wouldn't be threatened that the first friend she had made in over three years was a man. But I wasn't the jealous type, certainly not with Bree. I wanted her to have a life full of friendships and adventure; the happier she was, the happier it made me.

"And where did you meet this gray-haired old man?"

"On our front porch! He came to the door."

My Spidey-sense tingled a little because I didn't know what kind of person would come knocking on a stranger's door in the middle of a workday, but I tried to keep an open mind.

"Selling cookies?" I guessed.

"No, but he did bring a honey cake." She was flipping chicken with one hand and seasoning it with the other, so she indicated the cake on the edge of the island with her chin.

"I don't know that I've ever had honey cake."

"It's Russian. His wife made it." She leaned into the word "wife" like she wanted me to know he was married. But it was his Russianness, not his maleness, that made my skin prickle.

"How do you know he's Russian?"

"He told me. I was playing Tchaikovsky, I guess he thought it was relevant." Her voice was singsongy and bright as she told me about how he practically begged her to play a duet with him. "He was pretty terrible, but he knows music. I'd rather talk to him than play with him, but we'll see where it goes."

"So you got his number?" I hoped I didn't sound jealous—that's not what this was about.

"It's on the honey cake. There's a little card."

I didn't want to look. I didn't want this new friend my wife was so excited about to be anything other than a nice neighbor who shared my wife's passion for classical music. Because she needed a friend. And I needed to turn the page on a shameful chapter of my life.

We ate out on the deck, at the folding table I'd brought from my office. We'd shop for proper patio furniture in the coming days, maybe this weekend. Bree asked about my day, and I told her about the job I'd bid on in Calabasas and bringing in a bookkeeper to clean up my cash flow report.

"That's great that you got help," she said. "I know you were stressed about having our taxes in order." She smiled at me, and I immediately regretted that I'd made a big deal about the money she'd made teaching. Yes, making thousands under the table is illegal, but what I had done was much worse—I had no right to project my guilty feelings onto her.

She cleared the plates with a "Be right back!" and then I was alone in our backyard for the very first time since we'd moved in. A few blocks away, in downtown Beverly Hills, people from all over the world were sipping martinis in fancy hotel bars, but here it was luxuriously peaceful, with only the songs of a few night frogs to cut the silence.

"OK, time for dessert," Bree said as she returned with that honey cake, still wrapped in plastic and cinched at the throat with a bow. A card that said "To my neighbors" was hole punched and threaded through the ribbon. *"Neighbors," not "neighbor."* It was meant for me, too.

I suddenly couldn't help myself; I laughed. This Russian Tchaikovsky lover could have been anybody. I was being totally paranoid. Such is the work of a guilty conscience.

"What's so funny?" Bree asked as she unwrapped the cake.

"I've been living in the city too long," I said, shaking my head.

"What, you think he poisoned the cake or something?"

"Well, if he wanted to poison us, I don't think he would write his phone number on the card."

I plucked the card off the ribbon and opened it. "Welcome to the neighborhood," I read aloud. "Hope you enjoy the cake." He'd signed it "Alex." And my breath caught in my throat. Because I recognized not just the signature but also the phone number that was scribbled beneath it.

"Don't throw away the card—I want to write down his number. Just in case we run out of milk or something." My wife winked at me. And I didn't have the heart to tell her that her surprise visitor wasn't interested in her music and didn't want to be her friend.

CHAPTER 30

SOPHIE

My parents took us to Italy when Carter and I were in high school. A cousin of my dad's was getting married in Tuscany, so he decided to make a trip of it. We toured the Colosseum in Rome, zipped around Venice in water taxis, climbed a tower in Verona, ate gelato on Lake Garda. We had never gone on a family vacation where we stayed in hotels every night and ate every meal out, and as I watched my dad swipe his credit card three, five, ten times per day, I came to the stunning realization that money really does make the world go around.

Of course, money moved mountains long before you could transfer it with a swipe or a tap. Standing in the Vatican, the epicenter of the great and powerful Holy Roman Empire, surrounded by frescoes painted with real gold, it was impossible not to feel the connection between wealth and power. As my dad shelled out a hundred euros so we could join the throngs of tourists tromping through the Apostolic Palace, I couldn't help but wonder: How did the church come to own so many priceless treasures? Were they commissioned? Won in battle? Gifted? Stolen? How many people had suffered so kings could accumulate so much? Like the millions who came before us, we paid twenty-five euros apiece for the privilege of seeing the "priceless" art hoarded by the Holy Roman emperors of yore, which, as it turned out, did have a price after all.

From Rome we traveled to Florence, considered by many to have the best leather in the world. The streets were like a giant flea market, jammed with some of the most exquisite purses I had ever seen—shiny carryalls in inky black, messenger bags in supple mahogany, leather totes that looked like woven baskets. They were all handmade there in Italy. I knew that because I could see the people making them: stamping patterns onto the outside with their hot-presses, sewing colorful silk linings into the insides with skilled hands. At one hundred euros each, these handmade, one-of-a-kind purses were orders of magnitude less expensive than the Gucci bags up the street that were mass-produced in China. *"Something's only worth what people will pay for it,"* my dad said, when I asked him why. And with that answer began my obsession with money.

Unlike most teenage girls, my obsession was not with having money, but understanding it. I wanted to know who was making it, how it moved, how its value was created and destroyed. I wanted to know how people leveraged it, manipulated it, grew it, stole it, hid it, spent it, washed it. I came to understand money not just as the means to power and influence but also as a tool of oppression. I found it absurd that a ham sandwich worth five dollars in normal times would be priceless if it were the last one on earth. Because at the end of the day it's still just a ham sandwich. I realized that money is an illusion, and scarcity is a game rich people play when they want to screw the masses. And I didn't like watching people getting screwed.

Memories of Michelangelo's "priceless" masterpiece swirled through my brain as I pored over Luke's files. The bank statements for the last twelve months showed huge payouts—some over six figures—to a company called All American Building Corporation (AABC), which I googled to discover was a construction company, just like Luke's. *Why would Luke pay another company to do what he could do himself?* It made no sense. Even more puzzling was that he hadn't asked me to show the payouts to AABC on the profit and loss statement I was preparing. These were huge expenses that would have offset his taxable income, yet they were completely off the books.

I thought for a second I might be looking at bank accounts for a different business, but upon scrutiny, I recognized many of the transactions from the cash flow report I'd just prepared—$26,855.00 to Westlake Hardwood, $7,808.00 to Home Depot, $1,661.00 to Pioneer Plumbing—which indicated he didn't have two accounts or two different businesses. So why were receipts for the payouts to AABC not included in the folders he gave me?

It was none of my business, and there might have been a simple explanation, but I was bored. Plus I smelled a rat and I was a forensic accountant—maybe it was time to put that degree to good use?

I worked my way backward through statements from the past five years. This past year was all about money going out—tons of it, the vast majority to AABC. But the four years before that were the mirror image; the statements showed not money going out, but money coming in—gobs of it, in big chunks. It was almost as if he had two separate operations: one legitimately remodeling kitchens and bathrooms, converting garages, building additions, for reasonable amounts; the other taking huge sums of money to do very little. Seventy thousand to install a new garage door, fifty thousand to plant a few trees. I knew construction prices were high, but these were astronomical.

I got my phone out and started taking pictures of the bank statements. I would add it all up later—right now I was just collecting data. At that point I wasn't planning on telling anyone what I'd found; I just wanted to solve the mystery.

As I was putting the bank statements back with a little prayer that no one would notice that I'd riffled through them, I saw the house folder. I had no idea that the Rodeo Drive house was the key to this whole money mystery—I was just curious. The last picture I took was of the deed, made out to Luke and Aubrey Sprayberry. I made a mental note to find out if the wife was as cute as her name, then locked up the cabinet and texted Luke that I was finished. He Venmoed me with instructions to add the payment to the spreadsheet, then lock up and put the keys through the mail slot.

As I was driving home, I realized my dad was right: I did have too much free time. I had a professor who liked to say "Curiosity is the engine of achievement," but we all know it's also what killed the cat. I didn't know yet if I was destined for greatness or if I was the cat.

CHAPTER 31

———

LUKE

Did my flooring come in yet? I texted at six the next morning, while Bree was still asleep. Alex would be expecting to hear from me—that's what the honey cake was for, to get me to reach out. His response was predictably brusque.

Meet me at the showroom in one hour.

We always texted in code now. There was no showroom, and I didn't need flooring. Now that my legitimate business was a front for a criminal one, I couldn't be too careful.

It started how every job starts: with an incoming call asking if I was available for hire. The guy on the phone said it was a "big job"—a "to the studs reno." So I dropped everything to go meet him at the property.

"Hi, I'm Alex," the man said when I got out of my truck and walked up the driveway that hot afternoon in July. The house was in an up-and-coming neighborhood in the South Bay, near where the Rams and Chargers play. It wasn't the nicest house on the block, but it wasn't the worst.

"Luke."

"Are you the owner of the company?" Alex asked, even though he already knew that I was.

"That's right."

We shook hands and he escorted me inside. It was a modest house, probably about two thousand square feet, with four bedrooms and two baths. The kitchen was from the nineties, and the bathrooms were Home Depot basic with glassed-in tub-showers and boxy vanities.

"This is what the owner wants," Alex said, handing me pictures cut out of a catalog: new cabinets and countertops in the kitchen, new vanities and shower stalls in the bathrooms, hardwood floors throughout. It was a little unusual for the owner to have a representative for a job of this small scope, but what he said next was even more of a red flag.

"We'll pay you five hundred thousand. I can give you the whole amount now."

Normally it's the contractor who sets the price, not the client. So I told him: "I can't tell you how much the work will cost until I take measurements, and price out the labor and raw materials." But he was intent on doing it his way.

"The owner wants the work started right away."

I looked at the pictures. What he was asking for was pretty basic. The house would never be luxurious with its low ceilings and cookie-cutter floor plan; it didn't make sense to put super high-end cabinets and fixtures in it. Eyeballing it, I figured I could probably do a nice face-lift for between $150,000 and $200,000.

"For five hundred grand I could build you a brand-new house," I told him. I figured it was best to be honest. Not because I thought he was testing me or anything, just because that's how I rolled.

"That won't be necessary," he said, then did something that should have been another red flag: he reached into his wallet and pulled out a check already made out to me, for $500,000.

In retrospect, it's clear that Alex had done his research on me. He knew the amount was too high for what he was asking me to do, but not so high that I would dismiss him as some sort of scam artist. He knew it had been a slow year and that I needed the money. He probably knew how much I would net on the job, and that it would be generous, but not so generous that I couldn't justify it. I wasn't a crook, so the thought that I was being treated like one never entered my mind.

"Typically I take a deposit and collect the fees in stages," I said, not taking the check from him. But he was ready for that.

"My client is out of the country and doesn't want to be bothered with having to make a bunch of payments while he's traveling." He put the check down on the counter. "Why don't you have a look around and I'll meet you outside."

I walked through the property trying to figure out what the catch was. I looked at the electrical panel. It was adequate for the square footage and didn't need to be upgraded. I ran the water, flushed the toilets: no obvious plumbing problems. I hopped up on the roof, which didn't need to be redone, then checked the hot water heater and the HVAC system, which were also in good shape. In the end, I let myself believe the hefty profit margin was a matter of convenience for the owner and that it was OK to be overpaid just this once.

I cashed the check, and once it cleared, I got to work. I decided to pass some of my profits on to my workers, giving them bonuses for staying late and working on weekends. I was a single guy with no real dating life, so I made this project priority number one. I finished it in forty-three days, which was pretty good considering the cabinets were on back order and I couldn't do the floors until the cabinets were installed. The job cost just over $200,000, plus a $30,000 contractor fee for me. The $270,000 profit was not only the biggest I'd ever made from a job—it brought my company bank account to an all-time high.

I met Alex at the property to give him a tour. I had all the receipts with me in case he wanted to see them, but he brushed off the folder with a brusque "The work speaks for itself."

I went back to my world of bidding for jobs I wouldn't get and haggling over a few hundred bucks on the ones I did. I was in the middle of a particularly contentious pool installation (complicated by unforeseen bedrock in what was supposed to be the deep end) when Alex called again. "My client is very pleased with the work you did and would like to hire you for another remodel."

This second job was similar to the first: an older home in decent condition that needed updating. Once again he wrote me a check for $500,000, and once again I brought the job in for right around two. I felt a little guilty about making such a huge profit, but Alex assured me the "convenience" was worth it to his client and in his world such markups were not so unusual. "Do you know how much profit McDonald's makes on your Big Mac?" he'd asked when I insisted on showing him what the work had cost me. "Not everyone lives on the fringes."

As my bank account swelled to over $500,000, I thought about what it meant to be "on the fringes." As someone who bought wholesale materials, I knew the markups some of these companies charged the public were sometimes 200 percent or more. I knew how top brands created value by projecting the illusion of scarcity, selling to only a handful of retailers, or limiting production to a fraction of the demand. It was rare that a material was expensive solely because of its high quality; there were a lot of high-quality materials to choose from—part of my job was finding good value. Because that's what my clients demanded.

But what if I was courting the wrong clients? What if in always looking for a bargain I was branding myself as the contractor to the frugal? There were plenty of contractors who turned up their noses at jobs in modest neighborhoods, and it wasn't because their work was any better than mine. Hell, we hired the same electricians, drywallers, installers, and roofers, and I knew from talking to them that we paid them the same hourly rate. Yet what these fancy contractors were charging their clients was an order of magnitude higher than what I charged mine. Who decides what a fair price is? Why is what's fair for a schoolteacher different from what's fair for a CEO? It's just as much work to install IKEA cabinets as it is to install custom Italian ones, so why is it reasonable to charge three times as much for the latter?

Working for Alex, hearing him talk about his "client" as someone "too busy" to fret over the details, willing to pay a premium for convenience, convinced me that it wasn't price gouging if the person you were working for was accustomed to paying more. I imagined my benefactor as a rich real estate developer, buying up properties like I buy groceries. These were disposable investments to him. He was a CEO, not a schoolteacher, and I was damn lucky that he plucked me out of my daily grind.

Once I decided I wasn't doing anything wrong, I started looking forward to Alex's calls—and was grateful he kept calling. Over the next three years I did close to a dozen jobs for him. Some of the properties barely needed any work at all—just a new roof or new doors and windows. But the fee was always the same. And my bank account grew and grew.

I didn't have to continue to take other jobs, but Alex's were so quick and easy, I would have been bored if I didn't. Plus I figured it was good for my karma. If I was getting cushy work in one hand, I should give good deals with the other. I didn't think I was doing anything criminal, until what happened next.

"It's time for you to buy a house," Alex said when I met him at a jobsite in Rancho Palos Verdes. I was a year into my marriage to Bree, and I definitely wanted to upgrade our living situation—I just hadn't figured out how to do that. Yes, I had money in the company, but if I transferred it to myself, I'd get hit with a huge tax bill, so I'd just left it there.

I couldn't remember telling Alex anything about my personal life, but he was right, so I agreed. "Yeah, I know, I will soon."

"You can have your company buy it; just expand your business model to include real estate development and pretend it's an investment property. Then when it's done, you can just sell it to yourself."

I knew investors did all sorts of tricks to avoid big tax hits—I just never had the occasion to use them myself. "I'll look into it."

We talked about neighborhoods, and I told him how my wife loved the flats of Beverly Hills and had likened walking the eclectic tree-lined streets to going to Disneyland. "She's never been to Disneyland, and I can't take her now because if she thinks it looks like this, she'll be disappointed," I joked, and I thought that would be the end of it. But a few weeks later I got a text asking me to meet him at a Rodeo Drive address.

"We bought this house for you," Alex said when I pulled up to the dilapidated ranch-style house in the middle of the block. It was a true teardown, but I knew the land to be worth several million. I figured this was just another job for his absentee client, until he added, "Your company can buy it from us."

"I wish," I said, "but this neighborhood is out of my league."

"We'll loan you the money."

I started to object, "I don't want to get in over my head. I'm not quite ready—I need to talk to my wife," but he cut me off.

"Luke, there is no free lunch."

"I'm sorry?"

"Surely you didn't think you would be allowed to keep all that money," he said, not really as a question.

"I renovated your properties."

"Ha!" he laughed. "Yes. That's the cover story. And you were smart to keep your other clients; they're what make you credible." *Cover story? What is he talking about?*

"I . . . don't understand."

"It's time to pay the money back, Luke."

I felt like I was both falling and frozen in place, just like when I found out my mother had died. Alex must have gleaned that I was still confused, so he explained: "We overpaid you, now you give the money back by buying this house from us." He pointed at himself: "Win." Then at me: "Win."

And that's how I became a money launderer for the Russian mob.

CHAPTER 32

———

LUKE

"Your wife is lovely," Alex said when I walked into the garden center at Home Depot, a.k.a. "the showroom." We always met outside, where it was noisy and my truck blended in with all the others. Now that I had graduated from hapless dimwit to full-fledged coconspirator, we couldn't be too careful.

"I didn't know you played the piano," I said. There was no point pretending I didn't know why he had gone to my home and introduced himself to my wife, but it didn't hurt to be cordial.

"Oh, it's been years since I've played; she was very forgiving."

"Yes, that's one of the qualities I admire most about her." I hadn't told Bree about the mess I'd gotten myself into. Yes, she was forgiving, but my having joined a criminal cabal of arms dealers and human traffickers might have been a bridge too far.

"How are you enjoying the house?" He loved to ask me about the house, as if it were a reasonable consolation prize for being duped into a life of crime. I liked having a house in Beverly Hills, but Bree and I would have been happy in a refrigerator box at the side of the freeway as long as we had each other.

"Still settling in." I'd foolishly thought paying an inflated price for the property they'd bought for me would make us square. I had taken close to $3 million from them in the form of big profits on small jobs, and they had sold me a parcel of land for $3 million more than what they had paid for it. I thought that would be the end of it, but turns out it was just the beginning.

"I have some good news," Alex said, and I braced myself because Alex and I had a very different definition of what news was good. "We're giving you a raise." Any normal person would have been thrilled to hear they were about to start making more money, but to me a raise meant I was about to get dragged deeper into the operation, and I wanted out.

"Alex, I appreciate the opportunity, but this is not the life I want," I whispered, over the din of seventies soft rock playing through overhead speakers. "You can have the house; I'll sell it back to you at whatever price you want." At this point I didn't care if I was in debt to them for the rest of my life—I just wanted my freedom back. But his response was chilling.

"That's not how it works, Luke."

And that's when I fully understood what I'd become: I was not a poor schmuck who'd made a few shady deals; I was a long-term asset cultivated over many years, doomed to keep helping them as long as I was useful. Those first few jobs when I'd been overpaid, those were the appetizer. The continuous flow of money through my business, that was the meal—a never-ending buffet that they would feast on for life. They had led me to believe that rich people routinely overpaid for convenience and that a 200 percent markup was perfectly reasonable— *"Hell, Starbucks charges 300 percent of their cost for your morning coffee!"* Alex had said. And I'd been gullible enough to fall for it.

The operation was as simple as it was devious. Alex would hire me to "renovate" properties. I would turn around and use the money they poured into my business to pay their fake construction company, ironically called All American Building Corporation, or AABC, to do nothing. Of course there was nothing American about AABC, and it wasn't building anything. It was a shell; my company was doing all the building, and for much less than what it said on the purchase orders.

It was a very tidy scheme. Alex's "client" bought houses that needed little to no work, then overpaid me to do it, leaving me with a sizable "profit." I would funnel the "profits" to the nonexistent AABC builders by "hiring" them to do work that I was doing myself. That's how my house was built. I took two hundred grand from Alex to dig a pool at 123 Main Street. But 123 Main Street already had a pool. So I redirected the pool guy to the Rodeo Drive house. He was still getting paid to dig a pool, just at a different address, and it didn't cost two hundred grand, only fifty. Once the pool was finished, AABC would bill me as if I'd subcontracted them. And I would transfer the remaining one hundred and fifty grand back to them. We did this over and over, with plumbing, electrical, roofing, flooring, framing, drywall. The end result was clean money for them, a brand-new house for me, and a debt that would never be paid.

Alex was clear that in order for this to work, I had to keep doing legitimate jobs. I had to file my taxes on time and have a clean set of books. That's why I'd hired Sophie—to make sure my books would hold up to an audit. As for the money flowing to and from AABC, Alex said not to worry about it. They had books for "all their contractors," which I guess was supposed to make me feel better, but only made me feel worse. How many of us were there? How big was this operation? Where did all this money come from? And how could I ever escape?

I never threatened to quit, but Alex was not shy about dropping hints about what would happen if I tried, telling me things like: *"We hired a very nice contractor to do a job for us down in San Diego. He has twin girls who both play soccer. I go and watch them sometimes. Lovely girls."* It was not a coincidence that he'd waited until I had a wife to reveal that his client was not the benevolent investor he had made him out to be. If it weren't for Bree, I would have gone straight to the FBI and confessed to my part in their illegal scheme. But I wasn't willing to put Bree's life on the line to expose their crimes, and he knew it.

"Bree doesn't know about this," I said as we strolled through a row of tomato plants. "And I don't know what she'd do if she found out." I didn't mean it as a threat, exactly. But they had to be concerned about snitches.

"My wife thinks I'm a financial adviser; it's never been a problem."

"I don't know what I'd say if she started asking a bunch of questions about you." *"So don't come to my house anymore"* is what I would have said next, if I'd had the nerve.

"You flatter me," he said with a grin. "I doubt I left a lasting impression. But if you wish, on my next visit, I can solicit a recommendation for a good contractor; then you don't have to pretend you don't know me." *Next visit? Good God.*

"Whatever you think is best," I muttered because there was no winning this fight.

"Who's that girl you have working for you?" he asked, abruptly changing the subject, and for a second I didn't know who he was talking about.

"What girl? Oh, you mean Sophie?" She was a grown woman, probably around the same age as Bree. Had he seen her from a distance? Or was he at that age where anyone under thirty looked like a child to him?

"We find it's best to keep the circle small." I had long suspected that spying on me came with the territory, but the thought that he knew I had hired someone was still unsettling.

"Don't worry about her. She's the daughter of one of my longtime clients. She's getting my cash flow report cleaned up. I only gave her the legit transactions. The AABC ones are separated out." Sophie's dad was a colleague, so I figured she would assume my business was on the up-and-up and interpret any discrepancies as careless mistakes. And there would be mistakes—misfiled receipts, missing invoices—there always were. I was a fine craftsman but an abysmal bookkeeper.

"Watch her."

Of course, he was projecting. They were already watching her, sealing her fate and mine. In retrospect I wonder if on some level I'd invited Sophie into my books and my life because I wanted to get caught. Because I called her again at the end of the month, and again the month after that, even though tax season was over and my need wasn't pressing. Yes, the incriminating files were in a locked cabinet, but the key was right there on the desk. I never told her she couldn't see my bank statements, but she had to wonder why I never offered them to her; we both knew she needed them to do the job properly. I told myself if Sophie was smart enough to figure out what I was doing, she was smart enough to know what to do about it.

It was becoming clear that my handlers had eyes everywhere. If I called the FBI, I'd be dead before I answered the door. But maybe that was for the best? All I cared about was protecting Bree. If I was gone, the risk of me squealing on them would die with me.

I would have given my life for her. And I had a sinking feeling the moment was fast approaching that I might have to.

PART 3

October

CHAPTER 33

—————

CARTER

"She slept here," I said to the detective who was sitting across from me at the kitchen island with his notebook open.

"Who?"

"The woman who killed my sister," I blurted, knowing I was jumping to conclusions on two fronts. One, that Bree was capable of murder—just because she had dissed me didn't mean she was a killer. And two, that the body on the side of the pool belonged to Sophie. I hadn't glimpsed it enough to know if it was male, female, or even human. Three dozen of Sophie's friends had come to the party—she could have left with any one of them. Except for Bree, because you can't leave with someone who never left.

"She might still be here," I pressed. I knew Bree was still in the house when I'd driven off; all the doors she could have snuck through were locked from the inside, and if she had left through the pocket doors, I would have seen her. "We need to search the house," I insisted, then jumped to my feet like I was going to do it myself. A uniformed cop moved to grab my arm, but the detective stopped him with a hand signal.

"We're treating this as a crime scene," the detective said, as if I couldn't see the dead body on the side of the pool with my own two eyes. "We don't want to trample through the house, because if there's evidence, we don't want to compromise it; does that make sense?" He was talking to me like I was a little kid, probably because I was acting like a pissy two-year-old. I forced myself to take a breath.

"Someone stayed here. After the party. A woman. She . . ." *Where am I going with this?* "She might know something," I said, because it suddenly occurred to me there was another possible explanation why my would-be girlfriend had disappeared. *What if the dead girl is Bree?*

"That's great—we'll definitely want to talk to her. But let's start with your sister. You said she was missing?" I could tell he thought I was overreacting, which I probably (hopefully) was.

"She didn't come home last night; her bed wasn't slept in." I suddenly felt self-conscious. She was my sister, but she was also a grown woman. It was a big leap from not coming home to being dead. "She's not with her boyfriend," I added, so he didn't think I was completely clueless. "I texted him this morning."

The detective wrote in his notebook, probably something about me being a lunatic. I decided not to mention seeing her with said boyfriend, or that I wasn't actually sure he was still her boyfriend, though I did wonder how that conversation had ended. Jared wasn't angry with her— quite the opposite. He loved her and wanted the world to know. Plus I knew him. He was patient and easygoing, and my dad and I trusted him unconditionally. But I knew nothing about Bree, except that my sister didn't want me going anywhere near her. I had assumed she thought I wasn't good enough for Bree, but maybe it was the other way around?

I loved my sister, but it wasn't easy being the dorky little brother of the most popular girl in school. I was only a grade younger than she was, but her friends treated me like I was a puppy tagging along for an attaboy and a pat on the head. I knew Dad favored her; my high school years were a constant refrain of *"Why can't you be more outgoing like Sophie? Why can't you get good grades / go to football games / have friends / get invited to parties, ski trips, and game nights like your sister?"* Sophie spent her spring breaks in Mexico with friends. I spent mine in my room. If she didn't come home after the party last night, it was most likely because she got a better offer—as per usual with her.

"Can you describe your sister for me?" the detective asked. "Hair color, eye color, age?" *Yes, that I can do.*

"Five foot five, skinny, brown hair. Darker than mine, but not curly. She just turned twenty-four." He asked about scars ("No."), tattoos ("None that I know about, but it wouldn't surprise me."), piercings ("Yes—left nostril, she usually wears a little gold hoop. Oh, and ears, four in one, I think her left? And one in the other. The fourth is in the cartilage—she wears a diamond stud in it."). He nodded as he jotted it all down in his trusty notebook.

"You're doing great, Carter. Any other identifying markings?"

"She has a mole on her upper lip, like Madonna." I didn't tell him how I used to make fun of her for it, and how she'd begged Mom to let her get it removed, but now thought it was cool, *because what did it matter?*

"This is really helpful, Carter," the detective said, and I got scared again. *Helpful because he knows that it's her now? Or that it isn't?*

"So? Is it her?" I asked, my voice rising with anger because it was cruel of him to string me along like this, and I wasn't afraid to let him know it.

"The coroner will do the ID," he said, a little too matter-of-factly. "If she needs your help, we'll let you know."

Rain was pummeling the roof and pool deck. I suddenly noticed we were sitting in the near dark. No lights, no hum of appliances, no neon-green numbers on the microwave clock. And I remembered that this was the reason I had come here: to check the power.

"The power's still off." I said it like I thought it was significant. And turns out it was.

"What do you mean 'still'?"

"It went off last night. During the party."

The detective's eyes got wide like Frisbees. "Do you know what time?"

I thought back to the party: meeting Bree in the kitchen at around ten fifteen . . . guests arriving between ten thirty and a quarter to eleven . . . looking for Bree, not seeing her anywhere . . . then being lured inside by the sounds of Coldplay and finding her playing the piano like she was the pied piper and we were mice.

"Around eleven, I think?"

He wrote it down.

"I'm supposed to get it back up," I informed him. "That's why I came here."

"You're the owner?"

"Yes. No! My dad is. But he sent me to find out why it went out."

"We're looking into the power issue," he said, like I wasn't allowed to "look into" it myself.

"When is the coroner coming?" I needed to call my dad. *Good God, what am I going to tell my dad?*

"Hard to say. She's a busy lady." He handed me that same glass of water, but this time I took it.

The coroner finally showed up at ten thirty. I knew it was the coroner because I heard someone say "The coroner's here" over the walkie-talkie, and then she appeared. I watched her through the glass door as a uniformed cop escorted her across the lawn, holding a big black umbrella over her head like she was royalty and he was her valet. The officer standing guard took a respectful step back as Her Highness pulled on a pair of powder-blue gloves, crouched down next to the body, and pulled back the yellow tarp.

By this point I had begun to hope there was a logical explanation why Sophie, the belle of the ball, hadn't come home. So when I saw the tangle of jet-black hair spill out from under the tarp, I felt relief. *My sister doesn't have black hair!* But then I remembered the costume, the gold sandals, the wig . . . and my chest tore wide open.

"No, no, no!" Sobs exploded from my mouth like projectile vomit. I don't remember falling off the stool, just the feeling of my knees hitting cold tile when I'd tried to stand. The police officer stationed inside stepped in front of me to block my view, but it was too little, too late.

Guilt seized me like quicksand. I shouldn't have left without her last night. I should have asked if she needed a ride, insisted on giving her one. But instead, I'd left like a bad dog with my tail between my legs. *No wonder Dad liked Sophie better.*

Tears and mucus poured down my face as I gasped to catch my breath. I don't know how long I cried like that, but I suddenly became aware of a hand on my shoulder. A woman in a green pantsuit and ballet bun was staring down at me. The bald detective was a few feet behind her.

"Hi, Carter," she said. "I'm Agent Morales with the FBI. I need to talk to you about what happened here last night."

"I gotta call my dad," I said, taking my phone out of my pocket with trembling hands.

"I'm afraid I can't let you do that just yet," she said. "This is bigger than your family, and we need your help piecing it together."

"But my sister—" I blurted, and maybe I've seen too many cop shows, because I didn't know if what she said next was meant to mess with me or entrap me.

"What makes you think that's your sister?"

CHAPTER 34

SOPHIE

Gloved hands gripped my ankles and pulled me into the back seat. I tried to scream, but as soon as I opened my mouth, someone stuffed a rag in it and taped my lips shut. I pushed my tongue into the balled-up cloth to keep from gagging.

"Let's go," a gruff voice commanded.

Thump, thump! Two car doors closed and the engine turned over. I heard the transmission pop into gear. A half second later the car lurched forward. And then we were bumping down my street.

"Sit her up."

I felt hands on my shoulders: one set pulling, the other pushing. I jerked my head up to get a look at their faces, which is apparently what they'd anticipated I'd do, because the bag was over my head the instant I was vertical. I raised my arms to yank it off, but I guess they'd anticipated I'd do that, too, because a second later my hands were zip-tied behind my back.

I could feel hot tears streaming down my face. I tried to slow my breathing so I wouldn't pass out. My nostrils gaped as they begged for air.

"Take it easy, we're not going to hurt you," the voice soothed, and I kicked my legs against the seat in front of me in protest. It was a futile gesture, but with my hands tied and someone's old sock in my mouth, it was the only thing I could do to let them know I had no intention of making this easy for them.

I knew when I started snooping around Luke's files that he was involved in something shady, but it took me a while to figure out that it was criminal. I started by taking pictures of everything: bank statements, receipts, purchase orders, profit and loss statements, even tax returns. When I couldn't make sense of the numbers on their own, I started calling vendors, who told me stories of delivering goods to one address, only to be told when they arrived at the jobsite to take them to another. While those things were odd, I hadn't suspected I was dealing with a money laundering operation until I did some digging into AABC . . . only to find out it didn't exist. That's when I got scared. I knew I should destroy every scrap of evidence I'd collected and lie low for a while. But that's not what I did. *Obviously.*

The car curved around a corner and accelerated onto the freeway. I knew it was the 405, because that was the only on-ramp near my house, and that we were going north, because south would take us straight up a hill and the stretch we were on was flat. As the car accelerated, I tried to count the minutes in my head—one minute equals one mile—to mark the path like a modern-day Hansel and Gretel. Not that I had any illusions about making it out of this alive. These guys were criminals, and I was the one who'd blown the whistle on their operation. I'd tried to be stealthy about my evidence gathering, but I must have asked too many questions. I should have known which side of the law those vendors were on and that they would rat me out to the bad guys just as I'd ratted them out to the good ones.

Money laundering in real estate was personal to me because my dad was in the business. White-collar criminals using real estate to cheat their taxes or hide illegal earnings not only drives up the cost of business for my dad, it also makes it hard for honest people to buy into the market. With the gap between the haves and the have-nots growing ever wider, when I saw hints that Luke was one of the dirtbags ruining it for the rest of us, I had to make a choice: turn a blind eye, or turn him in. I was tired of living a purposeless existence. I wanted to do something impactful with my life. I don't know how Luke found out I'd turned his records over to the FBI, but it didn't much matter now.

Fifty-seven, fifty-eight, fifty-nine, sixty. I counted out the seconds as the car thumped over uneven pavement. Five minutes turned into ten turned into twenty. We would be on the 5 freeway now, or maybe the 14? *Ugh.* That curve could also have been the merge onto the 118. I was losing track of the turns and the minutes. I cursed myself for my sorry secret agent skills and my hubris: *Maybe I couldn't cut it as an FBI agent after all.*

The car slowed, then made a series of sharp turns. Pavement turned to gravel, and I felt my head start to spin as panic attacked. I tried to control my breathing, but it was hard with that damn sock in my mouth. I didn't realize I was audibly crying until my captor told me to be quiet.

"Shhhh. Easy now, almost there."

Time was moving in slow motion as my head continued to spin. Where were they taking me? And what did they plan to do with me when we got there? *A-B-C-D-E-F-G . . .* I tried to distract myself by singing the alphabet song in my head like I did when I was riding the sky-high chairlift in Mammoth or getting a cavity filled. My thoughts turned to Jared. How sad he looked when I wouldn't (couldn't!) give in to his ultimatum about going public with our relationship. I'd felt a flicker of regret on that Uber ride home, because of course I wanted to be with him. But any doubt that I'd done the right thing was long gone now.

H-I-J-K-L-M-N-O-P . . . This car ride was endless. My legs were cold, my throat was as dry as chalk, I had to pee. I tried not to think about what was going to happen next, and that my discomfort was the tip of the iceberg.

The ground got bumpy, and we slowed to a crawl. I heard the sound of branches against the roof—*Good God, are we in the woods?* The roar of gravel gave way to a silent glide, and I realized we had rolled onto a paved surface. *A driveway? A garage?*

The car stopped. The two front doors opened and closed. I felt a whoosh of cool air. And then my door was open, too.

"Let's get her inside," that gruff voice said. I felt a pair of hands reach under my armpits. I was too tired to resist now; I let the thugs slide me off the seat and stand me up. My legs dangled toward the ground like wet noodles.

"Hold her up," the ringleader said, and a moment later I was being dragged away from the car like an injured soldier off the battlefield. My feet slid across smooth cement. *A garage, we're in a garage.* I could tell by the way the man's voice echoed. An empty garage, by the sound of it. *Maybe I could have been a secret agent after all?*

I heard a door open. My toes bumped over a threshold. The door closed with a heavy thump. That was a formidable door. A fire door, probably, if we were coming in from a garage. My sandals broomed across carpet. The grip on my arms tightened as I was lowered onto a chair.

"Take off the bag."

I felt a puff of cool air on my cheeks as my eyes blinked the room into focus. I was in a conference room with a long wooden table and plain white walls. There were snacks on a credenza: SunChips and granola bars and bottles of water. There were no windows, pictures, or decorations of any kind. The ceiling was dotted with can lights, but they were dimmed, giving the room an almost cozy vibe.

"Take off the gag and cut her hands free," one of the men said.

"Sorry about this," another one said.

My cheeks burned as the tape was ripped from my mouth. I spit out the balled-up sock and gasped for air.

One of the goons crouched down beside me and cut the zip tie with a box cutter. I whipped my arms around my body and hugged my legs to my chest, then took in the faces of my captors. There were three of them, all clean shaven and wearing dark suits. As the one who cut my tethers stood up, his jacket wafted open and I saw his GLOCK holstered to his chest. If these guys were gangsters, they were the most J.Crew gangsters I had ever seen.

"Who the hell are you people?" And the answer was as obvious as it was surprising.

"FBI."

CHAPTER 35

SOPHIE

"What is this place, what's happening?" I said as I rubbed the grooves left by the zip ties on my wrists. The three men *(or FBI agents, I guess?)* were all staring at me. They didn't flash ID, but I could see their badges on their belts. I must have been a sight to behold in my crooked wig and make-up-streaked face. I looked down to see my cleavage spilling out from my homemade Cleopatra dress, which was ripping at the hastily stitched seams.

"Get her a blanket," the tall, good-looking one said to the young one. I figured he must have sensed I was self-conscious, because isn't that what FBI agents are trained to do? Read the room?

"Where am I?" I repeated. I knew my tone was hostile, but I was too terrified to play polite. I had no reason to doubt these guys were who they said they were, but they had kidnapped me. *Why the hell did they kidnap me?*

"It's a safe house," Agent Tall, Dark, and Handsome said. Perhaps the word "safe" should have made me feel better, but it only made my heart beat faster.

"What am I doing in a safe house?"

The young one returned with a gray army blanket that was scratchy but did the job. I wrapped it across my shoulders, then crisscrossed it in the front to cover my chest.

"Agent Morales will explain everything in the morning. We were just sent to extract you." *Extract me? Sherman Oaks is a war zone now?*

"Do you want something to eat?" It was such an absurd question I almost thought I'd misheard.

"No, thank you."

"Then Agent Tasker will take you to your room." My panic morphed to confusion. *I have a room?*

Tall, Dark, and Handsome nodded to the young one, who I guess was Agent Tasker? He stood and opened the door for me. I waited a beat, hoping that someone would say something more to explain why the FBI would throw an innocent civilian in the back of a car and drive her out to God-knows-where in the middle of the night, but no one did. So I got up and walked through the door that was being held open for me.

I hugged the blanket around my body as I followed Tasker down a short hallway as bright as the bar at closing time. The chocolate-brown herringbone carpet looked straight out of a Holiday Inn and smelled brand new. My feet were cold and sore, and my head was spinning. While I was relieved to learn I'd been abducted by the good guys, that car ride was the most terrifying hour of my life, and I had to bite the insides of my cheeks to keep from crying.

"We set you up in here," Tasker said, indicating a door midway down the hall. There were two other doors beyond the one to "my" room, both closed, and a wave of panic washed over me.

"Are there other people, like, staying here?" I asked, because the thought of bumping into a fellow abductee was unsettling to say the least.

"Just me and Agent Bartleman." I didn't know who Bartleman was, but I relaxed a little at the word "agent."

Agent Tasker opened the door and indicated for me to go inside. I tightened my grip on that scratchy blanket as I stepped over the threshold of the tidy ten-by-ten room. There was a tightly made bed (white sheets and pillowcases, same army blanket), one round nightstand with a reading lamp bolted to it, and a lowboy dresser with toiletries laid out like the personal care aisle at CVS. The walls were blank and painted camel brown. The same herringbone carpeting covered the floor. The place smelled vaguely like Pine-Sol, which was gross but also comforting, because at least I knew it was clean.

"There are towels, pajamas, and a robe in the dresser," Tasker said from the doorway. "You're welcome to any of the toiletries; your bathroom is across the hall." I peeked across the hall. The bathroom door was open partway, and I saw a rectangular pedestal sink under a flat oval mirror.

"Thanks."

"I'll be right next door if you need anything." He indicated a door, which I took to be his room, and I suddenly wondered if we were sharing the bathroom, but I didn't ask.

I nodded to let him know I understood, then watched him as he disappeared into the room next to mine, as promised. Then I shut my door. Which I noticed had a lock on it . . . that you locked from the outside.

"What the hell?" I muttered. I kicked off my shoes, then tested the firmness of the mattress with my butt: *hard as a rock.* I knew what a safe house was from the movies but never in my life expected to be in one. As I looked around the Spartan accommodations, I couldn't help but wonder who else had slept in this room. *Drug dealers? Human traffickers? Thirteen-year-old girls sold into prostitution?* I wasn't a woo-woo weirdo who believed rooms held on to the energy of their previous occupants, but the thought of getting into a bed slept in by meth heads and whistleblowers was not very relaxing. *Maybe a shower would help?*

I pulled off my wig as I crossed to the dresser to survey my soap and shampoo options. There were travel-size bottles of TRESemmé shampoo and conditioner, three varieties of bar soap, a selection of toothbrushes, and a full-size tube of Colgate, which I hoped was not an indicator of how long I would be here. I opened the top dresser drawer and extracted the robe—a fluffy, white Hammacher Schlemmer special folded in a neat square with its belt tied like a bow. There were slippers in that drawer, too—utilitarian white scuffs—so I dropped them to the ground and slid my feet into them. Then I slipped out of my dress and into the robe, dropped my chosen toiletries into the pocket, grabbed a towel, and padded across the hall to get cleaned up.

I stood at the sink and looked at my reflection in the mirror—not really a mirror; it was made of some sort of reflective plastic, not glass, and warped my face like a fun house. I tried not to think about why they wouldn't use glass, and what kind of down-and-out people stood exactly where I was standing wondering the same thing. I pulled off my fake eyelashes and dropped them into the cylindrical plastic wastebasket. At first I thought they'd forgotten to put a bag in it, but then it occurred to me that a plastic bag, like a glass mirror, could be used for other things. I guess if they were going to go to the trouble of bringing you here, they wanted to make sure you came out alive.

I hung my robe on the hook (more like a nub, with no point on the end), then climbed into the shower. When I was clean and my limbs were thawed, I got out and put on the robe without drying off. I used the towel to swipe the remnants of mascara from under my eyes. I didn't know what to do with the towel now that it was wet and pockmarked with "Jet Black by Maybelline," so I hung it on the nub. Then I slid into my slippers and headed back to "my" room.

I had been tipsy when I left the party, but I was stone-cold sober now. I knew I should try to get some sleep, *but holy hell, what a night!* I was in a freakin' safe house, like Denzel in that movie. How long was I going to have to stay here? What were they going to tell my family? That they had no idea what happened to me? That I had died? Could they really be that mean?

My last thought before drifting off to sleep was of Carter. If we were twins, maybe I could have sent him a message telepathically, as twins do. But, alas, we had never been that close, and I had no such superpower. So I just had to trust these guys and the system that I had willfully walked into, because there was no turning back now.

CHAPTER 36

—

BREE

"Hey! You can't be back here, sir!" I heard a booming voice say as I peered through the sliver of space between the twin pool house curtains.

"No, no, no . . . ," the man cried out. I couldn't see his face, but I recognized the voice.

"Let's get him inside."

I watched as a uniformed police officer grabbed Carter's arm and led him through the sliding glass door into the kitchen. I was still standing there half-naked in that wet T-shirt, shivering like a tree in an earthquake. Rain was falling steadily, and the sky was as mournful as my heart. I didn't know Sophie, but she seemed like a kind and caring person; poor Carter must have felt like someone ripped his heart straight out of his chest. I knew the feeling all too well. I said a silent prayer that in time, he would find comfort in her memory and not be haunted like I was every day and night.

I knew it was foolish to be hiding ten meters from where a woman was found dead, but it's not like I had anywhere else to go. My window-less car had been sitting in the rain all night, and even if the plastic had done its job, it was deafeningly loud in there on a cloudless day. Plus my pants were hanging over the sink, dripping with pool water, and I had no shoes. *How would I even get to my car? Streak down the street in my underwear and hope the swarms of police don't notice?*

I crept over to the couch-bench and lifted the padded lid. There were two blankets in there—one fleece, one fuzzy. I plucked the fleece one out and wrapped it around my body, then sank down on the floor. I was shaking so much from the cold that at first I didn't realize I was sobbing. How had my life come to this? Hiding in the pool house on a property that had once been mine . . . ducking the police because I didn't want to face my past . . . I knew the thought was sinful, but I couldn't help but wonder if I might not be better off dead, too.

I lifted my head and looked back through the slit between the curtains to see a man and a woman in black raincoats and shiny shoes exit the kitchen and start walking—no, jogging!—in the direction of the pool house. *Good God, they're coming in here!* There was no back door, and I couldn't hide in the bathroom because what if they wanted to use it? Panic shot up my spine as I realized I had five seconds to disappear, and nowhere to disappear to.

Five seconds became four as I snatched my wet towel off the floor and my dripping joggers off the side of the sink. *Three, two . . .* I flipped up the lid of the couch-bench and tossed my wet things and myself inside. *One . . .* I lay down, pinched the frame of the lid between my thumb and finger, and pulled it down flat. As my countdown hit zero, I heard the curtains open and two sets of feet—his and hers—step onto the hard tile floor. It was pitch black in my sarcophagus-bed, but my ears had always been better than my eyes.

"You want to tell me what the FBI is doing at my crime scene, Agent Morales?" the man said, confirming what I suspected—*this wasn't an accident.* I guessed he was a police officer, because what else could he be?

"I didn't want to talk in front of the kid."

"The kid's not here."

I was stretched out flat like a surfboard. The balled-up wet towel was pressing into my back. It was crazy uncomfortable, but I didn't dare move. My nose was an inch from the underside of the lid, and my breath was bouncing back at me, tickling my eyelashes.

"Crazy weather," the female agent said, but the man didn't want to talk about the weather.

"If you want my cooperation, you need to give me something."

Swoosh! I heard the curtains close. Footsteps clopped across the floor. And then stopped. I heard the squeak of a heeled shoe pivoting across wet tile. And then with a whump the bench lid shuddered from the weight of the woman's backside dropping down onto it. Agent Morales was literally sitting right on top of me. I squeezed my lips together, then turned my head to the side to keep my hot breath from seeping out between her legs.

"The house has a bit of a history," the FBI woman said. And I wondered if she knew about me and what I'd done.

"What kind of history?"

"I'm not at liberty to say more than that."

Agent Morales shifted her weight, and the bench lid groaned above my head. My heart was beating so loud that if not for the pouring rain I was sure she would have heard it.

"So, what? Someone murdered someone here over a grudge about the house?" the policeman asked, and I felt a little sorry for him that he thought it was as simple as that.

"I know you want to solve your homicide, Detective, but this is an open federal investigation. I'm hoping you will help us without being coerced." Agent Morales abruptly stood, and a needle of light leaked in as the lid exhaled.

"Can I tell the kid it's not his sister?" *Wait, what?*

"Not yet." I flashed back to my view from the upstairs window: the white dress, the black fan of hair. *If it's not Carter's sister, who is it?*

"The poor kid is in there sobbing his guts out. If I can't tell him the dead woman we pulled out of the pool is not his missing sister, you're going to have to tell me why." And then I remembered. *There was another Cleopatra at the party. Same dress, same hair. Sophie had laughed about it: "Who wore it better?"*

"I'm not supposed to tell you this, so don't repeat it," Agent Morales said, and I held my breath in anticipation of hearing something I shouldn't. "We have the sister."

"What do you mean, *have* her?"

"She's a CW." I had no idea what a CW was, but luckily the detective spelled it out for me.

"Cooperating witness?"

"Yes. We think the hit was meant to be on her and they got the wrong girl."

"Helluva mistake." My brain was spinning. Pool water from my hair rolled down my temple into my ear, but I couldn't move to wipe it away. I flashed back to last night when Sophie introduced me to her brother. *"This is Aubrey,"* she'd said. Even though I was sure I'd introduced myself as Bree. How had she known my name? What else did she know about me? And what was she "cooperating" with the FBI about?

"We don't want anyone to know just yet that they got it wrong," Morales continued.

"What about the kid?"

"He's going to have to tough it out for a little bit."

"What's 'a little bit'?"

"We're chasing a big fish here, Detective. There are a lot of moving pieces."

"So what do you want me to tell him?"

"I don't know—tell him you can't make an ID yet, like you would if he were a suspect."

"So he's not a suspect?"

"No."

"Do you have a suspect?"

"Like I said, the house has a history."

"So someone connected to the house."

"Why is the power out?" Morales asked, presumably to evade the question. And the detective's answer was bone chilling.

"Main was cut."

"How?"

"I don't know, an axe maybe? The conduit was sliced clean through. Probably to disable the security system. That's just a guess." The thought of an axe murderer roaming through the party sent terror up my spine. I didn't know how the puzzle pieces of this mystery fit together, but someone had killed Sophie's doppelgänger, and there was no telling who they would come after next.

"So the victim was murdered here?"

"We don't know for sure she was murdered," the detective hedged. But Agent Morales wasn't buying the act.

"But you're proceeding as if."

"The coroner will make the determination; you know the drill."

"I think we can assume it was a murder," the FBI lady said.

"Do you know something I don't know?"

"I'm part of a years-long federal investigation, Detective. So yes, quite a bit."

I heard a phone chirp. "Morales," the FBI lady said, presumably to the caller. "OK, I'm on my way."

Her shoes clicked across the tile floor. "I'll need that coroner's report," she said. And then the curtain whooshed open, and her footsteps disappeared into the rain.

"Bloody hell," the detective muttered. And I couldn't have agreed more.

CHAPTER 37

———

SOPHIE

I woke up to the sound of rain. I had no idea what time it was—there was no clock in the room, and if they'd picked my phone up off the ground when I'd dropped it, they hadn't given it back. All I knew was that the sun was up, and wherever I was, the weather was awful.

I didn't know if I was allowed to get up (and where would I go?), so I just stared at the ceiling and contemplated my situation. I had basically been kidnapped, but by the good guys, who for some reason didn't want to tell me why.

I was thirsty and had to pee, so I slid out of bed in my plain-Jane scrub-like "pajamas" and tried the door. To my relief, it was unlocked. I opened it to see Tasker sitting in a folding chair right outside my room.

"Good morning," he said as he stood.

"Morning."

I wasn't wearing a bra, so I crossed my arms in front of my chest and indicated the bathroom door with my head.

"Just going to the bathroom."

I peed and splashed some water on my face, then used that mascara-stained towel on the back of the door to dry off. When I stepped back into the hall, Tasker was gone. So I went back into "my" room, gulped down half a bottle of water, then peeked in the drawers to see if there was anything else to wear. There wasn't.

I didn't have a phone to fiddle with, or anything to do, so I just sat down on the bed to wait for something to happen. I wasn't normally an anxious person, but when I looked down at my hands, I saw they were shaking. *Breathe, Sophie, breathe.* I reminded myself that I didn't do anything wrong, and if the FBI were mad at me, they never would have given me that nice robe. Five, ten . . . who knows how many minutes later, there was a knock on the door.

"Miss Britten?" I don't know why I was surprised to hear my captor speak my name, but I startled and stood up.

"Come in."

It was Tasker. "I can take you to breakfast if you like."

I wasn't cold, but those pajamas were kind of see-through, so I slipped on the robe and slippers and followed Tasker down the hall and into the same conference room from last night. But this time, instead of SunChips and granola bars, there was a carafe of coffee, single-serving cuplets of nondairy creamer, a basket of pastries, and a bowl of fruit.

"Please help yourself," Tasker said, then left and shut the door behind him.

I wasn't a muffin person, but the coffee was hot, so I poured myself a cup, then sat down to peel an orange. It was weird being left in an empty room without so much as the back of a cereal box to distract me. I once considered going on a silent retreat to "know myself" but decided not to because the thought of being alone in a strange place seemed too scary. I didn't imagine it would seem scary now, after being dragged to one zip-tied and blindfolded.

I had finished the orange and was picking pith out from under my fingernails when the door opened and Tasker reappeared with a woman in a high bun and an Alexandria Ocasio-Cortez red lip: Special Agent Morales. I shot to my feet, equal parts eager and terrified to find out why I was here.

"Hello, Miss Britten," she said with a smile. "Did you sleep all right?"

"Yes, thank you," I said, jamming my hands in the pockets of the robe to keep her from seeing my nervous fists.

"It's nice to see you again." I had met the special agent briefly back in mid-July as she was reviewing the tip I'd provided. She'd called me in to ask me how I'd come to work for Luke, and I told her about discovering the deed to the house and all the accounting shenanigans I'd stumbled onto. I was hoping she would want to talk to me again, but I never imagined it would be like this.

"Nice to see you, too, Agent Morales."

"We'll get you some clothes," she said, and I suddenly felt self-conscious in that poofy robe and my wild-child hair. I told myself she wouldn't dare judge me for my appearance, given she was the reason I looked this way.

"Please have a seat." She sat as she indicated that I should do likewise. But I remained on my feet.

"Look, I don't know what's happening here," I said, a little too forcefully, because I feared if I talked normally my voice might shake. "But I need to call my brother. He's going to worry if he can't reach me." I knew my brother. Once he discovered I was missing, he would freak out.

"We'll take care of Carter," the special agent assured me. "Not to worry."

"So he knows I'm here?"

"He will soon."

"What's going on?" I asked. "Why did you bring me here?" I remained standing and crossed my arms in front of my chest. I was trying to show her I was tough, but Morales just smiled at me, then pushed out my chair with her foot, which I understood meant she wasn't going to talk until I sat my butt down.

"We track the movements of a suspected contract killer used by the ROC," she said as I sank into the chair. "We suspected you were a target of a hit, so we had to extract you."

"ROC?"

She looked at me like she was disappointed I didn't know what that meant.

"Russian organized crime. I thought you knew."

I got a panicky feeling in my chest. I had suspected Luke was washing money for someone but never in a million years thought it was an organization as ruthless as the Russian mob.

"We determined it would be best to make it look like you didn't come willingly," Morales said, and once again I was confused.

"Wait, does that mean someone was . . ." It was almost too outlandish to say. "Watching me?"

"We thought it best to act as if." I felt the bottom drop out of my stomach. My disbelief turned to anger. If I was in danger, why didn't she tell me before I threw a freakin' party?

"So that's why your coworkers put a bag over my head and threw me in a car?" I wanted to make sure she knew how it all went down, in case she wanted to apologize. She didn't.

"You were a target the moment you set foot in Luke Sprayberry's office. The fact that your family now owns the house made you even more troubling to them, because it indicated you were more than just a random bookkeeper." The funny part is, I was a random bookkeeper. When my dad sent me there, it was just to help a friend.

"I still don't understand why you had to kidnap me," I said, my courage returning now. I mean, they were the frickin' FBI—surely they knew more humane ways to bring in a witness. For example, they could have texted, or sent someone dressed as a flower delivery boy; at least I'd have gotten a dozen roses out of it.

"We want you to have plausible deniability when we put you back into the world. If they saw us taking you by force, they're less likely to think you're cooperating."

"Wait," I said, processing the implications of them putting on a show, "does that mean you think someone was waiting for me at my house last night?"

"Like I said, we've been tracking a contract killer." And then she just smiled, like I was meant to finish that thought for myself.

"My brother is at the house," I said, because the thought that Carter was home alone with an assassin lurking in the bushes was as terrifying as it was absurd.

"Carter will be fine," Morales said coldly. "They have no reason to return to your house." *OMG. Return?*

"So, what, I have to hang out here until . . . ?"

"Until we know their next move."

"So, what. Another day? Two days?" And she was maddeningly evasive with her answer.

"You did a very brave thing, coming to us. We didn't tell you at the time, but we were already aware of the operation. Your evidence is one of many pieces of the puzzle. We're close now."

I wanted to help, but her nonanswer annoyed me. "What if I don't want to stay?" I asked. "I mean, you can't just keep me here. I'm not a criminal."

She opened her camera roll, then turned the phone toward me to show me a photo. At first I didn't know what I was looking at. The photo was blurry, like the camera was wet. But then I made out the image: arms, legs, an amorphous white gown, a head of jet-black hair . . .

"Oh my God."

The grief was immediate and crippling, a boulder that slammed down on my chest, crushing my heart into a million pieces. I wanted to scream but I couldn't breathe. Hot tears tumbled down my face and into my open mouth.

"Her body was found in the pool early this morning."

Samantha was a year older than me in school and the captain of the cheer team until she handed the reins over to me. My mentor. My teammate. *My friend.* Why would anyone want to kill her? It made no sense. *And then I realized . . .*

"Was that supposed to be . . ." I choked on the word. "Me?"

Morales didn't answer. She didn't have to. A sob caught in my chest. I put a hand over my mouth to stop myself from crying out. Poor, sweet Samantha, my high school hero, was dead because of me. *Good God, what have I done?* Through the flood of horror and shame, I felt a stab of fear. Because the person who'd murdered my friend was still out there. And it was only a matter of time until they realized they got the wrong girl.

CHAPTER 38

BREE

I was starting to get hungry.

It was plenty warm in my little crypt-couch, and once I moved the balled-up wet towel out from under my back, it was even almost comfortable. It was cramped—I couldn't move my arms to scratch my nose—but not airtight, and I think I may have even dozed off for a few hours.

I had no idea what time it was when I woke up, only that my stomach was convinced it was mealtime, because it was churning like a storm. I felt safe, but I couldn't stay here all day and night—I had to get out and find a bathroom and some food.

Before making my move, I closed my eyes and listened. Rain was falling, pattering against the roof of the pool house, making it difficult for me to hear if I was alone or there were still people milling around. I took a chance and pushed up on the lid of my coffin, opening it just an inch, then pausing to listen. But all I heard was rain and more rain.

I listened for a full minute, then a minute more. I finally took a chance and opened it wide enough to peer out. It was still daytime, but the light was flat and gray as ash. The curtains to the outside were open, which was good because I could see the whole backyard, but bad because the whole backyard could see me. The body had been removed, and there were little orange cones marking the spot. I didn't see any people, but that didn't mean there weren't any on the premises. Chances were there was someone standing guard somewhere. A woman had died; this was a crime scene. The detective had said it explicitly. They wouldn't just leave . . . *would they?*

I sat all the way up and snaked out of the bench, being careful to stay low in case someone was standing guard. I lowered the couch lid back down, then crawled on hands and knees into the galley kitchen. The fridge had no power to it, but it was still cold inside. There was a pitcher of mojitos, a bowl of limes, two jars of salsa, a six-pack of club soda, and a Tupperware container of meatballs. I ate the meatballs two at a time, barely stopping to swallow between bites, then washed them down with a swig of bubbly water. I burped as quietly as I could, put the Tupperware back, then crawled toward the bathroom. It was either go on the toilet or on the floor, so I chose the former, but without flushing. I dared to wash my hands and face. My hair was stiff with chlorinated pool water, so I dipped it under the tap, then squeezed it dry.

I crawled back to the kitchen and drank some more club soda, then slid the empty bottle against the baseboards so I wouldn't trip on it. I was desperate for some dry clothes, but there was no way I could risk going into the house. I was going to have to make a run for my car, which I'd stupidly parked two blocks away when I thought I'd have shoes to get me there.

I knew once I left the pool house I would never come back. It's one thing to sneak out of a crime scene, but something quite different to sneak back in. I was sad to leave. This little pool house was the closest thing to a proper shelter I'd had in months. Even if I could stay hidden, there was no more food, and no more Sophie to bring me any. No, she wasn't dead, thank God; but I was pretty sure she wasn't coming back.

Before it happened to me, I used to see unhoused people and wonder why they didn't go get jobs and clean up their lives. I quickly learned it's not so simple. You need a job to get an apartment, and an apartment to get a job. I had the added complication of needing a work permit. A big university like UCLA or LACM could sponsor me, but I would need a permanent address and a place to wait it out, because these things take time. There were music schools dotted through Canada, but most were on the East Coast. It would take a lot of gas to get to Toronto, if my tires would even make it that far. Plus winter was coming, which is a totally different experience two thousand kilometers north of here. At least in LA I could be unhoused and not freeze to death.

I dipped into the couch bench and extracted my sopping-wet sweats. They were heavy and cold against my skin, so I pulled the cinched bottoms up to my knees to at least spare my shins the discomfort. Then, with a quick glance left and right to be sure the coast was clear, I snuck out into the yard. There was yellow police tape across the back door, but no police, at least not back here. I took a gamble that the back gate wasn't monitored and crept around the side of the pool house toward it. Passing the shower stall, I flashed back to how this all started—standing nose to nose with Sophie, returning to find the care package, stupidly accepting her invitation to a party that turned my life from sad to catastrophic.

As I'd hoped, there was no one guarding the back gate, so I slipped through and let it lock behind me. The soles of my feet slapped against the wet pavement as I jog-walked down the narrow alley toward my car. I had parked in front of a cream-colored Mediterranean two blocks down and around the corner, under the cover of a leafy maple tree. At least I thought I had.

Rain pelted the top of my head as I stood there staring at the spot where I was absolutely certain I had left my car. But the spot was empty. I know because I ran across the street and stood smack in the middle of it. My eyes combed the block, looking east, then west, then back across the street. *Where the hell is my car?*

Panic seized my chest. This was definitely where I'd parked, and my car definitely wasn't here. Had it been stolen? Or towed? Either way, I would have to go to the police . . . *and tell them what?* That I'd just spent the night in the murder house and now couldn't find my car? *Oh, and by the way, I'm the suspect you interrogated in the crime that claimed my husband, but please just help me find my car and forget about all that.*

The will to live is a funny thing. Because even in this, my darkest moment, all I could think about was how to survive. It must be programmed into living things at a cellular level, because at this point I had no one and nothing to live for. Shoeless, soaking wet, no money, no future, shameful past, and yet I didn't want to die. I was too stunned to cry, too stunned to do anything except stand there letting the cold rain wash away whatever remained of my dignity.

"Bree?" I heard a voice call out, and I was certain it was in my head, because who would want to talk to me?

"Bree, is that you?"

I turned my head toward the sidewalk to see a man under a big black umbrella.

"Are you OK?" he asked as the little dog he was walking sniffed my bare feet.

I didn't answer. Because I really didn't know.

"My goodness, you're soaking wet! Here, come under my umbrella."

I didn't move, so the man came to me, holding that umbrella over the two of us as he took in my disheveled appearance.

"You're not wearing any shoes," he observed, and for some reason I looked down at my feet as if I hadn't known.

"I . . . ," I started, because it would be impolite not to say something. "I lost them," I lied, because in that moment I couldn't remember why I wasn't wearing them and I had to say something.

"You poor girl," he soothed. "Come on, let's get you dried off and warmed up."

I looked up at the face of my Good Samaritan. Gray hair curled out from under his black fedora, but it was the Russian accent that triggered my recognition.

"Alex?" I said. "You're Alex. You came to my house."

"That's right."

"We played Schubert."

"You played. I tried to keep up." He smiled, like he meant it as a compliment.

"You brought me honey cake."

"I did." The memory of honey cake and music and a loving man to share it with was too much. My heart burst like a dam breaking.

"My house is just up the block," Alex said, putting a gentle hand on my shoulder. "Come, let's go."

And my survival instincts must have switched off, because I went with him.

PART 4

———

JULY

(THREE MONTHS AGO)

CHAPTER 39

BREE

I loved my house.

I loved the shiny brushed nickel handle on the front door, how smooth it felt in my hand.

I loved the creamy wide-plank oak floors, as inviting as vanilla pudding.

I loved the huge columns of light that fanned out from windows that opened to the whole wide world.

I loved the floating staircase, the sparkly Caesarstone counters, the marble fireplace, the graceful flow, the tranquil lines, the soothing simplicity.

But most of all, I loved that my husband had lovingly built it for me. I tried to imagine him fretting all the details—*What color countertop in the bathroom? Will she want a drying rack in the laundry room? Accent wall here?* I didn't know if my mom was watching over me, but I checked in with her every day to let her know she could rest in peace now. "Look at this house," I would close my eyes and say out loud. "It's everything you wanted for me. Rest easy, Momma—I am safe, I am happy, I am loved."

It took nearly three months, but Luke and I finally got the place furnished. We didn't shop at the super fancy stores on Robertson, but we didn't bargain hunt, either, choosing tables and chairs from Crate & Barrel, a sofa from Room & Board, pillows and accent furniture from Z Gallerie. We browsed farmers' markets for wall art and decorations for the mantel. Luke was partial to the seascapes and sunsets, while I preferred more abstract pieces. I loved the swirl of our dueling aesthetics, how it made the house uniquely ours: a lighthouse in the bathroom, a crisscrossing geometric print in the living room. The vibe was eclectic and whimsical and distinctly us.

LA emptied out on the Fourth of July, so we decided to join the mass exodus and go up to Ojai to visit Luke's childhood stomping grounds. Canadians have a halfhearted holiday called Canada Day on July 1, but it was nothing like the blowout bash America has for its birthday, and even though this was my seventh one, I was still awed by the spectacle.

We decided to camp, because why stay in a hotel when you have the world's most perfect house? Luke had everything we needed: a two-person tent, twin sleeping bags (that zipped together to make one big one), flashlights, lanterns, cookware, collapsible bowls, a spacious cooler, a compact Coleman stove. He kept it all in a trunk in the garage, ready to go. All I had to do was shop for food. I knew the supermarket would be busy the day before the holiday, so I went early, right when it opened. I didn't normally need a trolley, but I was buying food and water for two days and nights, so I broke my rule (don't buy more than you can carry!) just this once.

I loaded my cart with sausages, pasta curls, lunch meat, sliced bread, apples, oranges, hot cocoa, marshmallows, a flat chocolate bar, and a box of graham crackers for s'mores. I got a block of dry ice on my way out, which I put right into the cooler where it would stay all weekend. It would be hot during the day but cool at night, so I packed shorts and sweatpants and a featherweight down parka. Luke had packed before he'd left for work, so when he got home, we ate a quick dinner (flatbread pizzas I made in the air fryer), then got on the road.

There was traffic getting out of town, but we didn't mind. Sometimes we listened to an audiobook—I loved a good mystery, and Luke and I would always come up with crazy theories about whodunit; I don't think we ever got it right. But Luke wasn't in the mood for a book, so we just played music. I always had a playlist at the ready—some of the classics I'd performed with my band mixed with indie hits that I'd inevitably try to learn.

Ojai was up a steep, windy road, but the days were long now, so we had plenty of light to get us up the mountain. We didn't camp at a campground; as a local, Luke knew all the secret spots where we could be alone with nature and each other. I always got a little verklempt on our camping trips because it made me think about my mom—how she'd taught me how to pitch a tent, then stretch the fly out over the tent poles so that if it rained you wouldn't get wet. I never liked doing dishes in our crusty porcelain sink at home, but I didn't mind washing them under the spigot at the campground because Mom was right next to me to dry and stack them: pasta pot, plastic bowls, spoons with little ridges on them that she called "sporks" because they doubled as both fork and spoon. Camping with Mom was as intimate as it was expansive. I loved cozying up to her while gazing up at an infinite, starry sky. Being in nature, knowing I was seeing the same stars as strangers in every corner of the world, made me feel connected to everyone and everything. It's a feeling I struggled to get back to after I moved to New York. I always found it ironic that it was in the bustling city of eight million people, not the vastness of the Canadian wilderness, where I felt most alone.

Luke pulled off the main drag onto a gravel road that wound through trees and scratchy brush. California was so dry and brown compared to British Columbia, which was green as far as the eye could see. The dusty landscape reminded me of the old cowboy movies they used to play at the drive-in near our house. Mom and I used to sneak in and watch from the hood of our car, eating popcorn we'd popped at home and drinking Cokes or orange Fanta out of the can. I never told Luke, but the day we went to see *The Rocky Horror Picture Show* at the Cinerama Dome in Hollywood was the first time I'd ever been to a movie theater. I loved it so much, I made him take me back at least once a month, to see anything that didn't have superheroes in it—those were too chaotic. I preferred stories of struggle and triumph; seeing ordinary people do extraordinary things always made me think of my mom, whose extraordinary act was to surrender to an ordinary life so I could pursue my music. I knew Mom wanted to get out of the Okanagan, go back to school instead of cleaning houses. I caught her sketching a few times when I was little, when she still hoped she'd find a way. But it takes seven years to become an architect. And with two mouths to feed, there was no time or money. So she doubled down on my potential, because if she couldn't be an artist, she'd be damned if her daughter didn't become one in her stead.

The sun was setting as we pulled up to our improvised campsite. As expected, we were the only ones there and had our pick of where to set up camp. Luke backed the truck into a flat spot between a giant pine tree and a little stream, then turned off the ignition.

"Is this OK?" he asked.

"Perfect."

I leaned over and kissed him. He didn't really kiss me back, but I figured he was just in a hurry to set up camp before it got dark. We worked in silence, him unloading the truck and pitching the tent, me setting up the "kitchen" to make dinner. I thought Luke was quiet because he was honoring the sacred silence of being in nature, but as we sat down to eat by the river, I sensed there was another reason he hadn't really spoken since we'd gotten here.

"Luke, baby?" I asked as I handed him a plastic bowl of pesto pasta. "Is something wrong?" He poked at his fusilli, and I knew the answer without him having to say it.

"Whatever it is," I said, "you know you can tell me." We'd been here before, and had made a pact not to keep our worries bottled up.

"Would you ever go back to Canada?" The question was so surprising I almost laughed.

"Why would I want to go back to Canada? Our life here is more perfect than I could ever imagine."

He set the bowl down on a rock and put his head in his hands, and for a second I thought he might cry.

"Luke, what is it?" I got a nervous feeling in the pit of my stomach. In my mind, things were perfect. Luke's business was booming; he was busy every day—so busy that he had finally hired an occasional bookkeeper to help keep track of it all. We had a showpiece home and a happy life together. The only thing missing was a baby, but we had only been trying for two months. I wasn't worried, and I didn't think he was, either.

"I was just thinking that maybe we should try living in Canada for a while," he said.

"Why?"

"Our life could be simpler there." In three years of marriage, Luke had never once expressed interest in so much as visiting Canada . . . *and now he wants to move there?*

"I love our life in LA," I said. "Every single thing about it." And it was true. I loved exploring the far corners of the city—the murals in East LA, the museums on Miracle Mile, the bike path in Santa Monica. I loved trying all the different kinds of food: dim sum in Chinatown, fish and chips in Malibu, Ethiopian food on Fairfax, tacos at the central market downtown. The thought of returning to the endless green corridors of British Columbia wasn't repugnant, but it held zero allure compared to the playground that was Los Angeles.

"I love it, too," Luke said, "but sometimes it just feels so . . . complicated." I didn't know what was so complicated about our LA life. Packing up a house and moving to a foreign country was ten times more complicated. He wasn't making any sense.

"I think it would be more complicated to move, don't you?" I tried to ask it as a question, so he wouldn't think I was pushing back. I would do anything my husband asked me to, but I had to understand why he wanted it.

"I suppose," he said noncommittally. To my knowledge, Luke had never been to the Okanagan, which meant he wasn't feeling drawn toward this other life, but rather away from the one we'd built here.

"Luke, did something happen?" I reached into my imagination to try to come up with a reason he might want to leave, but I drew a blank.

"No," he answered a little too quickly. "Forget it." He took my hand and gave it a squeeze. "I was just thinking out loud."

I got an uneasy feeling. I knew there was something he wasn't telling me. What I didn't know was that our "perfect" life was far from perfect, and about to unravel in the worst way.

CHAPTER 40

LUKE

It was a strange choice, going to Ojai for Fourth of July weekend, given the circumstances. I had plenty of old friends—former classmates, teammates, neighbors—who would have welcomed us into their homes, but I didn't want to see them. That would mean facing their questions, including the dreaded "How's work?" How could I tell them my success was literally criminal and I had betrayed everyone and everything I ever cared about?

When I'd had to make the tough decision to put Mom in a care home, then go to LA to find a way to pay for it, all my mom's friends came out to say goodbye and wish me well. To reconnect with them would be to subject myself to a chorus of "We knew you could do it!" when in fact all I'd done was ruin my mother's good name. Luckily I had married that rare, adventurous woman who preferred a campground to a "stuffy" hotel, so I was able to continue the pattern of isolation I had adopted since becoming a person who had to hide the truth from everyone, including himself.

Bree was predictably bewildered when I suggested we move to Canada. Even as I was saying it, I knew it was a preposterous idea. *Who knows if we'd even be safe there?* The Russian mob was an international crime syndicate; if they wanted to find me, surely they'd have the means.

Just because I went to another country didn't mean that I'd be safe. As they say, I could run, but I couldn't hide. It was selfish of me to delay the inevitable just because I wanted a little more time with Bree.

I slept surprisingly well for a tortured soul and woke to the sound of a pair of acorn woodpeckers knock-knock-knocking on a giant Jeffrey pine. I peeked out of the mesh tent door to see a river otter lounging on the bank, drying himself in the rising sun. Bree was curled up against my chest, nose pressed against my ribs. As I watched her sleep, the thought that I couldn't protect her made my throat constrict in agony. I hated having a secret from my wife, but I knew telling her the truth would be more than cruel—it could get her killed. If Alex and company thought she knew anything, she'd be a loose end. And people like Alex don't like loose ends.

There was another risk to confiding in my wife. Bree was not an American citizen. If I got caught, and the government found out she knew what I was up to, they would deport her and likely tell her she could never set foot in the US again. As torturous as it was, if I wanted to keep my wife safe, I had to keep her in the dark.

There was of course something obvious I could do to keep Bree from becoming a loose end or unwitting coconspirator: I could leave her. As I gazed down at her perfect heart-shaped face, felt her warm breath against my skin, I tried to imagine what I would say. *"I don't love you anymore"?* Even if I could get the words out, she wouldn't believe me. She wasn't just someone I loved; she was love. I knew the moment I saw her on that stage that my life would never be the same. At the sight of her, the room got wider and brighter, like I'd closed my eyes in Kansas and opened them in Oz. Even the music sounded fuller, like I'd ditched my mom's old record player for Dolby surround sound. I can honestly say I didn't know what it felt like to be truly alive until Bree slipped her hand in mine. With that first kiss, my heart found its purpose: to beat with hers.

There was a time when I thought I might never get married. I wasn't afraid of commitment; I just didn't think I had anything to bring to a marriage. My father split when I was twelve. I had no family traditions to share. My girlfriends would bring me home for Christmas, and I would feel like an impostor sitting around the tree opening presents. Mom was a gate agent for the airlines, so she often had to work on holidays. It sounds sad that she would leave me home on Christmas Eve with a new train set to build or book to read, but I never knew anything else, so I didn't feel like I was missing out. Like a lot of only children, I was good at being alone. I was happier building castles in my imagination than I was tossing a baseball with friends. None of my girlfriends understood my need for alone time, or how creating made me feel like me. Except Bree.

I never had to apologize to Bree for not having any holiday traditions, and she never expected me to smile my way through hers. When we talked about having a family, we understood that, as two people practiced in creating things from nothing, we would figure it out as we went—together, with no preconceived expectations or pressure to conform to someone else's ideals. For the first time, I felt like I could bring something to a marriage, because all Bree wanted was my enthusiasm to start from scratch. She lived in the moment, like people with difficult pasts learn how to do.

I tried to wiggle out of our shared sleeping bag, but as soon as I moved, Bree's hands reached for me, and as quick and smooth as that river otter slipping into the stream, we were making love like there was no one on earth but the two of us. If someone cried after, it was usually her, but this time we reversed roles and she was consoling me.

"Hey," she soothed, "whatever it is you're feeling, it's all good."

I should have corrected her, because it was not good at all, but it felt so right to have her arms around me, one hand pressing into my back and the other stroking my hair, that I gave in to it, let myself enjoy her loving embrace like I knew it was the last time.

CHAPTER 41

——

BREE

We rinsed our bodies in the river, then made some oatmeal, which we topped with brown sugar and thinly sliced Honeycrisp apples. I'd snuck the French press into the "kitchen" box, and we drank our coffee black and strong just like we both liked it. Our "table" was a big, flat rock by the river, and we sat on a fallen log and let the rushing water remind us that life is ever changing. A petal falls, a shadow forms, sunlight does an improvised dance across the water. If you're not present, you'll miss it; nature never gives you the same show twice. If only we could be so present for each dance step of our own lives—be the rainbow that peeks through a cloud, not the worry over never seeing it again, or the regret that it was gone too soon.

By midmorning I was itching to go exploring, so we zipped up the tent, stowed our groceries, and climbed into the truck to drive into town. Luke was still distant, but I didn't pry. I had never seen him in such a somber mood. I knew he'd open up when he was ready, so I just rested my head on his shoulder as he drove and let him use the silence to work through his thoughts.

We parked on the outskirts of town, which was already bustling. Locals had their American flags on full display—on their cars, front porches, even painted on their faces. The parade wasn't until tomorrow, but people were already starting to put out chairs to mark their ringside seats. It was a festive, joyful atmosphere, which made my husband's dark mood seem that much more marked.

We hadn't been to Luke's hometown since we were married there, so perhaps the memories of his bumpy childhood, or being abandoned by his father, or his mother's drawn-out illness were what brought on his melancholic mood. Was the fact that we were trying to start our own family making him nostalgic for his? I hadn't been "home" in seven years; would I be similarly sad if I went back there?

As I observed the locals chatting and hugging as they greeted each other in the street, I wondered to myself, *What makes a place home? Is it where you grew up? Went to school? Go to work? Lay your head?* Because sometimes those are four different places. When Luke and I traveled and people asked me where I'm from, I always said Los Angeles now. Not because I'd spent the most time there—of all three places I'd lived, I'd been in LA the shortest. It was my home because I chose it to be my home. It was the place where I watched the sun set over the ocean, where my cat prowled for mice, my students lived, my herb garden was planted. And it was where the man I loved had built a home for me and where we planned to raise a family.

I knew Luke didn't love LA like I did; was coming home to Ojai making him long for a different kind of life? He had said LA life was "complicated" and that Canada would be "simpler." We had never talked about living anywhere else—his musing about moving was so completely out of the blue, I didn't think he was serious. I would follow him anywhere—to the woods, or to the moon. I made a mental note to tell him the next time we talked, not knowing there would be no next time.

There was a farmers' market in the middle of town, so we waded in to sample organic strawberries and farm-fresh goat milk soap. Somewhere in the distance, a bluegrass band was playing. I heard a banjo, an acoustic guitar, drumsticks on a tin can tapping out a simple 4/4 beat. After we shopped, I planned to drag Luke over to watch them for a while. I knew what it was like to play to a disinterested crowd, and how seeing even just one or two people listening and smiling made the effort feel worthwhile.

It was getting hot, and I could feel the July sun baking the back of my neck. I had a tube of sunscreen in my shoulder bag. I would ask Luke to reapply it once we got out of this stall, and I would insist he put some on himself, too. Seeing little kids in strollers and on shoulders, wearing bucket hats and too-big baseball caps, made me excited for the day that I would be that mom buying them kettle corn and carrying them on my back when their feet got tired.

I was filling a wicker basket with peaches, indulging in the fantasy of a future I hoped would soon be ours, when—

Pop! A whip-sharp cracking sound pierced the air.

It was so close I felt my eardrum vibrate. But before I could so much as gasp, Luke was on top of me, driving my body to the ground.

My basket sprang from my hand. Peaches bounced out onto the pavement. I felt my chin graze the ground as Luke smothered me with the full weight of his body.

"Luke, you're hurting me!" My lungs ached as I tried to breathe. The asphalt was hot against my bare chest and thighs, and my elbow burned where it was scraped raw.

"Oh my God, Bree, I'm so sorry."

He rolled off me and crouched down by my side. My knee was crisscrossed with road rash, and my chin was bleeding.

"I'm sorry, Bree. I'm so, so sorry."

Luke slipped his hands under my armpits and helped me to my feet. All around me, people were staring. Blood dripped onto the front of my tank top, and it took me several seconds to realize it was my own.

"Here, sweetie," a white-haired woman said as she handed me a napkin, then pointed to her own chin so I knew to wipe mine.

"What just happened?" I asked, not really to anyone.

"It was a firecracker," the white-haired lady said, looking at Luke, then saluting him with a stiff hand to forehead like he must be a military veteran with PTSD, because why else would he behave like that?

"Of course," he muttered, shaking his head in embarrassment. "I'm an idiot."

Someone else came up to me and handed me a bag of ice.

"Thank you." I winced as I pressed it to my throbbing chin.

"Bree . . . ," Luke said, making prayer hands and putting them to his lips. "I'm so sorry. I don't know what came over me."

"It's OK," I assured him. "I'm OK." And I was. But I didn't know what on earth was wrong with him.

CHAPTER 42

SOPHIE

The hardest part of being an FBI informant is not the clamming up and pretending you're some clueless dumbass only interested in fashion and TikTok-ing. It's the waiting. I thought blowing the whistle on a crime would bring on the cavalry to haul the perpetrators off to jail that same afternoon. But it's not like that. There are a lot of ducks to line up. Finding evidence, even damning, irrefutable evidence, is just the appetizer. To indict someone, you need to build a case—pinpoint a motive, a victim, a chronology. Then you need to convince a judge that your case is strong by calling witnesses (e.g., me) to testify about all the reasons indictment is warranted. That's a multicourse meal. A lot can happen between nibbling on the hors d'oeuvres and sitting down for a steak dinner. Suspects can run, they can hide, they can die—at their own hand or at the hand of coconspirators. That's why I needed to keep quiet. If perpetrators don't know they've been found out, they won't try to cover their tracks. And, as I would learn the hard way, criminals like the ones I stumbled onto will go to deadly extremes to silence witnesses to their crimes.

It had been six weeks since I'd marched into the local field office to accuse my former boss of fraud, yet despite my treasure trove of evidence, no one had followed up. "I'd like to report some suspicious activity," I'd said to the security guard posted at the entrance of the aging, unimpressive Federal Building in West LA. He'd directed me to put my phone in a basket, then walk through a metal detector, which I set off because I forgot gold bangles are metal and that I should have left them at home.

They kept me waiting for two hours. As my butt grew numb on that cheap metal-and-vinyl chair, I wondered if the state of California got a deal on those twelve-by-twelve chalky-gray floor tiles because every government building had the same ones. I didn't have my phone—they wouldn't let me bring it in—and I hadn't brought a magazine, so I just sat there staring at my cuticles, wishing I'd been born with better nail beds or at least gotten a manicure.

As unimpressive as the place was, I still felt crazy excited to be there. I would work in a dungeon to do the job I was called to do. I knew this was where I belonged the same way a baby bird knows it's born to fly. I was ready to take flight, and this dated office building was my sky. I'd even visited the shooting range a few times, because even people who work desk jobs at the FBI are expected to know how to fire a gun, and I wanted to be ready when the time came.

"I'm a trained forensic accountant," I said to the junior field agent when I finally got invited into his cubicle. "And I think a client of mine is cooking his books." He listened with a face of stone as I laid out my case just as I'd rehearsed. "I have all of his bank statements showing the flow of money," I'd said. "As you can see, the movement is highly unusual."

He took my documents with a halfhearted promise to "pass it on," and that was it. Hours of photocopying, tabulating, spreadsheeting, and analyzing . . . just for fifteen minutes with some low-level administrator who may or may not tell anyone what I had found. Walking in there I'd felt like a boss; walking out I'd felt like a fool. When a week of radio silence turned into two, three, and now six, my inferno of confidence was reduced to a few smoldering embers. I couldn't believe I had dared to hope the FBI would not only act on my intelligence but also be so impressed with me that they'd offer me a job on the spot. *How stupid can you get?* I was beginning to think my parents were right—that a job at the FBI was out of my league. I wish I could say that I was certain I'd done the right thing. But as I peeled potatoes for my mom's "famous" potato salad that hot July 4 morning, I mostly felt dejected and useless.

"Don't overcook them," Mom said as I put the last of the potatoes into the pot of boiling water. "We don't want them to get mushy."

"I won't."

Mom had stopped nagging me to get a job, but I had enough self-loathing for both of us, and without the distraction of constantly sparring with her, I felt even worse. *Why the hell would the FBI hire me?* I had zero real-world experience. And they probably got thousands of tips every day that were way more pressing than mine: an active shooter, a bomb threat, mysterious white powder in your Bed Bath & Beyond coupon. A few irregular bank transactions were hardly worthy of sending in the SWAT team—*what the hell did I expect?*

As I stared down into the cauldron of potato water, it wasn't the steam that made my eyes shiny. As repugnant as the thought was, I knew it was time to start looking for another job. The most palatable option was to join a private firm, start helping dejected divorcées get their fair share of the money their slimy ex-husbands were hiding in foreign bank accounts. I wouldn't be fighting crime, not exactly . . . but I'd still be sticking it to the bad guys.

There were perks to taking a well-paying job in the private sector, even if it wasn't what I wanted to do. If I started working, I could finally move out, and consummate the flirtation with Jared, whose weekly visits to clean our pool were the only thing I looked forward to these days. I could also beg off some of those interminable Sunday dinners, as people with apartments to clean and lives to live sometimes legitimately need to do.

"I set a timer for twenty minutes," Mom said. "That should be enough." She left the room, and the implication was clear: I was the newly appointed potato salad czar. Which, tragically, was the greatest responsibility of my pathetic postcollege existence.

Later, when my parents, brother, and I climbed up onto the roof to watch fireworks bedazzle the sky, I closed my eyes and asked the universe to give me a sign. *Time to give up? Or hold the course?*

And wouldn't you know my prayer was answered the very next day. I felt a pang of guilt when I heard what happened to Luke—it wasn't my fault that he had chosen to get involved with criminals, but I couldn't help but feel partially responsible for how it ended for him. I always knew I would need thick skin if I was going to work in law enforcement; people get hurt, incarcerated, sometimes even die. If I couldn't handle it, best to learn that now.

If I had known how many lives were going to be destroyed, would I have kept my mouth shut? Hard to say. I had fantasized about a life on the edge, full of danger and intrigue. I wanted to make the world better and safer, put the greater good first. So even though what had happened to Luke was awful, in my heart of hearts, I was right where I wanted to be.

CHAPTER 43

LUKE

I knew what I had to do. I had gotten myself into this mess, and I wasn't about to drag my wife down with me. There were no easy choices. So I would take the simplest one. The one that would keep Bree safe.

They say you don't know what you've got until it's gone. I understand how that could be true for some people, but it had never been true for me. I had serious relationships before I met Bree. I was with my high school girlfriend for nine years. It was long distance for a while, when she was in grad school, but we lived together for six of those nine years, and everyone—including her—thought we were destined for marriage. I loved Christine—she was kind and easy to talk to. But when she left me because I "wouldn't put a ring on it," I didn't feel regret. I knew my forever person was still out there, and that I would meet her when I was ready.

When my mom first got sick, our pastor came to her bedside and tried to help us make sense of her suffering. He told us we wouldn't know joy if we didn't know agony; that's why God gave us struggle. If all you knew in your lifetime was happiness, he'd said, then how would you recognize it? There is no such thing as celebration without disappointment, triumph without failure, dark without light; one defines the other. If your life is nothing but smooth sailing, the gifts along the way are water droplets in the ocean—indiscernible and unimpactful. God gave us hardship so we would know peace, he'd explained. And created us in his likeness so he would know them, too.

It's not that I didn't believe Pastor Cordero—he was a wise man and taught me a lot over the years. But I didn't need my mother to die to know that I loved her. And I didn't need a failed relationship or a decade of loneliness to appreciate the extraordinary connection I had with Bree. I recognized it like a lightning bolt in a storm. I knew we were meant to be like you know you need a drink of water on a hot day.

I thought Bree would want to go home after I tackled her to the ground in the farmers' market parking lot, but she insisted she was fine and there was no reason not to camp another night as planned. In retrospect, I'm glad we stayed. If I was going to go through with this, I wanted our last night together to be in a beautiful place so at least she'd have happy memories of our final days.

Pastor Cordero also had preached that all good things come to an end. That I knew to be true—we are all mortal, after all. I glanced down at Bree's bloody knee as I helped her into the truck. As she smiled up at me to reassure me that she forgave me, I couldn't help but wonder if there might be an inverse relationship between how good something is and how long it can last. For three years, I'd basked in beauty most people never glimpse. Perhaps my pastor was right after all—I was just experiencing it all in reverse. I had been given love as expansive as a cloudless sky so that I could recognize agony now that it had seized me.

We got back to the campsite just as the afternoon sun slipped behind the mountain. I insisted on making dinner so Bree could wash up and rest. If this was our "last supper," I would make it a feast—sausages cooked over an open flame, salad made with fresh spinach and peaches we'd bought at the farmers' market, organic wine from the vineyard outside of town.

We would enjoy a weekend of great food and fireworks, and then it would all be over.

Even though I knew I was doing the right thing, I felt nervous that I wouldn't be able to go through with it. But, as fate would have it, I didn't have to do it myself. Because someone else did it for me.

CHAPTER 44

Bree

Luke made me the most perfect dinner that night—crispy, sweet sausages and salad so fresh it tasted like we were eating it right off the vine. I was fine, but I let him do everything, because while I didn't need to be taken care of, I knew he needed to take care of me.

After he washed all the dishes (by himself, while I read a book), we roasted marshmallows and ate s'mores under the stars. He wasn't chatty, but his dark mood had lifted, like he had come to peace with whatever had been troubling him.

We slept side by side but without touching, me respecting his emotional space, and him respecting my bandaged knee and elbows that were still tender to the touch. I woke to perfect, steaming hot coffee and pancakes as fluffy as cotton candy. We spent the day hiking and bird watching, then packed up early to watch the fireworks from his secret lookout spot above Ventura Harbor. It was a near-perfect day, and I felt hopeful his inner storm was clearing.

We listened to music as we drove home, then went to sleep in our bed without unpacking—I would do that in the morning, as Luke had an early start. The next day, when he kissed me goodbye, I had no idea it was for the last time, so I barely kissed him back.

I didn't have any lessons scheduled, so I spent about an hour putting the camping gear away. Most of it stayed in the garage, but I hung up the sleeping bags to air out and threw the dirty dishes in the dishwasher.

I had the whole day, so I decided to make a lasagna. I found the recipe on Instagram, made a shopping list, then pulled on a T-shirt and jeans and drove to the supermarket. There was a nice Pavilions a few blocks away, but I preferred the Gelson's in Century City for how they always turned the labels out so you could read them.

I didn't like the underground lot because driving down there made me feel disoriented, so I always parked in the same spot next to the exit. I had to walk farther, but I was only buying a few things—vegetables, four kinds of cheese, lasagna noodles, crushed tomatoes—so I could easily carry it all without a trolley.

As I perused the pasta aisle for the perfect noodle, my phone rang in my pocket.

"I'm going to make a lasagna!" I sang, assuming it was Luke calling to check in on me like he normally did around this time. And I was right about half of that.

"I'm so sorry," he blurted, and then he did something I had never known him to do. He sobbed.

I thought back to the weekend, about how strange he had acted. Was he sick? Had he just gotten test results? Had he been in an accident? Hurt somebody? Hurt himself? In that half second of silence, my mind raced through the possibilities.

"Luke, babe, where are you?" And his answer knocked the wind out of me.

"This is not how I wanted to say goodbye."

"What are you talking about? Where are you going?"

"You're going to be OK. I love you." And the line went dead.

I didn't hear the basket hit the ground. Mushrooms rolled everywhere as a block of cheese bounced off my foot.

"Miss?" I heard someone say. "Are you all right?"

My eyesight was blurry as I ran toward the exit. I groped for my parking ticket and fed it into the machine with shaking hands. The gate wafted open and I accelerated underneath it and onto the boulevard, cutting off an SUV that reprimanded me with an angry honk of its horn.

Red light, stop sign, then a straight shot toward home. The tears were rolling down my face so fast there was no point wiping them.

I turned onto my street. The swarm of black sedans was like a dark stain on a white shirt, zigzagging in front of my house like train tracks at Grand Central station.

I pulled up and jumped out of my car. I counted two, three, four squad cars as I ran past them toward my front door.

"Luke!"

I called out at the top of my lungs as I stumbled toward my house. There was a man in a dark suit standing guard at my front door. He put out a hand to stop me as I lunged for the handle.

"I'm sorry, ma'am. But I'm afraid you can't go in there."

"This is my house! I need to get inside!"

He stepped in front of me, blocking my path.

"You can't stop me from going into my own house!"

I felt a hand on my shoulder. I spun to face a trim woman in a tight ballet bun and red lipstick like she was at the opera.

"What's happening? Where is my husband?"

"Are you Mrs. Sprayberry?"

"Yes!"

"I'm Agent Morales of the FBI."

She flashed a badge. I waved it away. I didn't care if she was the president of the United States. All I cared about was finding Luke.

"Where's my husband?" I demanded. I didn't understand why they wouldn't let me into the house. "Has something happened to him?"

Morales looked at her hands. Her silence was like a blow to the ribs. Sobs ripped through my chest as I fell to my knees. Because I knew what it meant when people looked at their hands like that.

I flashed back to my mother's wake. The hushed whispers, the red-rimmed eyes, how our landlady dabbed her cheeks with the back of her veiny hand. Were they crying for Mom because it hurt to think about how she'd suffered? For me because I was an orphan now? Or themselves for all the loved ones they had lost?

I didn't know what was going through the heads of all those cops swarming around my house, and I didn't care. Because my husband was gone, and my whole heart died with him.

PART 5

OCTOBER

CHAPTER 45

BREE

Raindrops bounced off the pavement as the three of us walked down the sidewalk in silence—me, my inexplicably kind neighbor, Alex, and his little white dog, who was tugging at his leash like he was sick of getting rained on.

"Yes, Leo, we're going home," Alex said, but it only made the little dog tug harder.

Alex tried to shield me from the rain with his big black umbrella, but it was a wasted gesture—I was already soaked to the bone. I didn't think this block was "permit only" when I parked my car here last night, and I was right: it wasn't. But the man who stole it, who was also the man walking beside me, assumed (correctly) that I'd be in no condition to go to the police, given the circumstances and my history . . . both of which he not only knew about but also had helped to create.

My bare feet were numb, but somehow they took me the two blocks to Alex's house as the powdery light of dusk gave way to the charcoal glow of pending night. I was freezing and dizzy with hunger, and no wonder—it was dinnertime, and I had used up my reserves months ago.

"Here we are," Alex said, stopping in front of a princely English Tudor with twirls of ivy clinging for dear life on the bumpy stone exterior. The hip-high gate was flanked with white roses, and just beyond it, a front door fit for a castle left me looking for the moat.

Alex opened the little gate, and I followed him up the slippery slate path that cut through a manicured lawn the color of money.

"Can you take him for a moment?" Alex asked, handing me the leash so he could close the umbrella and unlock the front door.

"Please, go on in," he said, holding the door open for me like I was worthy of the gentlemanly gesture. The sharp bristles of the welcome mat tickled the soles of my feet as I followed Leo the dog into the house.

"Wait here; I'll bring you a towel," Alex said, leaving me standing there holding Leo's leash and dripping cold rainwater onto the smooth marble floor. The place reminded me of the Magic Castle with its rounded archways, heavy drapes, and a giant wagon wheel chandelier that looked straight out of King Arthur's court.

"Here, wrap this around you," Alex said, handing me a fluffy white bath sheet. "Then I'll take you upstairs to find some dry clothes."

He took the leash from me and dried Leo's paws with a hand towel while I used the bath sheet to blot my hair and wet T-shirt. The pants were hopelessly waterlogged, but I wrapped the towel around my body to tamp the dripping. I guess Alex was satisfied enough with my efforts, because he smiled and nodded and said, "Follow me."

He led me toward a wide mahogany staircase that curved up to a landing with views of the open living room and foyer below. Little Leo tagged along, his nails clicking on the hardwood as he brushed past my wet pant leg.

"Yes, Leo, you can come," Alex said, patting his leg to beckon the dog to get out from under my feet. As we reached the top of the staircase, I saw the whole upstairs was encircled by a banistered landing like the mezzanine of a grand opera house. That medieval chandelier looked even bigger now that I was eye level with it, and the chain suspending it from the ceiling was thick enough to moor an ocean liner.

"This was my daughter's room," Alex said as he opened a bedroom door in the middle of the hallway. "She's at university now, on a semester abroad." He indicated for me to go on in. I hugged my towel across my chest as I stepped over the threshold.

The room was tidy and sparsely decorated with a few framed photos on the dresser and a bookcase of textbooks and YA lit. It smelled a bit like lemons and floor cleaner, and I suddenly became self-conscious about the rancid mix of rain and pool water that was dripping off my pants.

"Let's see what we can loan you for a bit," Alex said, crossing to the dresser and extracting a pair of sweatpants by PINK and an assortment of tank tops and tees.

"You're welcome to choose any undergarments you wish," he said shyly. "If she didn't bring them with her, she doesn't want them anymore. Help yourself."

He set the sweats and tees on the bed, then opened her underwear drawer, taking a step back so I could peer in.

"I trust there's something in there that will be to your liking."

"Thank you," I managed. I hadn't come here for a handout, but I desperately needed one, and was too exhausted to be proud. Even if I had known Alex's hospitality was a trap, I probably still would have accepted it. I couldn't tell him what he wanted to know, so the give-and-take he was pursuing would only amount to him giving and me taking.

"Shoes are in the closet," he said, opening the door to reveal a shoe caddy with a dozen different brands of sneakers. "She went through a sneaker phase; you'd be doing me a favor by taking a pair or five."

He smiled, like he thought that was funny. And maybe it was. It had been so long since I'd laughed, I'd forgotten how.

"Bathroom is right there," he said, pointing to another door. "Help yourself." And then with those words he started toward the bedroom door, pausing at the threshold to say, "I'll go make us some tea."

Leo lingered by the foot of the bed, seemingly uncertain if he should leave me there by myself. He was right to want to keep an eye on me, if my past behavior was indicative of my future trustworthiness.

"Come on, Leo," Alex commanded, snapping his fingers at the little dog. "Let's give the young lady some privacy."

Leo reluctantly did as he was told, and Alex nodded and smiled at me as he shut the door behind them. And then I was alone in this strange woman's bedroom, surrounded by her clothes, shoes, and memories. I had no idea why the neighbor I had met only once had invited me into his home, but even if I had suspected malevolent intentions, I wasn't in any condition to turn down his help. I was penniless, homeless, carless, shoeless, starving, and soaking wet. By that point, I would have taken a handout from the devil himself.

I plucked a pair of bikini briefs and a sports bra from the underwear drawer, along with a pair of white ankle socks, then scooped up the sweatpants and pile of T-shirts and lugged my haul into the en suite bathroom. I would have loved to take a shower, but I didn't want to overstep Alex's hospitality, so I used the toilet, rinsed my hands and face, stripped off my wet clothes, then got dressed. I found a hairbrush and a scrunchie on the vanity, which I used to pull my hair into a low ponytail. Not glamorous, but a vast improvement from the wet-rat look I'd sported on my way in.

The numbness was fading from my feet, making them ache a little, so I decided to help myself to a pair of Nike Air Force 1s, which, as luck would have it, were only a half size too big. It was a small luxury putting on cushy new sneakers, but after three months in the same pair of worn-out Reeboks, it damn near put a spring in my step.

There was a mirror on the back of the door, and I almost didn't recognize the woman staring back at me—the hollows under her eyes, how the crisp, clean clothes hung on her withered frame. I felt like I was looking at a stranger. And in a way I was. Because I didn't know who I was without Luke or music, or why I was trying to survive a world that brought me nothing but pain.

I put my hand on the knob. As I pulled the door open—

Pop!

I had never heard a real, live gunshot before, but the biting urgency of it halted me in my tracks. I might have thought the sound was something else—a twig breaking, a whip snapping, a hardcover book falling on that unforgiving marble floor—if it weren't for the violent spatter of blood that appeared like a flame on the downstairs foyer wall.

Pop! Pop!

Two more shots rang out. Through the open bedroom door, I saw a body crumple to the ground. Blood was oozing out from under it like ink from a broken fountain pen. A tanned hand reached up and squeezed the empty air, then flopped down like a wounded pheasant falling from the sky. And I knew from the shiny Rolex around the wrist that the dead man was Alex.

For a second that felt like eternity, I couldn't move or breathe. I just stood there, gripping the doorknob, peering down at the carnage below. And then came the noise that turned me from a horrified onlooker into a target.

"Arf!"

I hadn't seen Leo there when I'd opened the door, but there he was—all ten pounds of fur and curiosity—staring up at me with fangs bared.

"Arf-arf-arf-arf-arf!"

There was a swish of movement from below. In less than a heartbeat, a man in a black hoodie was standing at the foot of the stairs. The gun that had killed Alex was tucked in his waistband. His eyes widened as they flicked up and locked onto mine. As his right hand reached for the gun, I slammed the door shut and locked it with shaking hands.

"Arf!"

If the dresser had been full, I never could have toppled it, but thanks to that semester abroad and all the belongings that had made the journey with their owner, it went over with a full-body heave.

My survival instincts kicked into overdrive. I ran over to the window, flipped the lock, and yanked it open. If it was twenty feet down, it might as well have been a hundred—there was no way I could jump.

But the roof, with all its pointed edges, had a little eave that I could reach. I couldn't go down, but if that windowsill could hold my weight, I could go up . . . ?

Pop!

A gunshot blew the doorknob clean off, and I was out that window and up on the ledge quick as a finger snap.

My hands grabbed the drainpipe. My grip was strong and my body light, so I pulled with my arms and pushed with my legs, trusting my fingers to hold on as I monkey-climbed up onto the roof.

Wham!

I heard a sound that must have been the door hitting the dresser. *No turning back now.*

I clawed my way up and over a pointed turret. The shingles were slippery with rain, so I slid down the back of the house, onto the garage roof. Then I crouched like a catcher behind home plate and launched myself into a rosemary bush, thick with stubby needles. The branches heaved with my weight but stopped me from hitting the ground. I rolled to one side, scrambled to my feet, and took off running.

Tears and misty rain burned my eyes as I tore down the street. Instinctively I ran toward the one place I knew I could hide, not knowing the man who killed Alex knew that's where I'd go.

CHAPTER 46

————

CARTER

The coroner had taken the body "into custody," yet I remained. The cops wouldn't tell me that the corpse they pulled out of the pool was my sister, but they also wouldn't tell me that it wasn't. So I was trapped between hope and despair, eager for news, but also grateful to not know because what if knowing was worse?

A dozen people dwindled to a handful as the hours ticked by. By midafternoon, it was just me, the detective, and a pair of bored-looking uniformed cops. And then it was time for us to go, too.

"We should know more in a few hours," the detective offered as he walked me to my truck. "Go home and get some rest." I couldn't go home just to sit around waiting for the phone to ring, so I did what any other rational person would do under the circumstances. I went looking for my sister.

I drove to all her favorite hangs—the sushi place on Ventura and Cedros, the coffee spot on Riverside, the deli at the top of Beverly Glen, her favorite happy hour on Sunset. "Have you seen Sophie?" I asked her waiter and waitress friends, and they all shook their heads no. I know it sounds crazy, but I couldn't help but believe my sister was still alive. Maybe it was a sibling thing. *Because wouldn't I know if she were dead?* Or maybe I was just in denial. Whatever the case, I clung to hope like a buoy in a hurricane, praying there was a simple explanation why she hadn't texted or called all day and circling the town like a shark who might die if he stopped moving.

I filled my tank at a gas station in West Hollywood as the sky drew dark and my mood grew darker. I couldn't go home; Sophie's absence would suffocate me. It would be another six hours until my parents got back—they had just left New York after cutting their trip short when I called and told them I couldn't find Sophie and I needed them. I hadn't told them about the murder because Mom was already an anxious flyer and there was nothing either of them could do at thirty thousand feet—might as well let them fly in peace.

The cloudy afternoon had smudged into a cloudy night. I was a traffic jam away from home but a stone's throw from Rodeo Drive, so I decided to head back to the crime scene. I knew I wasn't supposed to disturb anything, but it was our house; I had every right to be there. I was no Sherlock Holmes, but if there were clues about what happened to my sister, I wouldn't find them here at this stupid gas station. I couldn't understand why the cops wouldn't tell me who the dead body belonged to, because if they were waiting to inform the family, as her brother, I should be the first to know. *So does that mean it isn't Sophie?* By telling me it wasn't Sophie, they wouldn't be telling me who it was, just who it wasn't. But maybe they weren't allowed to say who it wasn't until they told the family who it was. *So does that mean it is Sophie? Or it isn't?* I couldn't get my head around it.

I arrived at the Rodeo Drive house to see a crisscross of police tape on the front door but no police cars or anyone standing guard. I knew I wasn't supposed to be there, so I parked around the corner, even though it was still drizzling and I didn't have a raincoat.

My garage door clicker didn't work because the power was still out, but I had learned how to manually open an electric garage door from one of our contractors on a jobsite, and I always carried a coat hanger in my truck should the need arise.

Under the cover of rain and nightfall, I slipped the makeshift fishing rod over the top of the garage door and trolled for the release mechanism. It took a couple of sweeps, but I finally snagged the handle and gave it a tug. I heard a click as the locking mechanism released. The front of the door was slippery, but I was able to ease it up with the palms of my hands. A second later, I was standing at the threshold of the garage, staring at a truck and a Porsche that for some unknown reason came with a house that had more mysteries than a *Knives Out* movie.

I eased the garage door closed and used my phone light to survey the space. Along the side wall were two sleeping bags hanging from the rafters, a tool bench, a pegboard with a vast array of hammers, screwdrivers, and socket wrenches, and a chest with the lid off and propped against its side. I peered into the chest to see a Coleman stove, a Jetboil, and a few assorted pots and pans. I knew where there was camping gear, there'd likely be a lantern, and a quick search through the box proved my hunch was right.

I flipped on the lantern. The beam was powerful enough to light up a whole room, so I decided to go inside and start searching them one by one.

I didn't have to worry about the alarm going off, because no power to the house meant no electronic surveillance, which, as I would later learn, is precisely why someone had cut it. It would take the events of the next hour for me to believe that there had been an assassin trailing my sister the night before; had I known, I'm not sure I would have ventured into the Rodeo Drive house by myself in the dark. But my ignorance emboldened me. Plus I had two questions bouncing around my brain that were more burning than why the power had gone out. What happened to Sophie was obviously the big one, but what happened to Bree was a close second, because I couldn't help but think they were connected. I was still convinced that Bree had spent the night, which meant she had been here when this place went from a party house to a crime scene. *Witness? Victim? Or murderer?* She had to be one of the three.

I figured the police had already searched the downstairs, so I decided to start with the up. My sneakers and socks were wet, so I slipped them off, then held the lantern over my head as I tiptoed to the floating staircase and took the steps two at a time.

The upstairs landing had space for a pool table or a small library but was unfurnished except for a little pedestal table with a vase of fake flowers—*orchids, I think?* Rain pattered on the skylight, creating an ominous soundtrack to complete the horror movie mood. There were four doors off the hallway. The three closest to me were closed. But the one at the end of the hall was ajar, so that's where I headed first.

Light from my lantern bounced off soaring ceilings and smooth plaster walls as I made my way across the wide-plank white oak floor. I nudged the bedroom door open with my elbow, then held my lantern above my head to illuminate the space.

I knew from the size and prime placement at the back of the house that this was the primary suite. It was decorated sparsely but tastefully with matching teak furniture—a lowboy dresser, twin nightstands, a sitting chair overlooking the pool. The king-size bed was unmade, but only on one side. I found that curious, so I walked around the foot of the bed for a closer look at the slept-in side.

I wasn't looking down, so was startled to feel something lumpy beneath my feet. I stepped back, then shined my lantern on the floor to see a jumble of clothes: white peasant blouse, black leggings, and a scarlet cape. I got a tingle up my spine as my suspicion was confirmed. Bree *had* slept here. The question was, *Why?* What business did she have in this house, this room, this bed?

I gazed at the nightstand. There was a reading light and a pile of books: a book club thriller, *The Art of Happiness*, a biography of some composer with round spectacles and a double chin. There was a hair clip—the kind my sister used to sweep back her bangs when she washed her face. A fine layer of dust that twinkled in the light of the lantern told me this room hadn't been lived in for a while, by Bree or anyone else.

I turned and walked toward the dresser. There was a scented candle, a book of poetry, and a wedding photo in a silver frame. The groom was laughing like he was so happy he couldn't keep it in. And when I saw the bride's face, I knew why.

Bree looked like a Disney princess at the end of the movie, all sparkles and radiant joy. If you had asked me ten seconds ago, I would have said tiaras are a ridiculous accessory and have no place outside of kids' cartoons, but on her it looked as natural as wings on a butterfly. In her lace and pearls, she was grace personified, and even under these most precarious of circumstances, I couldn't help but feel a slap of disappointment that she was married to someone else.

I slumped down on the bed. My head throbbed with confusion as I tried to process what I had just found. Why was there a picture of Bree here? Who was the man in the wedding photo, and where was he now? Was this our house? Or her house? *What the hell is going on?*

I got up and peeked into the en suite bathroom. The shower floor was wet, as was the towel on the back of the door. So she had showered here. *And then what?*

I exited the suite to explore the rest of the upstairs—behind the other closed doors were an office with built-in bookcases, a guest bedroom that looked untouched, and an empty room painted yellow like it was destined to become a nursery. As someone who built houses, it was clear to me that this was a family home. *Bree's family.* So where was she? And why was my dad's name on the title?

I retreated downstairs. Turns out the answers to all my questions were there waiting for me. Because as I stepped onto the ground floor landing, the wide eyes of that picture-perfect Disney bride were staring at me through the back door.

CHAPTER 47

BREE

The rain had slowed to a drizzle, but it still blurred my vision as I ducked into the alley behind my former house. The interval between being kind to me and winding up dead seemed to be growing ever shorter, and I couldn't help but wonder if I was approaching the ability to get someone killed with a handshake.

The back gate to my Rodeo Drive house was locked, but that wheelie bin was perfectly placed for a literal hop, skip, and jump into the yard. The grass was a waterlogged sponge, and mud oozed up over the soles of those brand-new Nikes as I plopped down onto it, soiling the crisp white leather.

I crouched-ran toward the pool house. I was about to duck inside and hide myself like the last time someone died under my nose when I saw a flash of light inside the main house. Not a flash—an orb. *A flashlight?* No, more like a lantern, descending at an angle like the person carrying it was coming down the stairs. I didn't know who it was, and I didn't care. I was sick of running, sick of hiding. I needed help. A man was dead. It was time to come clean about everything—what I'd seen and what I'd done. I wasn't sure I believed in karma, but I believed in telling the truth, and I'd been choking back mine for far too long.

I skirted around the pool and ran up the deck stairs. I could see the lantern bearer's face now. And it was time to reveal mine.

Bang, bang, bang! I slapped the glass door with my palm. Carter looked over with a start.

"Carter," I shouted into the wind. "Carter!"

He stared at me for a beat, and I thought for a second he might run away, as was my habit. But after a second of studying me through the glass, he finally set the lantern on the counter, made his way to the door, then reached above his head and—*click-clack!*—unlocked it.

"What are you doing here?" he asked, cracking the door open but blocking the entrance with his body.

"Please, Carter . . . let me in."

He hesitated, like he didn't want to, then finally stepped aside so I could get through.

"I should call the police," he said. And I didn't disagree with him.

"Yes! Call the police! Tell them to come here." He looked surprised at the suggestion but quickly pivoted back to interrogating me himself.

"What did you do to my sister?" he asked. His voice trembled a little, and I didn't know if it was rage or fear, just that I was glad I hadn't told him I'd just fled another murder scene, because how could he not think I was a serial killer?

"Nothing!" I insisted. "I barely knew her." I don't know why I added that last part, except for that it was true.

"I know you slept here," he said. "I saw your Halloween costume on the bedroom floor." I didn't care that he knew; I planned to tell him everything, right then and there.

"I can explain. I will explain." I was trying to decide where to start—with getting the house on my anniversary? Or losing it because of my lies? But he had a more pressing question.

"First you need to tell me what happened to my sister."

I flashed back to the morning . . . peering out into the yard from behind the pool house curtain . . . seeing him arrive . . . then collapse in shock and grief. But that was hours ago. Was it possible the FBI hadn't told him that his sister was still alive?

"That wasn't her," I said cautiously. I didn't know if he had gotten a glimpse of what was under that yellow tarp, so I added, "It was the other Cleopatra." He scowled, like he didn't believe me.

"What do you know about it?"

"You're right; I slept here," I said. "I woke up to see a body in the pool. I saw the hair, and the dress . . . I thought it was Sophie, too!"

"How do you know it wasn't?"

"I heard them talking—"

"Heard who? Who was talking?"

"Police, FBI, whatever they were. I hid in the pool house after I called 9-1-1. They didn't know I was listening."

"You called 9-1-1?" he asked, and I nodded. I thought he would ask more about why I was hiding from the police, but in that moment he only cared about one thing.

"So where is my sister?" There was urgency in his voice. I wanted to reassure him, but I didn't know if what I'd heard would make him feel better or worse.

"They said they had her."

"Who? Who has her?"

"I'm not sure. But I think the FBI." He shook his head, like what I was saying was absurd.

"The FBI doesn't kidnap people." But of course I knew differently.

"Yes, they do."

CHAPTER 48

SOPHIE

There was a knock on "my" bedroom door.

"Come in," I called out as I popped to my feet.

The door opened a crack, and Agent Tasker, my roommate at the safe house, peeked his head in.

"We're leaving," he said.

"Where are we going?"

"Courthouse."

He opened the door wider and handed me a shopping bag from H&M.

"I hope these are adequate," he said, then shut the door before I had a chance to ask why on earth we were going to court.

Earlier in the day they'd brought me some magazines (cooking, fashion, *Reader's Digest*), but I couldn't look at them. I was worried about Carter, but I spent most of the day thinking about Samantha. What did they tell her family? What would *I* tell her family? That she was collateral damage in an investigation I'd stuck my nose into? That I'd willfully put her and all my friends at risk by throwing a party because I was lonely? That her beautiful life was snuffed out because I was a selfish jerk? If this weekend had been a test of my self-discipline and judgment, I failed. I had to do better. I had to *be* better. I vowed that if I got the chance to join the FBI, every case I worked on would be to honor the friend I'd led to the slaughter with my selfishness.

Tasker knocked again. "Ten minutes," he said through the closed door, and I understood that I was meant to put on the clothes he'd brought me, so I did.

The white button-front shirt was stiff, but a good choice given that they'd neglected to get me a bra. There was a three pack of high-waisted white panties that sat just above my belly button. The flat-front chinos were too big, but the boxy double-breasted blazer they bought me to top it off camouflaged the waistband that puckered under the slim leather belt. They didn't get me shoes, so I put my sandals back on, then stepped out into the hall to find Tasker waiting for me.

"I need to use the bathroom," I announced, hoping he would take the hint and move down the hall. But he just stood there, as immovable as the King's Guard at Buckingham Palace.

"I'll be right out."

I peed and washed my hands, then tried to check my appearance in that wavy fun house (not) mirror. I didn't have any hot tools, ponytail holders, or product, so there wasn't anything I could do with my hair even if I could see it, so I just pulled it back, twisted it like a cinnamon cruller, and tied it in a knot. I didn't care about looking good, but I wanted my appearance to reflect the respect I felt for the court and the remorse I felt for getting someone killed.

"OK, ready," I said as I stepped out of the bathroom. Tasker escorted me down the hall toward the back door, where another agent was waiting with his hands folded in front of his fly.

"Hello," I said, and he just nodded.

They let me put the bag over my head myself this time—"for my own protection," I was told. They didn't want anyone knowing the location of the safe house, not even an aspiring future agent. *You can't be tortured into telling if you don't know.*

I sat in the back, behind the driver like last time, but minus the zip ties and terror. As we rolled out of the garage, the image of my dead friend played in my brain like a broken record. It was supposed to be me lying lifeless on the side of the pool, which strangely didn't make me feel scared, maybe because I was too busy feeling heartbroken that someone else had died because of my ambitions.

Working in law enforcement was more than some ego trip or lust for power. It was my calling. I'd known it ever since I'd come back from Italy. While everyone else was raving about the art, the food, the architecture, all I could think about was the injustice—how the Crusaders had ripped across the continent in the name of the Holy Roman Empire, taking everything they could get their hands on for their king. How a thousand years later, not much had changed. Rich people continued to work the system to get richer, blaming "supply chain issues" and "inflation" for price hikes they created by widening their profit margins and taking bigger salaries for themselves. The pain of "tough times" was always passed on to the consumers, because why should a handful of owners suffer when everyone else can suffer for them? It was sickening, and I was determined to do my part in fighting it.

We rode in silence as the car bumped along the dirt road. I was glad I had a bag over my head because I didn't want my FBI escorts to see the tears that were leaking out the sides of my closed eyes. I wanted them to think of me as a peer, not a crybaby. I knew they would already be biased to see me as weak because I had girl parts. I didn't want them to think I couldn't handle working for the FBI, because maybe then I'd start to think it myself. You can't be a crime fighter without encountering criminals. And criminals, by definition, do bad things. If I wanted to be part of their world, I would have to toughen up . . . *starting now*.

I'd watched enough police procedurals to know that being in law enforcement takes its toll. The portrayal of cops and federal agents turning to a bottle or a bar fight to battle their demons might be a cliché, but that doesn't mean it doesn't happen. I was already learning it's impossible to get close to anyone. I couldn't be with a man I adored. My friend was dead because I'd thrown a party after ratting out a money launderer. Regret welled up from the pit of my stomach, and I wrestled it back. This was no time for regrets. It was time for action.

The dirt road gave way to pavement, and the car accelerated. I had no idea what time it was, but it didn't matter. I had committed to testifying the moment I walked into that field office with a folder and a crazy theory. Which turned out not to be so crazy after all. Quitting wasn't an option. I would help bring these bastards to justice if it was the last thing I did. Not for me. For Samantha. Who never signed up for this but paid the ultimate price.

"You can take the bag off now," Agent Tasker said.

As I pulled the thin black sack over my head, I turned my face toward the window so he wouldn't see my swollen eyes. We were on the freeway. To my surprise it was dark out. Had I really been in that tiny bunker all day? After breakfast, they had put out sandwiches, but I don't like sandwiches—not that it mattered. I had zero appetite and probably wouldn't have eaten even if they had offered me sushi and caviar.

"What time is it?" I asked.

"Eight thirty." *Eight thirty?*

"What time is our court appearance?"

"Whenever we get there." I didn't want to be annoying, but what kind of trial happens at eight thirty at night?

"Why so late?"

"Sensitive witness," he said. And I assumed he was talking about me. "The court makes special accommodations."

We got off the freeway and weaved our way through downtown, toward a floating glass cube with zigzaggy windows, a.k.a. the federal courthouse. Our "special accommodations" included an unmarked entrance to an underground parking lot that we drove into with a wave of a magnetic badge.

We curved around and down to the lower level, then parked near an elevator. Tasker got out and opened the door for me.

"Thank you."

Tasker and his coagent showed their badges to a security guard, who used a key to call the elevator. We got in, and the guard used his badge to send us to the sixth floor. The doors opened, and Tasker indicated for me to get out first. I stepped out into the grand atrium. The place was a glass palace, with windows in every direction, including above our heads. The unsubtle architectural message of "We see you" was as clear as a looking glass, and I felt it as soon as I stepped onto a marble floor so shiny I could see my reflection in it.

"To the right," Tasker said, then edged out in front of me to lead the way. There was a series of closed doors. We stopped at the last one, which was guarded by a deputy in a tan uniform.

Tasker flashed his badge, and the deputy opened the door. The walls were bright white but textured with little triangles to make the room feel modern. The overhead can lights were all on, but it wasn't overly bright. In the middle of the room was a rectangular conference table—white oak, to match the door.

Two people were already sitting at the table. One of them I recognized immediately. It was Agent Morales, still looking as fresh as she did when she'd come to see me that morning in that slick ballet bun and matte red lip. She stood when she saw me, then beckoned me over with a curt wave of her arm.

The other person remained seated. He was wearing what looked like navy-blue scrubs and was gripping a cup of coffee. Black, of course, because that's how he always drank it. He turned to look at me. A jolt of fear shot up my spine. I nearly stumbled. But then he did something unexpected: he smiled.

"Hello, Sophie," he said. And it occurred to me I might not be the only "sensitive witness."

"What are you doing here, Luke?"

CHAPTER 49

———

L U K E

My FBI handler warned me it would feel weird being back in the "real" world after three months in a high-security Protective Custody Unit, or PCU, as the suits called it. That's where I'd been since they'd arrested me the day after Bree and I got back from our Fourth of July holiday in Ojai. They don't put you in regular jail when you agree to cooperate in a RICO case (for a crime that falls under the Racketeer Influenced and Corrupt Organizations Act) because the mob has tentacles that can reach inside prison bars, and if you know too much about their operation, you probably won't survive there.

To be clear, I wasn't in WITSEC (witness protection). I was in federal prison like the criminal that I was. A PCU is not a country club or white-collar jail. The only thing that makes it different from regular jail is that no one can visit you, because no one can know where it is or that you're in it. Not even your family. Not even your wife. Because what if the mob is watching your loved ones and they accidentally reveal things about the DOJ's case against them? Not being able to see, or even talk to, Bree was the hardest part about getting sent away. I knew she was going through hell, and I couldn't comfort or help her. I deserved to be punished. But she didn't.

The timing of my arrest was as fortuitous as it was tragic. Fortuitous, because I had planned to turn myself in that very day, after I tied up a couple of loose ends for a client who had been waiting nine weeks for her kitchen cabinets and had run out of recipes she could make in her garage. Tragic, because it happened quickly and without warning, and an incoherent phone call with FBI agents bearing down on me is not how I'd wanted to say goodbye to my wife.

I'd had the whole day planned out. I got up and showered at the usual time, went to the wholesaler to check on the cabinet order, then onto the jobsite to give instructions to the crew. Before I left, I turned everything over to the foreman so that he could finish the reno without me. The FBI field office, where I'd planned to turn myself in, was already programmed into my nav, but I had two stops to make before I went there. First stop was my office to collect the evidence I'd prepared, which was neatly organized in a color-coded binder. Next was home, to say goodbye to my wife and beg her to wait for me while I did my time. But I never got to say goodbye to Bree. Because as soon as I pulled into my garage, the Feds swarmed my house like honeybees at the hive. They already knew all about my crimes, and Sophie had already given them all the evidence they needed to arrest me for them.

I smiled at my whip-smart bookkeeper as she sat down across from me so she'd know I wasn't angry at her. She'd done the honorable thing by turning me in. And let's be honest: If I didn't want to get caught, why would I have hired a woman whose proud papa bragged about how brilliant she was? If anyone had a right to be angry, it was Sophie. I put her life at risk the moment I invited her into my books. I knew the mob was onto her—Alex had told me as much when he'd asked me about *that girl you have working for you.* So yeah, the right to be angry belonged to her, not me.

"The judge is on her way," Special Agent Morales, a.k.a. my handler, said as she looked up from her phone. "Do you have any questions?" She was looking at me, but it was Sophie who spoke.

"I have a question," Sophie said, raising her hand like she was in school.

"Go ahead."

"If Luke is working with you guys, then what am I doing here?"

Morales looked sharply at the two agents who had escorted her in, like, "Didn't you tell her?" and they just shrugged.

"The murder at the Beverly Hills house prompted us to request an emergency hearing," Morales said. I got a sick feeling in my stomach at the mention of a murder. Morales had told me someone had been killed at my former home, but she wouldn't answer my questions about Bree, except to say that "to her knowledge" she was safe. If something had happened to my wife, I would never forgive myself. All I could do was pray Morales was telling the truth.

"As a convicted felon, Mr. Sprayberry is not a reliable witness," Morales added. "So we need your testimony to corroborate his."

"What's the hearing about?" Sophie asked. And I wondered the same thing. Since becoming a government witness, I was on a need-to-know basis. They told me what they wanted, when they wanted. The justification was that it was for my safety, because the less I knew, the less valuable I would be to the crime syndicate once I got out. Maybe it was true. Or maybe they just didn't trust me. I was a criminal, after all.

"We're seeking an arrest warrant for Alexei Popov, the man who enticed Mr. Sprayberry into the family business," Morales explained, indicating me with her head as she spoke my name. Since being arrested, I had come to learn that Alexei, or Alex, as he liked to be called, was a relatively small fish in the ocean of organized transnational crime, and the hope was to get him to cooperate just like they'd done with me. Minnow ensnares goldfish ensnares catfish ensnares piranha. That's how the DOJ does it. I was the fish food. The big fish was many meals ahead of me.

"Who's Alexei Popov?" Sophie asked. So Morales explained.

"He's a Russian mob asset. The guy who engineered all those deals you uncovered while working for Mr. Sprayberry."

I'd told the prosecutor that I hadn't known I was getting into business with the mob when I accepted their money, but he'd had little sympathy for me. I'd had the opportunity to come forward, but I hadn't, he'd said. So I was guilty as charged. The punishment for money laundering was up to twenty years in prison. But by pleading guilty and

offering to cooperate, I'd gotten what the DOJ calls "downward depar-
ture." If my cooperation led to arrests of bigger fish in the food chain,
I'd earn a reduced sentence. Results mattered in this high-stakes game
of dominoes, they told me. So if I wanted my freedom back, I'd better
be convincing. And hope Sophie was convincing, too.

"OK . . . ," Sophie said. "I still don't understand what I'm doing at
the federal courthouse long after closing time."

"We don't do these types of hearings out in the open," Morales said.
"Not with RICO cases, and not with sensitive witnesses." *Who might get
killed for testifying,* she might have added, if it wasn't already implied.
"The judge insisted on firsthand testimony, given the seriousness of the
charges. That's why we brought you in."

"So we testify . . . and then what happens?" Sophie asked. And I
was wondering the same thing.

"Depends if the judge grants the warrant," Morales said, evading
the tough questions as was her habit. Her phone buzzed, and she looked
down at it. "She's in the building; you both ready to go?" She stood up
like we were going whether we were ready or not.

My life had been a living hell these last three months and three
weeks—not just because I missed Bree, but also because I'd learned the
DOJ had taken everything: our house and all our earthly belongings.
Turns out in crimes involving money laundering, the FBI has almost
unlimited discretion. They can seize homes, cars, bank accounts, even
the clothes on your back—just on the *suspicion* of a crime. For some
strange reason, so-called "civil" forfeiture is not a criminal proceeding, so "innocent until proven guilty" doesn't apply. To make matters
more complicated, asset forfeiture is a proceeding against the *property*
involved in the crime, not the *person*. So technically by taking your
things, they're not violating your rights, because it's the things that are
getting arrested, not you. Not that it mattered. I had confessed to a
crime, and they had my bank statements and Sophie's research to prove
I'd done it. The house had been bought with dirty money. Which meant
not only could they seize it, but I was also not getting it back.

As for the money that I'd earned legitimately before I'd met Alex, that hadn't been seized, but my bank accounts had been frozen on the assumption the money was all mixed up. A judge would have to rule on how much I'd get back, if any. I pleaded with my handlers to expedite the process—"I have a wife, she needs money to live on!"—but I still hadn't gotten a court date. The only concession the DOJ made was Bree's car, because it was registered to her, and she needed somewhere to put the small allocation of personal items they'd allowed her to keep. They couldn't prove she was an accessory to my crimes, but I couldn't prove that she wasn't; so she got swept up in the seizure right along with me.

In my first and last chaperoned phone call from the metropolitan detention center where I was formally charged and processed, I'd told Bree that I'd broken the law and was being taken away. When she'd asked *"What for?"* I didn't want her to think I'd committed a violent crime, and I knew better than to tell her the truth, so I'd said the first thing that came to me. *Tax fraud.* I figured that would explain why they came and took everything. In that moment, I'd forgotten that we actually *were* committing tax fraud. Her under-the-table teaching business was illegal, and she knew it because I'd told her. The infraction was minor—it never would have led to her or my arrest. But she didn't know that. As I rotted in jail, the only thing worse than being separated from Bree was knowing I had thoughtlessly led her to believe my incarceration was her fault. And I couldn't risk calling her to tell her the truth without putting her at risk.

I looked at Sophie, and she met my gaze. I understood that if Sophie and I did our jobs tonight, the same thing that happened to me would happen to Alex, and the Feds would be one step closer to shutting this ring down and saving more people from getting hurt. I had no idea that Alex was about to suffer a much worse fate than getting arrested, but it made sense. He was way more valuable than I was, and if the mob had clocked my disappearance, they knew the Feds were closing in.

"Let's put this bastard away," I whispered to Sophie. And her answer gave me confidence we were on the same team.

"I'm all in."

CHAPTER 50

SOPHIE

"All rise!" a deputy called out as the judge entered the courtroom through a hidden door in the wall. I stood on those wobbly sandals and clasped my hands in front of my waist to keep them from shaking. Luke, Agent Morales, and I were in the spectator area, which I later learned was called the public gallery, even though there was nothing public about this hearing or anything we were about to say here tonight.

"Be seated," the deputy commanded, and we all sat down. Besides the judge, deputy, and the three of us, there were five other people in the courtroom: the two agents who had escorted me from the safe house, a guy in a dark suit from the US Marshals office guarding the door, and two prosecutors, both of whom sat at a narrow table facing the judge.

The judge glanced down at her docket, which I presumed was just this one case, because no one else was in the courtroom, then looked up at the prosecutors.

"So you're here seeking an arrest warrant in a RICO case?"

The male prosecutor stood. "Yes, Your Honor."

"Are your witnesses here?"

"Yes, Your Honor." He indicated Luke and me. The judge glanced in our direction.

"OK. Tell me about this Alexei Popov."

I had no idea who this Alexei Popov was, so I listened with curiosity as the prosecutor told the story of how Popov had tricked Luke into taking jobs paid for with dirty money. I'd suspected the moment I saw the huge amounts of cash flowing into Luke's bank accounts that he was involved in something criminal, but it never occurred to me that he might be a victim, too. As the prosecutor described the flow of money from illegal arms and drug sales into US bank accounts via shady real estate transactions, the scope of the operation blew my mind. According to the prosecutor, Luke was one of a dozen players in the Russian mob's money laundering operation here in LA, and Alexei Popov was the bastard who'd ensnared them all.

The judge asked about Luke, and the prosecutor explained how they'd been alerted to his criminal activities by "the brave young woman sitting in the gallery." The judge looked at me, and I felt a rush of nervous anticipation that I might just get to use the speech I'd rehearsed every day since stumbling onto the crime ring the FBI had been investigating for over a decade.

The prosecutor told the judge that Luke had pleaded guilty and was serving out his sentence in a high-security PCU "due to the nefarious intimidation tactics employed by organized crime," and I got a chill down my spine as I connected Samantha's murder to my presence here today. The prosecutor wasn't exaggerating when he said the mob would stop at nothing to keep their scheme going, and I tried not to think about what would happen to me if the judge wasn't convinced. Being in that courtroom, on the side of justice, listening to the prosecutor detail how Mr. Alexei Popov had destroyed countless lives made my blood boil. My resolve to devote my life to putting these scumbags away grew so big it canceled out my nervousness, and when it was my turn to speak, my voice was steady and strong.

"Miss Britten," the judge said. "Tell me what led you to report what you found to the FBI."

I stood and told the judge how I'd come to work for Luke, and what I'd learned about AABC—the sham construction company operated by

Popov. "He's the CEO of an empty shell," I said. "Mr. Sprayberry was paying Popov to do work he was doing himself." I tried to be succinct but thorough. I described calling vendors and asking why shipments of lumber and shingles were requested at one address but rerouted to another.

When the judge asked, "What prompted you to investigate the anomalies in Mr. Sprayberry's books in the first place?" I boldly told her the truth.

"Your Honor, I got a degree in forensic accounting because I wanted to make a difference. Once I suspected I'd discovered a criminal operation, I felt it was my duty to report it." I didn't look at Morales, but I could feel her eyes on me. I can't say for sure what she was feeling, but I hoped it was respect.

I don't know how long I spoke, only that it was enough.

"Arrest warrant for Mr. Alexei Popov is granted," the judge said. "Is there anything else?"

There was something else, but it didn't concern me, so I turned to look at Morales.

"Now what happens?" I asked the FBI agent.

"We go pick him up."

CHAPTER 51

LUKE

The judge granted the arrest warrant, and Morales pumped her fist like we were at a soccer game and the home team had just scored a goal. I was happy for her that her case was moving forward, but nothing was going to change for me. I was still a convict with time left to serve, and going back to that PCU was going to be even harder now that I'd had a glimpse of life on the outside.

Days in the PCU were long, but nights were longer, and I hardly ever slept. I thought about Bree constantly and prayed to God that he was keeping her safe while I couldn't. I found myself thinking a lot about my mom—how she'd lived out her final years in a similarly isolated state. I'd felt awful that I couldn't take care of her when the double whammy of dementia and pain made it impossible for her to take care of herself, but her Social Security checks weren't enough to feed and house both of us, and the cost of her meds far exceeded what Medicare would cover. So I made the tough choice to put her in an assisted living facility, then go work in LA so I could pay for it.

In her younger days, my mother was a joyful, curious person who loved to shop, cook, garden, go exploring. I hadn't fully understood how jarring it was for her to have simple freedoms like getting her hair done, making coffee in the morning, going for a walk on a sunny day taken from her all at once . . . until it happened to me. I understood now how deflating it is to have your bedtime, meals, workouts, even bathroom visits scheduled at someone else's convenience. My mom had been in prison, just like me. The only difference was I'd earned my sentence from my poor judgment; hers had been forced upon her by illness. But the end result was eerily similar—days that all blurred together, the complete loss of spontaneity, autonomy, control, joy. Coming from Canada, Bree was shocked to learn how the American health care system discards people when they need it most. She was ready to pack up and go take care of my mom herself. And maybe Mom knew it, because she wanted a better life for my new wife and so let the angels take her just two short weeks after we were married.

I waited for the judge to retreat to her chambers, then turned and started walking toward the courtroom door where I knew the US Marshals who'd brought me from the PCU were waiting to take me back. I was halfway to the exit when the prosecutor called out my name.

"Sprayberry!"

He beckoned me over to his table. This man had complete control over my life, so I tried to be nice despite my sour mood.

"Congratulations," I said as I approached. He didn't thank me, just reached into his briefcase and pulled out an envelope.

"It's not much, but you won't have to sleep on the street," he said as he offered it to me.

"What's this?"

"The judge just granted your release. We were going to bring the motion at a bail hearing next week, but it felt right to ask for it now. You're not the kind of guy we want clogging up our prisons."

I peeked in the envelope to see it was full of cash.

"I don't understand," I stammered, because the DOJ doesn't give criminals money—they take it from them. That's kind of their job.

"The government provides a small stipend to help government witnesses transition back to the free world. But don't leave the state. We have a trial to prepare for."

"You mean . . ." I was almost afraid to say it. "I can go?"

"It's safe for you out there now that we're bringing Popov into custody," the prosecutor explained. "They won't be interested in you now that we have him. Agent Tasker will explain the conditions of your release, then take you wherever you want to go."

He indicated the young, clean-cut guy standing with Sophie; he nodded at me, like yes, this was happening, and no, I wasn't crazy.

My heart exploded in my chest as I felt every emotion all at once—joy, grief, shock, relief. I coughed out something that sounded like a sob—and I guess it was, because tears were streaming down my face. For nearly four months, day and night, I had thought about one thing and one thing only, and I could finally say it out loud.

"I need to call my wife."

When you're waiting to testify against the mob, your life is not your own. You can call your loved ones, but all calls are chaperoned and recorded, and anything a spouse says can be used against you or them—there is always suspicion that the spouse is an accessory. So it's safest just to stay silent. There is no public record of your arrest, and your whereabouts are not searchable on any database. They don't want the crooks to know where you are, because they might do things to intimidate you from testifying against them. You might as well be dead. I'd told Bree that's what she should consider me. For all I knew, that's how I would wind up. The various federal agencies—FBI, DOJ, US Marshals office—took steps to protect me, but they made no promises.

Agent Tasker reached into his pocket and handed me a phone, which he said I was to keep so they could reach me "at all times." I dialed Bree's number with shaking hands. *Does she even still have a phone? Would she answer my call if she did?* I'd left her with nothing; it was possible she never wanted to speak to me again. I'd written to her every day while I was in prison, but I'd had no idea where to send the letters, because by building her a dream house, I'd made her homeless. So they sat in a drawer, the ink fading along with my self-worth.

The call went to voice mail. Even just hearing the sound of her recorded voice felt like a miracle.

"Bree, baby, it's me. Where are you? I'm coming home." The word "home" just slipped out. I knew we had no actual home, but that didn't matter. Home for me was wherever she was. "You can reach me at this number. Please call as soon as you can. I won't rest until I see you." Tears were streaming down my face, but I didn't care. Fear, excitement, anticipation, gratitude . . . I can't tell you what I was feeling, only that it was overwhelming.

"The US Marshal has your things; you can change in the holding pen," Tasker said. The marshal stepped forward and handed me a clear plastic bag of clothes—*my* clothes, which I hadn't seen for more than three months.

"I need to find Bree," I said, trying to tamp the panic in my voice. But it wasn't the FBI who offered to help me.

"I know where she is."

I turned to look at Sophie.

"You do?"

"She's been staying at your Rodeo Drive house," she said, then clarified, "in the pool house."

"That's impossible," I said. "It's not our house anymore. They took it when I got arrested."

"I know," she said coolly. "My dad bought it."

"What? Why would he do that?"

"Because I told him to."

And in that moment I realized Sophie was even smarter than I'd thought.

CHAPTER 52

SOPHIE

"You did good today," Morales said as we stepped into the elevator and the doors closed behind us.

"What happens now?"

"We go make an arrest."

"Can I ride along?"

Morales looked at me like I had some nerve. And I guess I did. But so far my nerve had served me well.

I'd found out Luke had been arrested from my father, the day after it happened.

"You remember that guy I sent you to work for?" he'd said. "The contractor with the house in Beverly Hills?"

"Yeah."

"Apparently he's in jail now."

"No kidding?"

It's a shame I never played poker, because I have the best poker face of anyone you've ever met. That's not the reason I wanted to be a secret agent, but I imagined it would come in handy. As my dad detailed how there had been "some kind of raid" at Luke's house, I'd hidden my elation like candy eggs on Easter morning. I would have preferred to have heard about Luke's arrest from the FBI at my job interview, but it still felt good to be right. Maybe they didn't need me, but I still hoped they'd call and acknowledge that the information I'd provided had been relevant.

The call asking me to come in for a meeting came two weeks later, on July 18. The Feds had a lot of questions for me: *How'd you discover the deposits? What made you think they were unlawful? How many vendors did you call? What did you say to them? What did they say to you?* And I had questions for them: *Do you think there are others? Do you need me to testify? What happens now?* They wouldn't answer most of my questions, but they did throw me one bone.

"What happens to the house?" I'd asked the woman who'd introduced herself as "Special Agent Morales."

"It's property of the DOJ now."

"And what is the DOJ going to do with it?"

"Put it up for auction."

When she said the word "auction," I flashed back to how my dad had poked at his kung pao chicken when he'd told me about Luke having bought a house in Beverly Hills. Dad had worked hard his whole life. He wanted to retire but was frustrated that he couldn't figure out how to do that. My USC education, which he had generously paid for, had gobbled up a big chunk of that retirement fund, as had a couple of deals gone south. He always talked about finding that "one big flip" that would make him set for life. But building costs were high, his profit margins small, and the big-ticket properties out of reach.

"How does the auction process work, exactly?" I'd asked Morales, even though I already knew.

Morales had looked at me over the top of her glasses. I couldn't tell if she was puzzled by my curiosity, or annoyed.

"Typically, the DOJ goes in and tags the contents, sells what they can, then puts the house on the auction block."

"That's going to raise some eyebrows in that neighborhood. I mean, it's prime Beverly Hills." By that point, I had done a ton of research on RICO crimes. Enough to know that these networks of money launderers were like spiderwebs. And you only wanted the fly if he could lead you to the spider.

"We seize all sorts of properties," she'd said, as if that would somehow undermine my point.

"Are these auctions public?"

"Why? You want to bid on it?" I know she thought she was mocking me, because my answer made her eyebrows nearly pop off her face.

"Possibly. My father is a real estate developer. That's how I came to work for Luke—they've done some projects together," I'd said. Then clarified: "None of the dirty ones, of course."

"Well, sounds like you already know all about it," she'd said, definitely annoyed.

"It's a high-profile property," I'd pressed. "You can't let the grass turn brown and the pool turn green. There are tour buses on that street all day long; it won't go unnoticed." I didn't know for sure if that last part was true. But it was a logical assumption. Rodeo Drive was a tourist attraction. There were movie stars living all up and down that street.

"Yes, well, there are worse things than dead grass."

"How long does the auction last?" I knew the answer to that, too, but I wanted her to say it out loud.

"Six to ten weeks, typically."

"That's a lot of dead grass." I knew from listening to an interview with a federal prosecutor on YouTube that finding people to launder money for you was no easy feat. These relationships often took years to cultivate. And criminals being criminals, they tended to be irrationally optimistic about their chances of getting away with their crimes. And likewise were overconfident about their ability to keep their assets in check. If one of the people laundering money for them disappeared, they were inclined to believe he was taking personal time to visit family (preferred) or had quit and gone into hiding (not preferred, but tolerable). They were gangsters, after all, who were getting away with literal murder. Their people didn't get caught. Until they did.

"I don't know how you auction off all Luke's things without his bosses knowing he's in custody," I said. Did the mob know about the raid? Maybe. But maybe not. In this neighborhood, police could show up at a house for any number of reasons: a break-in, a false alarm, a marital spat . . . An arrest is an incident, short-lived and isolated; a move is an event. My dad only knew about the raid because his painter friend had been in the neighborhood bidding a job when Luke was hauled off in handcuffs. I don't imagine Bree was telling many people, and it certainly hadn't made the news—Morales had made sure of that.

"I don't imagine you want a bunch of moving trucks pulling up to the front door," I continued. "Talk about a red flag." Any criminal knows that if a cog in his machine gets arrested, there's a chance he'll flip. And if the mob so much as suspected Luke had flipped, evidence and witnesses might start disappearing.

By that point Morales was full-on annoyed. "Are you suggesting I tell the DOJ to skip the auction and sell Sprayberry's house and all its contents to your dad?"

"He'll water the grass. And keep it buttoned up until you give him the green light to resell."

And that's how I got my dad his "big flip."

I thought back to that conversation as my request to ride along hung in the air. My father had always told me to "ask for what you want." I had wanted the house for him, but the ride along I wanted for me.

"You want my job, don't you?" Morales said as the elevator arrived at the parking level. If any regular person had made that leap, I would have been surprised. But she was FBI—they are trained to read people.

"Not *your* job," I said. "But *a* job working for the FBI, yes."

She studied me a beat. I didn't blush or look away. I tried not to read too much into her answer, but yeah, I was pumped.

"Yes, you can ride along."

CHAPTER 53

BREE

"So you lived here?" Carter asked as we faced off in my former kitchen. My heart was pounding, and I was dripping with rainwater, sweat, and fear. I was desperate for him to call the police. A man had just been shot in cold blood, and his killer was likely on the hunt for the witness to his crime.

"I know what you're going through, what it feels like to think you've lost someone," I said, trying to keep my voice steady. "But we're in danger. You need to call for help."

"I'm not doing anything until you answer my questions," he shot back. He was angry. And no wonder. I had told him I would wait for him, and next thing he knew I was gone and a party guest was lying dead by the pool. I'd tried to tell him Sophie was still alive, but I had already established myself as a sneak and a liar. Why should he believe anything I said?

"Yes. My husband built this house. We moved in at the end of May, and it was seized by the Feds in July." The confession poured out of me. As shameful as it was, it felt good to finally say it out loud.

"Where is your husband now?"

I had avoided this question for three long months, but after what Carter had been through, he deserved the truth.

"Prison. He was arrested. Because of me." I wanted to tell him everything—how I'd cheated the government, how I'd tried to tell them

Luke was innocent, that I was the one who had hidden all that money, but they weren't interested in the truth.

"How do you know my sister?"

"I don't," I said. "Not really." I didn't want to tell him the next bit, but I didn't deserve to have secrets anymore. "She caught me sleeping in the pool house."

His face contorted like he just smelled something foul. "Are you homeless or something?"

I didn't answer. He already hated me for ditching him at the party—I didn't want him to pity me, too. But it turned out his disgusted expression was about something else.

"Did my family make you homeless?"

"What? No! I did it to myself. Your sister was trying to help me." He considered that a moment, and I couldn't help but wonder if his sister made a habit of helping people, or if this was out of character.

"My parents will be here soon," he said. "I need to tell them what happened to Sophie."

I was about to insist he call the police, tell him that it wasn't safe to be around me, but what happened next said it for me.

"Get down!" I shouted. I couldn't see the gun, but I knew from the shape of the silhouette that wafted out from behind the pool house that one was pointing straight at us.

Carter didn't move, so I grabbed his wrist and yanked him to the ground, just as the glass door exploded in a blizzard of jagged shards.

"Come on!" I shouted as another bullet ripped across the kitchen, piercing the wall above our heads.

"Go, go, go!" I yelled, pushing Carter toward the door to the garage, because the assailant would have a clear shot at us if we tried to run out the front. "Out the garage! Move!"

Our feet crunched on broken glass as we scrambled across the kitchen floor. I pulled the garage door open and pushed him through, yanking it closed behind me.

"Grab me that shovel!"

"What shovel?"

"There! Against the wall!"

Carter groped in the dark for the shovel I had neglected to put away after my spring planting. The metal spade scraped the concrete floor as he passed it to me.

"Open the garage door!" I shouted as I wedged the shovel under the doorknob. He sprinted toward the garage door and—

Thwwwwwwwack! Rolled it up. Light from a streetlamp wafted in, illuminating the car that I prayed would save our lives.

"Get in the Porsche!"

I opened the car door and slid into the driver's seat. Carter was still standing at the threshold, paralyzed with shock and fear. I knew the feeling all too well, but it was time for action, not empathy.

"Get in!"

I plunged my hand into the cup holder, extracting the key and holding it up so he could see. He still didn't move, so I opened the passenger door for him.

"Carter, come on!"

Fwump! The door to the house shuddered as the gunman rammed it from the other side. The shovel was holding, but it wouldn't for long. Carter finally snapped out of his trance and dived in the car beside me.

"Please start, please start, please start . . ." I jammed the key into the ignition. It had been over three months since anyone had driven this car; if it didn't start, we were dead.

I turned the key with desperate fingers. The engine roared to life. I slammed my foot into the clutch and popped the gear shift into reverse.

Clang! The shovel tumbled to the ground as the door flew open.

"He's in the garage!" Carter shouted. I gunned the engine, and we flew backward like we were being shot from a cannon.

The undercarriage scraped the driveway as we barreled onto the street. Our bodies lurched forward as I drove backward at full speed.

"Watch it!" Carter shouted as my rear tires clipped the curb. I slammed on the brakes, popped it into first, then made a big, arcing turn and sped off down the street.

"Call the police!" I shouted as I blew through a stop sign.

"My phone's at the house!"

"Where's the police station?"

"How the hell should I know?"

"Where am I going?" I was approaching the intersection of Rodeo Drive and Sunset Boulevard. The light was turning from yellow to red.

"Go straight! We'll call from my house!"

I sped up the hill toward the Valley, not knowing the gunman was already on his way there.

CHAPTER 54

———

LUKE

"I need all hands on deck for this pickup," Morales said as Tasker opened the car door for me in the underground courthouse parking lot. "Miss Britten is with me. You can drop Sprayberry off after we make the arrest."

Sophie and I got into our respective cars—me with Tasker and his partner, and Sophie with Morales and hers. My head was spinning. I could hardly believe that I was back in my old clothes heading for my old life. I peeked in the envelope and counted $2,000. It wasn't much, but I wasn't worried. I'd started from nothing before; I knew I could do it again. As we pulled out of the underground parking lot, I tucked the money in my pocket. I couldn't remember ever being so happy to see city lights, because it meant I was in the real world and on my way back to my wife.

Downtown was quiet, with light cross traffic and not a pedestrian in sight, and we were on the 10 freeway heading west toward my old neighborhood in a few short minutes. After growing up in a small town, it still blew my mind to drive freeways with five lanes in each direction. They were teeming with cars at 6:00 a.m., when I was going to work; at 10:00 a.m., when I was driving to a supplier to pick up materials; at noon, when I took a break for lunch; at dinnertime, when

I was heading home. As we joined the endless cars of people going who knows where at ten o'clock at night, I couldn't help but think of Bree. *"A traffic jam is a thousand souls trying to reconnect with their loved ones at once,"* she'd said, because wasn't it just like her to see something beautiful while the rest of us saw something inconvenient or annoying?

Tasker exited the freeway on Robertson and turned north toward Beverly Hills. I had only been gone for 112 days, but it all felt so foreign to me, like maybe I'd read about this place in a book or seen it on TV.

"Sorry I can't take you to In-N-Out," Tasker said as we passed the iconic fast-food chain with the best burgers in town. "I heard the food in those places is unrecognizable." I felt a tinge of gratitude that he avoided the word "prison," even though we both knew that's where I'd been.

"It's not so bad," I lied. I wasn't a foodie, but I missed Bree's cooking so much it hurt. Not the taste of it—the ritual of it. I loved sitting across from her, eating from each other's plates, telling each other what we did that day, making plans for tomorrow. Dinner at home was our time to reflect and reconnect. Without her sitting across from me, I'd barely been able to choke down my food.

My leg bounced with nervous anticipation as we drove west down Olympic Boulevard toward Beverly Hills. Tasker's eyes met mine in the rearview, and I put a hand on my leg to stop it from jackhammering against the seat. There were two squad cars already in front of Alex's English Tudor as we pulled up to it. Three pairs of agents in full tactical gear got out as we parked behind them. I flashed back to the last time I'd seen FBI agents in my neighborhood, and my stomach got tight as I pushed away the memory of the worst day of my life.

"Do I need to stick around for this?" I asked Tasker as he was pulling on his Kevlar.

"Don't you want to see us haul your boy in?"

I winced at the suggestion that Alex was "my boy."

"Not really." I would be perfectly content to never see Alex again, though I assumed it was inevitable. They would need me to testify at his trial, which everyone but the guy who'd just killed him thought was imminent.

"This shouldn't take long," Tasker said as he unholstered his pistol.

I remembered what Sophie said about Bree, how she was sleeping in our pool house. We were two blocks away. *Two short blocks!*

"If it's all the same to you, I'll just walk from here."

"Suit yourself." He opened my door. As I got out, he couldn't resist adding, "Stay out of trouble."

"I'll do my best," I said, then took off running.

CHAPTER 55

SOPHIE

"Stay in the car," Morales said as we pulled up behind the row of unmarked sedans on a residential street around the corner from our Rodeo Drive house. I peered out the window to see six agents in flak jackets and helmets, several of them with guns already drawn.

"Yeah, no problem," I replied, silently praying the windshield was bulletproof in case things didn't go as planned.

Morales closed my door, then slid into an FBI armband and gathered her agents behind her, using hand signals to direct her team members into position. It was like a choreographed dance—she was the soloist, and they were her backup dancers, following on her heels with footwork as precise as the Bolshoi Ballet.

I watched through the car window as the troupe fanned out on the front lawn. Morales, Tasker, and their partners continued straight down the walkway toward the front door, while the other four agents broke up into pairs, then snaked around the sides of the house and disappeared from view. I hadn't seen enough police procedurals to know for sure, but I guessed the agents off to the sides were positioned to catch the perp if he tried to run. They looked pretty fast, but I double-checked that the car doors were locked just in case.

Morales raised her arm and pounded on the door. Several tense seconds passed. She pounded again. Still no answer. Then she stepped aside, and an agent with what looked like a battering ram moved into position, and on her signal, broke down the door.

In a flurry of movement they charged inside, guns raised and shouting. I braced myself for gunfire. But there was only silence.

I didn't realize I'd been holding my breath until my lungs began to burn. I finally exhaled when I saw Morales exiting the house. Her gun was holstered. She looked upset, like something had gone wrong.

"What happened?" I asked as she opened my car door and I stepped out onto the sidewalk. The agents were all dispersing, but I still felt nervous. Until she told me why they were leaving without their suspect.

"He's dead."

"What? How?"

"Bullet to the head. Professional job." Morales looked pissed, like she was mad at herself for not anticipating this possibility.

"What does that mean for me?" I knew it was a self-centered thing to ask in that moment, but I didn't want to go back to the safe house . . . unless I wasn't safe.

"When they kill one of their own, it means they're shutting it down. My case has just gone cold." And by the way she slammed the car door, I knew she blamed herself.

"Sorry."

She shook her head, like there was nothing she could do. "They'll pop up somewhere else, eventually."

"So Luke and me . . . ?" I asked. "Are we . . ."

"Still potential targets?" she said, reading my mind. "No. Your usefulness died with him." And I didn't know whether to be relieved or disappointed.

"So I'm not going back to the safe house," I clarified.

"They went after you to protect him. But obviously that's not their concern anymore. They must have sensed we were closing in, decided to cut their losses." I knew this wasn't the outcome she wanted, but I took some satisfaction knowing that my actions helped shut the operation down, at least this small part of it.

"I need to call my brother," I said. I had no idea if anyone had explained my disappearance to Carter, and I knew he must have been worried sick.

"Tasker!" Morales called out. And a moment later my safe house roommate appeared with my phone in hand.

"Here you go."

I hesitated before I dialed. What would I say? How much did Carter know? In the last twenty-four hours, I had dropped my parents off at the airport, thrown a party, broken up with my secret boyfriend, gotten abducted, learned my friend had been murdered, testified in a clandestine hearing, and watched the FBI try to make an arrest only to discover the perp was already dead. *Helluva day.*

"What does my brother know about all of this?" I asked Morales. I wasn't sure what I was allowed to tell him but figured I should start by asking what he already knew.

"The identity of the victim was not released," Morales said curtly. "But you can tell him it wasn't you." *Um, obviously.*

"And the other stuff?" I asked. I hadn't said a word to anyone about stumbling onto an international crime ring. *Am I allowed to talk about that now?*

"Use your best judgment." Perhaps it was wishful thinking, but I thought her nonanswer might be a test.

"Copy that."

I dialed Carter's number. It rang, but he didn't answer. Which was strange, because *shouldn't he be desperate to hear from me by now?*

I ended the call. As I contemplated my next move, Morales beckoned to Tasker.

"Tasker will take you home."

"Thanks," I said, then raised a finger. "One sec." There was no point going home if Carter wasn't there. I wanted to go to him, not our house.

So I logged into Find My Phone and got a jolt down my spine when I saw where he was.

"Shall we?" Tasker asked, indicating his car.

"I'm good," I said. According to my tracker, he was right around the corner. Probably poking around a crime scene he had been told to stay away from. I didn't want him to get in trouble, and I couldn't think of any reason why I'd need an escort. "I need a walk."

And without considering the risks, I took off by myself toward Rodeo Drive to find my brother.

CHAPTER 56

LUKE

There was police tape across the front and side doors to the Rodeo Drive house, so I jogged around the block to enter from the alley. I probably should have been nervous about breaking into the house that got me arrested in the first place, but it was the excitement about seeing Bree that was making my pulse race.

I pulled on the back gate. *Locked.* The stucco was slippery and the wall a head taller than me, but with a little jump I was able to hoist myself pull-up style onto the top. I swung my legs around, then sat for a moment to survey the scene. It was strangely dark—no lights on anywhere—and I couldn't see anything except the surface of the pool shimmering beneath the gentle drizzle of rain.

Whump! I dropped down onto the grass. The wet sod gasped under my feet. The pool house was a few short steps in front of me. If the sound had startled Bree, I thought it best to announce myself.

"Bree?" I called out. "Baby, it's me."

No answer.

I walked around to the front of the pool house. The curtains were open a crack.

"Bree? Are you in there?"

I pulled back the curtain slowly, so as not to startle her if she was inside.

"It's Luke. I'm coming in," I said, a little louder now.

I stepped across the threshold. In the darkness, I could make out the silhouettes of the kitchen counter, the dining table, the six wicker chairs.

"Bree?"

I waded into the galley kitchen. I wouldn't have noticed the empty club soda bottle on the floor if I hadn't kicked it over. I bent down and picked it up.

On a hunch, I walked over to the couch-bench and lifted the lid. There was a jumble of towels in there, one of them wet.

"Bree, baby, where are you?" I said to the empty space. I was exhausted and rain soaked, but I wasn't going anywhere until I found my wife.

I retreated outside and gazed toward the house. The windows overlooking the backyard all glistened with rainwater. But the pocket door was a black hole.

It seemed odd that the windows would shimmer but the door would be an abyss, so I took a few steps closer. That's when I realized the reason there were no raindrops on the glass door was because there was no glass in it.

I jogged across the yard and took the deck stairs two at a time. Even in the darkness I could see the shards fanning out in all directions. My eyes combed the kitchen. It took me a few seconds to realize that that pockmark in the wall behind the island was a bullet hole.

My pulse accelerated. Everything in my body told me I shouldn't be here, but I didn't leave, *couldn't* leave. Not if there was a chance Bree was here.

I crunched across the glass, then groped for the light switch I knew was there because I'd installed it myself. But the lights didn't come on. As I stood there in the dark, I heard a rhythmic, high-pitched beeping sound. If it was an alarm, it wasn't one I'd installed . . .

I followed the noise down the hall to a pair of sneakers by the stairwell. I reached in one of them to find a phone sending out Apple's signature homing signal. Both the sneakers and the pair of socks balled up in them were wet. Which meant someone either just left . . . or was still here.

"Bree?"

I set the phone on the stairs, then started up them. I was halfway to the landing when I heard a knock on the front door, followed by a familiar voice.

"Carter!" the woman called out. "Let me in!"

I descended the stairs, then opened the door for a breathless, rain-soaked Sophie.

"Is my brother here?" she said as she pushed her way past me.

"Are those his shoes?" I said, by way of an answer.

She looked where I was pointing. She ran over to them for a closer look, then picked up the phone I had left on the bottom step.

"Carter!" she called out. She took the stairs two at a time. "Carter!"

I heard her footsteps above my head. I was about to join her upstairs when she reappeared on the landing. "He's not up here." She jogged down the stairs and picked up his shoes. "Why would he leave without his shoes or his phone?"

I had an uneasy feeling but no answer.

"What do you know about the murder that happened here?" I asked, flashing back to that bullet in the wall, praying Morales hadn't lied when she said Bree was safe.

"It was a drowning," Sophie said. I must have looked surprised, because she crunched her eyebrows. "What?"

"Not a shooting?"

She shook her head. "She drowned in the pool."

"So who did that?" I pointed to the kitchen—at the bullet hole in the wall, all that broken glass.

"This is not from last night," Sophie said.

"Then when?"

Sophie's hand flew over her mouth. "Oh God." I didn't know that Alex had just been shot by the same person who'd tried to kill her. But she did.

"Sophie? What is it?"

"He came back." I remembered what she'd said about Bree sleeping here, that wet towel in the pool house . . .

"Who came back?" I asked.

"The contract killer. And he knows where I live."

CHAPTER 57

———

CARTER

"Pull over here," I said to Bree as we turned onto my street and my house came into view. If someone had told me last night I would be pulling up to my house with Bree in her Porsche, I would have died of happiness. As long as they didn't also tell me she was married, this was no joyride, and if I died this weekend, it would *not* be of happiness.

"We'll call 9-1-1 from the landline," I said as she pulled up to the curb and shut off the engine. I opened my car door and stepped out onto the sidewalk in my bare feet, but she just sat there with her hands on the wheel.

"Bree, come on, let's go!"

"You call. I'll wait for you here."

"A guy just shot at us!"

"No. He shot at *me*."

I didn't know that to be true, or why it mattered. "What difference does it make?"

"I've caused you enough trouble." She tightened her grip on the wheel. I didn't like the idea of leaving her in the car—one, because she might drive away, and two, if she didn't, and we'd been followed, she might be in danger.

"Look, I wasn't supposed to be at that house any more than you were." I thought maybe she was afraid to talk to the police because she'd been trespassing, so I added, "The police aren't going to care why we were there when there's an active shooter on the loose."

She shook her head, like that wasn't it. "I'm bad news, Carter. You don't want me in your house."

I got back in the car and shut the door.

"What are you doing?"

"If you're not going in, I'm not going in," I said, because I could be stubborn, too.

"Carter, there's a lot you don't know about me."

"Did you try to shoot somebody?"

"What? No!"

"Then let's go!"

She opened her mouth like she was going to object, but I guess the fire in my eyes convinced her I wasn't going to back down, because she took the key out of the ignition.

"Fine."

We walked in silence up my front walk. My house key was in my truck, which was still parked on Rodeo Drive, but we kept a spare under the planter. She stood beside me as I reached down to get it. I always thought that the hide-a-key was in a stupid place; *isn't under the flowerpot the first place a burglar would look?* But today that hiding spot was the opposite of stupid, because as I stood up, I was at the perfect angle to see the reflection of the gun in the brass door knocker, barrel pointed at us.

"Bree! Get down!" I launched myself across the stoop, shoving her body against the sidewall of the house. The shooter must have used a silencer, because I thought the searing pain in my shoulder was from the impact of hitting the wall . . . until Bree told me otherwise.

"Carter, you're bleeding!"

I've been injured on many occasions in many different ways. I caught a baseball with my nose during tenth grade PE. I cleaved my calf climbing over barbed wire on a construction site. I filleted my finger on a lawn mower blade. But I had never bled as violently as I was bleeding now.

"Oh God," I muttered, looking down at my wound. Blood was coursing down my arm, dripping off my fingers, soaking my shirt.

Bree must have taken the key from my hand, because next thing I knew, the door was open and she was pushing me inside. The bullet must have passed straight through me because there it was, wedged below the door knocker that had saved Bree's life.

"One step at a time, Carter . . . that's it," Bree coaxed as she eased me toward the kitchen. She sat me on a stool, then grabbed a dish towel off the oven door and wrapped it around my shoulder.

"Press here, hard!" Bree said, taking my unbloodied hand and wrapping it around the wound. "Don't let go! I'm going to get us out of here."

She ran to the back door, but as she reached for the knob—

Blam! It popped off in her hand.

"Back to the front!"

I wanted to run, but my head was as floaty as my body was heavy. "I need to lie down," I said. And then I was on my knees.

"Carter, get up!" Bree commanded, slipping her hands under my armpits. I felt my legs straighten under me. "We need to hide. Where can we go?"

I had lived in this house my whole life and knew all the hiding spots. The best one was under the stairs. If Sophie couldn't find me there during our countless games of hide-and-go-seek when we were little, no one could.

"Stairs," I murmured, pointing with my elbow, leaning on Bree as she dragged me out of the kitchen and into the hall. My vision was a pinhole, but I knew it was a good hiding place because Bree almost walked right past it.

"Stop!" I said, then pushed on the hidden compartment with my foot. It levered up like an old garage door. I dropped to my knees to crawl inside, only to discover my sister knew about it after all, because it was filled with her suitcases. There was barely room for one of us; we would have to find somewhere else.

"Too small," I said. Bree knelt down to look.

"Get in! I'll find somewhere else!"

"No," I objected, but I didn't have enough strength to resist when she pushed me inside. My sister's hard-shell Samsonite pressed into my back as Bree shut the door and I was plunged into darkness.

My hand was sticky against the blood-soaked towel, but I didn't feel pain. And I was grateful for that, even though I knew feeling nothing was probably a really bad sign.

CHAPTER 58

BREE

I pushed the little door closed behind Carter, then took off running down the hall. The shooter had blown the knob to the kitchen door clean off, but I hadn't heard him come in. Was he in the back? In the front? Somewhere else?

My senses were on high alert as I dropped to my hands and knees and crawled past the living room windows toward what looked like a home office. I listened for movement in the house, but all I could hear was my breathing, fast and shallow through my open mouth. Carter was in bad shape; even if I did escape, he needed help, and soon. I had to find a phone. There was one on the desk. I reached up and snatched it.

I dialed 9-1-1, then slid the handset under the desk, praying the operator would send help without me having to ask for it.

I held my breath in hopes of hearing a whisper of movement, but there was none. I didn't know if the gunman was coming in through the front or the back, so I decided my best move was up. Maybe I could find a window to climb out, like I had at Alex's? Or a vantage point to spot him if he was circling outside.

I scurried up the carpeted stairs and paused on the landing. To my right was the primary suite, door open to reveal a king-size bed high off the ground with no dust ruffle for cover. I swiveled my head to the left. There were several doors, all ajar. I tiptoed toward the closest one—a girl's room, which I figured was Sophie's from the jumble of clothes on the floor.

I crouched down and crawled over the threshold. There were windows on the far wall with views of the backyard. I peeked under the bed. There was room for me. I had just dropped to my belly to slither underneath it when I heard it—the sound of metal against metal, like a latch being wiggled. I turned my head . . . to see a gloved hand opening the window. The gunman had come up the fire escape to surprise us from above.

I slid backward like a recoiling snake, away from the bed and through the bedroom door. As I reached the hall and sprang to my feet—

Whap! The window banged open, and heavy feet thumped onto the carpet.

I gripped the banister as I ran down the stairs two at a time.

The front door was a straight shot from the landing. I didn't want to be an easy target from the top of the stairs, so I scooted toward the back of the house, past where Carter was hiding, toward the kitchen.

The floorboards creaked above my head. I was about to make a run for the back door, but instead of walking down the stairs, the shooter flipped over the banister, landing like a cat ten feet from where I was standing. His back was to me as he peeked into the dining room, so I quickly banked right, toward the east of the house, praying there was an exit to the side yard. *Please let there be a door . . . please let there be a door . . .*

I sprinted into the sunken family room . . . to discover it was a doorless, windowless dead end.

It was too late to turn around.

He knew I had seen his face at Alex's. There was no way I was getting out of here alive.

The only thing I could do was hide.

Besides the L-shaped couch, TV console, and double-wide book-case, there was one other piece of furniture. An item that in many ways had already saved my life. At five feet ten inches, the Steinway baby grand was just long enough to accommodate me.

So I lifted the lid and slipped inside.

CHAPTER 59

———

SOPHIE

Luke's truck roared up Beverly Glen Boulevard toward the Valley. My phone was on speaker as the 9-1-1 operator picked up.

"9-1-1, what's your emergency?"

"There's been a shooting," I said, then spit out the Rodeo Drive address. Morales had said that I would be safe now that Alex was gone, that no one would have reason to come after me. It made sense and I'd believed her. But I had an instinct that this wasn't over yet. And if I had learned anything these last few months, it was to trust my instincts.

"Is this a report of an active shooter?" the operator asked. And I wasn't sure how to answer that.

"Yes," I said, because I needed her to take this seriously. "He fled the premises. We think he's on the way to my house." I gave her the address. I didn't know my brother was lying there bleeding, so I told her there were no victims "that I knew of," but that the situation was evolving. "Please just send cars to both places."

Luke's truck crested over the top of Mulholland Drive and plunged into the Valley. We were a few minutes from my house now. My brother wouldn't have forgotten his phone and shoes unless he'd left in a hurry. *So what was the hurry?* I had no way of knowing, but that bullet in the wall made me fear the worst.

We pulled onto my street. As we neared my house, Luke pointed to a white Porsche parked outside.

"That's my car."

"Keep driving," I said. I was starting to put a theory together. Carter had gone to the house, possibly to look for me. Bree was there, because she had nowhere else to go. The gunman blew out the door and they'd fled together, thinking they'd be safe at our house, not knowing the gunman had already been here in search of me.

"Which one is your house?" Luke asked.

"Blue one on the left. But don't stop or slow down."

My instincts were screaming, so I let them call the shots. *Drive by and scope it out. Park where we won't be seen. Maintain the element of surprise.*

"Park here," I said, pointing to a spot around the bend under the cover of a leafy tree. Luke pulled over as instructed.

"Do you have a weapon?" I asked.

"What? No!"

"We can't go in there with nothing."

"Tire iron?"

"Yes. Grab it."

"What about you?"

"I'll find something at the house." I had a better weapon than a tire iron, but I didn't want to say so just yet.

As we approached, I noticed the front door was open—just a crack, but enough for me to know something was wrong.

"He's in the house," I said.

"How do you know?"

It was a ridiculous thing to say, but I said it anyway. "I can feel it."

There were four entrances to my house: front door, back door, garage, and a fire escape that during my rebellious period I had used liberally.

"What's the plan?" Luke asked. I didn't have a plan, so I said the first thing that popped in my head.

"Don't get shot."

CHAPTER 60

LUKE

We decided to split up. I would go in through the backyard under the cover of trees; she would climb up the fire escape and scope out the scene from above. It wasn't much of a plan, but if Bree was in there, I couldn't just sit on the curb waiting for police who might never come.

The house was a modest two-story traditional with wood siding and a pitched shingle roof. It was a shady lot with fruit trees and flowers. I'd always imagined my house-flipper friend in a grander sort of place, but I guess his margins were as tough as mine.

I crept along the side yard, peeking into first-floor windows as I passed—a formal living room, a laundry room, a half bath. It was deadly quiet. No signs of life inside or out.

I rounded the back of the house and slipped onto a deck adorned with a Weber grill, a glass patio table, and six plastic chairs. There was a door to the kitchen with a window in it. My back pressed against the exterior wall of the house, I shimmied across the deck and peered through.

Empty.

I reached down to try the handle, but there was nothing but a gaping hole. At first I was confused. And then I realized: the doorknob had been blown clean off.

My heart did a backflip. *What the hell am I doing here?* I wasn't a crime fighter—quite the opposite. I was about to skulk back to my truck when I thought of Bree. *What if she's here? What if she needs help?* Yes, I might get shot, but there was nothing to live for without her.

I pushed the door open with the bottom of my foot. The tire iron dug into my palm as I held it at the ready. I heard a bird chirp. A plane descending into Van Nuys Airport. Wind rustling in the trees. But nothing from inside the house.

I took a deep breath for courage, then peeked my head in. There was a kitchen island a few feet ahead, so I crouched down low and ducked behind it.

It was an older house with a traditional floor plan—lots of interior walls, which blocked my view but also gave me cover. I crept out of the kitchen. I was about to turn the corner into the dining room when the barrel of a gun poked out from behind the doorway.

I raised the tire iron above my head and slammed it down on the gloved hand. The gun clacked to the ground. I kicked it across the room and cocked the crowbar back like a slugger at home plate. But I swung too high. The assailant ducked under my bat with the quickness of a boxer.

Thwunk! The tire iron sank into the wall.

I yanked it free. But before I could regain my balance, the shooter landed a kick in my ribs.

The gun was on the floor, halfway between him and me. But I was doubled over and he was already reaching.

I swung the crowbar at his knees. I heard the crunch of bone shattering as the iron rod connected with his kneecaps.

He tumbled onto his back. I didn't realize my palms were sweating until his gloved hands grabbed the tire iron and yanked it from my grasp.

I stumbled into a high-back dining chair. As he stood and raised the crowbar to bring it down on my head, I grabbed the chair and hoisted it in the air to block the blow.

Thwack! The crowbar connected with the bottom of the chair. He tried to retract it, but the c-curve caught the seat, and when he yanked on the rod, he pulled the chair out of my hands and into his own body.

The tire iron clanged to the floor as he flew back against the wall.

The curved end of the crowbar was inches from his gun. I reached out to grab the shaft so I could hook the gun and pull it toward me.

My hand connected with the tire iron. But as I extended it forward, the shooter's hand found the gun, and the barrel was pointed toward my head faster than a lightning strike.

Blam!

I heard the sound of a gun discharging.

I waited for the pain I knew would come.

Bree's face flashed in front of my eyes. I prayed to God for forgiveness, and to take care of my wife.

Blam! Blam!

Two more shots rang out. I felt no pain. I looked down at my chest, my legs, my hands . . . but there was no blood. *Does that mean I'm already dead?*

In front of me, the gunman crumpled to the floor.

Behind me, Sophie was standing at the threshold, pointing her gun at my assailant.

"Sophie?"

She lowered her arms.

"Are you OK, Luke?"

My ears were ringing, like someone struck a gong between my ears. But I could hear. I could see. I could breathe. "I . . . think so."

"Carter!" Sophie turned her back to me and ran out of the room. I felt weightless as I rose to my feet. When I looked up, I thought I must be in heaven, because right there in the doorway appeared the most beautiful angel God had ever sent to earth.

And I didn't care if I was dead or alive, because at long last, I was home.

CHAPTER 61

BREE

Blam!

The piano strings shuddered under my legs, back, and head.

Blam, blam! I squeezed my eyes shut. Grief was a sword through my heart. Those shots could only mean one thing: the gunman had found Carter. I tried to cry out, but horror gripped my throat. My body shook as I keened in silent agony. I was past trying to stay quiet. If the gunman was coming for me, then so be it; I deserved to die. If they found my bloodied body inside a piano, perhaps the person who found me would think it poetic that I died inside the very thing that had given me a reason to live.

"Sophie?" The sound of Luke's voice was like an apparition. It wasn't the first time since his incarceration that I'd thought I'd heard it. It was a hoot owl on a tree branch, a child's laugh on the wind, an airplane taking flight. Was I an optimist? Or slipping into madness?

"Are you OK, Luke?" I recognized that voice, too. But it made no sense. Luke and Sophie didn't know each other. She had been snatched by the FBI, and he was in prison. And what would they be doing here?

"I . . . think so." That voice again. All I could think was that I was hallucinating. Trauma can do that to a person. I wouldn't let myself be fooled again.

"Carter!" The urgency in Sophie's voice brought me back into my body—the smell of iron and wood, the piano strings etching grooves in my back.

"In here," I heard Carter answer. *Carter! Is he alive? What is happening here?* I pressed the piano lid up and maneuvered my body out of my cocoon. My feet connected with the floor, and I turned toward the doorway to see brother and sister melt into a hug.

"Help is on the way," Sophie soothed, then looked up and saw me staring. She motioned to the dining room with her head. I couldn't feel my legs as I walked toward it.

"Bree?" The sound of my husband's voice was like a dam breaking. When his eyes met mine, everything in the room fell away, like the whole world had been swallowed by quicksand and he was the only thing still standing. His face was both the most exotic thing I'd ever seen and as familiar as seeing my own. I opened my mouth to say his name, but before I could speak, his arms were around me and we fell into that quicksand.

And in that moment, I didn't care if we ever came out.

CHAPTER 62

—

BREE

The first thing we did was sleep.

Carter and Sophie's dad offered to let us stay in the Rodeo Drive house for a few days, but we preferred to take our camping gear and disappear in the woods for a while. Nights in the Ojai wilderness were cold this time of year, but we had the warmth of our campfire and our love and knew it would be more than enough.

We drove up the hill with our hips touching and fingers interlocked, neither of us able to let go of the other. After we set up camp, we crawled into our tent and coiled together like two trees whose branches are so intertwined you can't tell where one stops and the other begins. We woke with the morning light. Cold river water washed away our hazy disbelief that this was not a dream. We dried each other's bodies, then let the sun seep into our skin and warm us back to remembering the shocking day of Luke's arrest and the confusion, terror, guilt, shame, longing, and suffering that followed.

Luke told me everything, starting with how none of what happened was my fault, and I cried with relief as he cried with remorse. I understood that he had been tricked in the worst way, and the events at Carter's house made it clear why he'd had to disappear. I will never understand why people lie, cheat, and kill for money they don't need. If humanity has an incurable plague, it's our endless appetite for riches and our numbness to the suffering of others. I didn't know what Luke and I were going to do with our lives going forward, only that this episode had made us long for a simpler, more charitable existence that was closer to nature and to God.

Luke asked how I'd survived the last three months, and I told him about the Laundromat, the lessons, the searing loneliness. The days and nights blurred together as we recounted our respective struggles. Luke sobbed when I told him about the neighborhoods I'd slept in, bathroom stalls I'd bathed in, and all the ninety-nine-cent tacos I'd eaten in the Jack in the Box parking lot. And my heart broke when he described meals eaten off plastic trays and nights spent on a rust-stained mattress with a view of four concrete walls.

Slowly, after crying until our eyes burned, we let ourselves believe the nightmare was over. There was one last thing I had to do before I could put the events of the last few months behind me. Luke offered to drive me down the mountain, but this was something I wanted to do by myself. So after a breakfast of oatmeal and hard-boiled eggs cooked over a campfire, I got in the truck and drove toward LA. This was the first time since we'd been reunited that I was venturing off on my own, but after the initial shock of seeing other cars and faces, I felt confident in a way I'd never felt before. Gone was the urgency to get "home" as quickly as possible. I had discovered you can miss somebody without feeling like a part of you is missing, and despite the whiz of cars in front of and behind me, I felt grounded and calm.

It was a stunningly clear November day. The Pacific Ocean sparkled in my peripheral vision as I drove south down the 101, past breathtaking cliffs to my left and dreamlike white-sand beaches to my right. The earth looked more beautiful than ever to me; I guess that's what happens when you realize how lucky you are to be alive.

I pulled up to Carter's Sherman Oaks house a little after noon. I didn't have his number to tell him I was coming but hoped the chocolate chip cookies I had picked up in town were enough to compensate for my rudeness in popping in unannounced. Thanks to our 9-1-1 calls, police had arrived within minutes of Sophie's kill shot and got Carter in an ambulance a few minutes after that. He had lost a lot of blood, but paramedics promised his prognosis was good. Still, we didn't leave for the mountains until we were sure he was going to be OK. I imagined he'd be home by now, resting and on the mend.

I parked in the shade and hugged my pastry box to my chest as I walked through the front garden. I took deep breaths to try to slow my heartbeat, which was thumping in my ears like kettledrums. Trauma is a funny thing. I knew our assailant was dead—I had seen his lifeless body with my own eyes—yet I had to fight back the urge to look over my shoulder to make sure he wasn't still lurking.

I didn't know when I clacked the door knocker how that reflective brass hardware had saved me, but the bullet hole right beside it was a somber reminder that I owed Carter nothing less than my life. Thirty seconds passed, so I knocked again, a little harder this time. I was about to leave and come back later when Carter answered the door wearing flannel pajama bottoms and a look of pure astonishment.

"Bree!" he said, and I wasn't sure if the clap in his tone was surprise or anger. "What are you doing here?"

"I came to see you."

I felt foolish offering him that box of cookies, but he mumbled a halfhearted "thank you" as he took it with his good arm.

"Can I come in?"

He hesitated a moment, then stepped aside so I could slip through the door. I followed him past the dining room, keeping my eyes pointed straight ahead so I didn't have to confront the image of the limp corpse and bloodstained wall that was imprinted in my memory.

"How are you feeling?" I asked as we arrived in the living room and he indicated for me to sit.

"Tired, but OK. My mom's a nurse, which means no pity parties." He rolled his eyes a little, and I imagined being the son of a nurse who has seen every kind of horror is a double-edged sword.

"At least she can take care of you here at home," I offered, leaning into the upside.

"There's not much care required. They sewed me up, I'm on antibiotics. The bullet went clean through, so I shouldn't have any residual effects."

"Except a wicked-cool scar."

"And a wicked-cool story to go with it." He smiled a little, which made me smile, too.

"Look, Carter," I said, eager to get to the reason I came here. "I want to apologize."

"For what?"

"That bullet hole in your arm, for starters. You wouldn't have that if it wasn't for me."

Carter shrugged, like he didn't agree. "Sophie was the one who dragged our family into this; if I'm going to be pissed at anyone, it's going to be her." By the way he said it, I knew he was more proud than pissed. That Sophie owned a gun and knew how to use it shouldn't have been a surprise to her brother, given her aspirations, but even the cops were stunned by her heroics.

"She did the right thing, going to the FBI," I said, and I knew Luke agreed with me, even though it had ripped our lives apart.

"It was purely selfish, you know."

"How so?"

"She wanted a job there. Which she got. She started today. She's a bona fide secret agent now."

"Oh. Good for her."

"Your husband was her ticket." I thought maybe he felt bad about that, so I tried to reassure him.

"We were in an unsustainable situation. It would have blown up eventually. She might have saved his life." I understood now who those people who'd entrapped Luke were. He was always one wrong move from getting killed.

He nodded, then wiped his nose with the back of his sleeve. I thought maybe he wanted me to go, so I stood up.

"We're selling your house," he said, a little too loud and fast, like he thought it might upset me.

"It was never really our house," I countered. Yes, we were once the proud owners, but after I learned how Luke had come to buy it, I didn't want it anymore.

"I get to keep half the profits," Carter said, like he was confessing something horrible.

"Reparations for your pain and suffering."

He shrugged and wiped his nose again: his nervous tic. "Not how I wanted to earn my EVP title, but whatever. I'm getting my own place. I put an offer on a condo by the beach."

"That's great."

"It's a fixer. Because, obviously." Was he self-conscious about living at home? Trying to impress me? My heart broke a little as I realized what I'd done to his.

"I should let you get some rest."

"I had a huge crush on you, you know," he blurted. My cheeks got hot with embarrassment. But it would have been selfish of me to come and get closure for myself without giving him the opportunity to get his.

"Sorry," he said. "I shouldn't have told you that."

I met his gaze. I wanted to tell him he was kind and brave and worthy of a great big love. And that under different circumstances, if I hadn't given Luke my whole heart fully and forever, I might have gone on a date with him. And we might have been happy, in the way many are when they share their lives with good and kind people. But I didn't. Because I knew the best thing for him would be to forget about me.

We said our goodbyes with an awkward one-arm hug, both knowing it would be forever.

I had no reason to rush back to Ojai, so I exited the 101 at Topanga, then drove through the canyon toward the beach. As I hooked north onto the scenic Pacific Coast Highway, golden light fanned out from the midday sun, coating everything with lemony optimism. I was hungry and it was lunchtime, so I stopped for fish and chips at a roadside stand in Malibu. Most people don't realize what a luxury it is to be able to eat when you're hungry, or without worrying if there will be a next meal, but I would never take those things for granted ever again. Luke was already back to work; as soon as he'd put up those flyers in the center of town, his phone started ringing. The great thing about coming from nothing, which we both had, is that being broke doesn't scare you because you've been there before.

My food came, and I sat at a picnic table overlooking the ocean. Time stood still as I savored the salt on my fingers and the breeze in my hair. It was a new sensation. For the first time in my life, I wasn't "killing time" until I was reunited with my man or my music. I was alone with myself but connected to something bigger. Something unknowable. Something mine but not of me.

I didn't have a plan for my future, but I knew there would be music—lots and lots of music. I had dismissed the idea of going on tour because I didn't know what it would do to my new marriage. But if my marriage could survive this, it could survive anything. I hoped there would be kids, but just because my mom gave up everything to raise me didn't mean I needed to do the same. Yes, I would give them a safe place to call home, but I would also give them the world.

They say that the divine purpose of difficult things is to bring people together. And maybe in some cases that's true. But I had needed the opposite—to be OK with myself, without a mate or a cocoon of music or a fancy home to disappear in. I didn't know what the future would bring, only that I would be fine because I had me.

ACKNOWLEDGMENTS

First, a confession: five chapters into this book, I realized I was in over my head. I have as much experience solving crimes as I do flying fighter jets (hint: none), yet plunged my characters into a crazy-intricate one. I needed experts. I took a *Field of Dreams* approach—if you write it, they will come. And, just like in the movie, superstars appeared.

I shudder to think what this novel would be without the help of former FBI agent–turned–tech consultant–turned–grand wizard Mike Panico, who took me behind the curtain of how the FBI catches bad guys, including some methods that are not in the training manual. Turns out it's like you see on TV, only wilder. To learn what happens after perpetrators get caught, I turned to former federal prosecutor John Kroger, who knows not only how prosecutions work (he's done a few) but also how to write a book. (He's done that, too.) I owe Laura Eimiller of the FBI Los Angeles office a big thank-you (or at least a sandwich) for helping me flush out critical moments; knowing what FBI agents wear to a raid is not something I learned in school (or anywhere else). If I got the details right, it's because of the generous counsel of my advisers. If I got something wrong, it's because I failed to ask the right questions or misunderstood their answers.

Where there's a dead body, there's a call (or five) to Dr. Judy Melinek, who always generously helps me with the gory details of the gore. Thank you, Dr. Judy, for sharing your expertise with me time and again.

Once I got my facts straight, I needed to make sure I told a good story, and for help with that, I turned to my trusted posse of beta readers. Thank you, Debra Lewin (first and fastest), Miranda Parker Lewin (asks great questions), Avital Ornovitz (always sees something I missed), and Tyler Weltman (gets the big picture). The writerly support I get from colleagues W. Bruce Cameron, Ken Pisani, Gary Goldstein, Diane Driscoll, Barbara Davis, TJ Mitchell, and Alethea Black, all wonderful authors who inspire me every day, is incalculable, and I am supremely grateful to all of them for extending a hand when I reach for one.

Lake Union Publishing is an amazing place to learn and grow. I am beyond grateful to Christopher Werner for believing in this story and me when we were mere seeds. Thank you to my (new!) editor Melissa Valentine for jumping in with enthusiasm and grace (and seriously fantastic notes) and Danielle Marshall for making this perfect match. This manuscript was elevated by so many talented professionals: my brilliant developmental editor, Jenna L. Free (who always knows better); Haley and her whip-smart copyediting team; proofreader Kellie; and Gabe D., Jen B., and Kyra W., who hold all the pieces together.

Thank you to the world's best agent, Laura Dail, for your razzle-dazzle and creativity. Katie Gisondi and all the extraordinary professionals at the Laura Dail Agency, I see you and appreciate you! Special shout-out to Suzanne Leopold at Suzy's Approved Book Tours for connecting me with readers, and everyone everywhere who loves to read. To my fellow Facebookers, TikTokers, and Bookstagrammers: Your fan art and reviews are the pot of gold at the end of the rainbow. I've found so many great books thanks to you, and your thoughtful posts inspire me to dig deeper and write better.

Putting your stories out there can sometimes feel like standing on top of a mountain and inviting people to throw snowballs at you. Thank you to Andy Cohen for pushing me up that mountain, and Victoria Sainsbury-Carter for reminding me those snowballs are all in my mind.

Thank you to my daughters: Sophie, who let me use her name (even though I warned her bad things might happen to her namesake), and Taya, who is not afraid to tell me when something's not working (sorry if I'm a pill about it). To my husband, Uri: thanks for believing in me every day and in every way; your support means the most.

This book is dedicated to Maila Walter, who gets up to cheer me on, even on the hard days. I love you, Mom. You are my shining star.